FRAGMENTS OF TIME

J.W. CAPEK

BLUE FORGE PRESS
Port Orchard, Washington

Blue Forge Press is the print division of the volunteer-run, federal 501(c)3 nonprofit company, Blue Legacy, founded in 1989 and dedicated to bringing light to the shadows and voice to the silence. We strive to empower storytellers across all walks of life with our four divisions: Blue Forge Press, Blue Forge Films, Blue Forge Gaming, and Blue Forge Records. Find out more at: www.MyBlueLegacy.org

Blue Forge Press
7419 Ebbert Drive Southeast
Port Orchard, Washington 98367
blueforgepress@gmail.com
360-550-2071 ph.txt

*Dedicated to my lifelong muse, Jim,
my inspiring son, David, and to the people
and experiences that emerge in this
collection of characters and events.*

ACKNOWLEDGMENTS

My greatest appreciation for the encouragement throughout the *Prompt* project: Thanks to Wendy Roedell, Patricia Sheehan, and Paul Tice for beta reading with discerning eyes to improve the monthly stories. Remembrance goes to Helen Snyder for imagining characters and sharing the excitement of writing. I am grateful to the Blue Forge staff for their reassurance through the design of the *Prompt* publishing process.

Prompt: The Second Generation became a learning experience, a mental stimulation, and most of all, a rewarding involvement with Kitsap authors and publications.

TABLE OF CONTENTS

FRAGMENTS OF TIME

J.W. CAPEK

TO SAVE ONE MORE LIFE
TIME FRAGMENT 2020 CE

Crouched on the hillside, like the derelict it was, the old hospital buildings were dark and deserted; a new medical complex had sucked all services to itself in a nearby town. This morning, the Emergency Room with its adjacent parking lot and helicopter pad was the solitary source of illumination and activity. The whole emergency wing would succumb in a few weeks' time.

Walking through the ER foyer, Doctor Rebecca Howard adjusted her facial mask and went towards the medical locker room for her personal protective equipment and into another day of crisis. The mask and PPE were only the first of the many she would wear that day. Her shoulder length blond hair was tucked into a paper net, petite body encased in protection, shoes bagged at her ankles. Her day had begun.

Walking to her station, Rebecca's glance showed her the waiting area was occupied. Hospital waiting rooms can be unique in their sameness. Stark beige walls with nondescript pictures; a vinyl couch with a ripped seam, beige tile floors with hospital-standard shine, and a dripping coffee percolator in the corner, courtesy of the Ladies' Auxiliary. Various red-printed signs called for social distancing and repeated the need to wear masks.

The children's floor waiting room was no different. Its thumbed magazines lay unread on Formica end tables as a young couple just sat. Fatigue was evidenced in their slumped bodies and bloodshot eyes. They didn't even look up when another parent entered. A courtesy nod in their direction was ignored and the newcomer quickly poured a paper cup of coffee but took it to another hallway. Obviously, the man and woman were not to be disturbed.

There was an underlying tension in the room. The man was unshaven, and his right arm stiffly surrounded the woman's shoulders protectively. He stared at a fixed point on the floor and seemed beyond awareness of what was going on about him. The woman's fingers traced nervous patterns on the man's pant leg as she shifted her position slightly.

"Don, what time is it?" she asked her husband. They wore matching plain gold bands. "The doctor should return soon, shouldn't she?"

"I don't know, hon," he answered without looking up, his voice a monotone. "They'll tell us if there has been any change. They said to just wait here."

"Why doesn't she move? It's been hours and with all the stomach pumping and those other machines, why doesn't she do something?" Mona's voice rose, nearing hysteria just below the surface.

Her tone brought Don out of his stupor and he hugged her to him as he patted her knee. "Hold on, honey! Listen. Why don't you go home for a little while, take a warm bath and a nap? Maybe you could even eat something. I'll wait here and then do the same when you get back."

"No, I can't. She might come to and want me. Oh, Don! If only she would...." She stopped speaking as tears filled her eyes.

Rebecca paused by the doorway window and looked in at the parents. In her middle thirties, she unconsciously checked her hair net with her hand and smoothed her rumpled scrubs. By habit, she secured the position of her medical-grade mask. Taking a breath, she entered the room.

Immediately the man jumped up, nervously pulling his mask into place. "Doctor, is she all right? It's been so long." He looked back and forth between his wife and the doctor. "So long."

Rebecca stayed a few steps back and crossed her arms as if to protect herself from their agony. "Mr. and Mrs. Martin, nothing has changed. We're watching Emily very closely and her blood work will tell us what we need."

"Is she still vomiting? I didn't know there was anything wrong. Emmy just said she had a stomach ache. That's all, a stomach ache. But when she just started vomiting and I gave her some... oh, what do you call it? The stuff the pediatrician recommended. But then she had diarrhea and we took her to Prompt Care and they sent us here..." The words tumbled from the mother's mouth. "...and... and...."

Rebecca wanted to touch the mother, to pat her arm, but instead asked, "From her symptoms, I just wonder if you remember anything new. Do you know what she ate, what pills she may have taken?"

The parents looked back and forth hurriedly. "We didn't find anything. I do have a prescription for iron pills but they're kept on the top shelf of the medicine cabinet," Mona said hesitating. "We've locked away all the aspirin since Emily started walking and climbing."

"This happens. Kids are very creative about getting

into things. We've started basic treatment and the tests will direct us. I need to get back." With a nod, the doctor left.

At the central station, Rebecca paused to look at Emily's chart. Next to her, Taylor, the floor nurse, was feeding information into a computer and humming. Taylor paused and motioned to the computer, asking, "Do you need this?"

"No, the data hasn't changed. I'm just waiting for the blood labs." Rebecca stretched and moved her arms and neck. With the onslaught of respiratory patients, there were still emergencies like children taking forbidden meds. The doctor looked with admiration at the nurse beside her, a friend as well as a co-worker. "Taylor, how do you do it? You look refreshed whenever we start a shift."

The older of the two, Taylor confided, "And you, Doctor, look positively beat!"

Rebecca grinned. "Thanks a lot!" she acknowledged. "These kids get to me, but there's always a surge of new patients, shift changes of personnel, and perpetually being tired." Rebecca blinked her eyes to better read the monitor. "Even at home, when I relax, I'm thinking and staying awake. I'll be glad when we get to move into the new hospital. There should be enough room for the electronics and the people."

Thoughts of Emily continued. "They brought the little girl in last night but even with the stomach pump and respirator there hasn't been much response. It's really serious. And they're such a young couple. It makes me feel helpless. I wonder if I've made the right choice for the case." She sighed. "But you, Taylor, you just keep going like you have a battery recharger."

Taylor laughed gently and returned to humming. Her

fingers moved over the touch screen. With a pause, she reached over to her little Daily Thought calendar near the monitor. She always took one day of wisdom at a time. Looking at the current date, she ripped off the note and handed it to Rebecca with a nod.

Taking the note, Rebecca recited, "'Things turn out for the best for those who make the best of the ways things turn out.' John Wooden." Quizzically, she looked at the page then folded it into her scrub pocket. Returning to the monitor, she asked, "How are the respiratory devices holding up?"

Taylor changed the screen to equipment inventory and gestured to it.

"Seriously," Rebecca spoke to Taylor while perusing the data. "How do you do it?"

"Do what?" Taylor asked. Both women kept their eyes on the technical lists on the monitor as they talked. It was difficult to tell doctor and nurse apart with their protective clothing.

"Keep so even-tempered and calm no matter how hectic it gets on the floor?" There was admiration in the question.

Taylor winked and replied, "With everything else in the world being so crazy, I rely on those old sayings and my own experience. Besides, you're the doctor! I just pass the stress on to you." Her eyes smiled warmly above her mask and she turned to answer a call light at one of the beds, humming gently.

Taylor stopped suddenly as a team poured into the ER. A flailing woman was fighting the paramedics all the way, struggling against the restraints keeping her on the gurney while vile and vulgar words were thrown at every encounter.

She was bleeding from a superficial head wound and partially bandaged, which did not hinder her struggles to get free. The team looked exasperated as the EMT handed Taylor the woman's chart.

"We were called to the bar on 18th where the patient was in a broken-bottle fight over some guy. We started treatment but hesitated to give her a sedative until you could figure out how much alcohol she's had," the medic explained as he wiped the patient's spit from his face. "She's all yours! The ID was all we could get."

He moved the gurney toward a curtained station but the woman's raucous screams echoed throughout the floor. Starting to escape, the team backed out of the ER as quickly as they could. "We've got another call; we'll retrieve the gurney in a few minutes!"

With the racket and cursing, Rebecca moved towards the patient but Taylor was there ahead of her, next to the drunken woman.

"That is enough!" the nurse commanded and the patient paused momentarily in surprise. For only a moment!

Glaring at the nurse, the cursing and comparisons to female dogs poured out of the woman's mouth: "She had my man and I'm not gonna let that slut touch my man's dick! You let me outta here, you masked paper doll!" She continued to strain against the straps, never pausing in her profanity, shaking the heavy gurney on its wheels.

Approaching the quivering gurney, Rebecca thought of the old ER adage: 'The more noise a patient makes, the less serious their ailment.'

That did it. Taylor put her hand out to stop Rebecca's advance, pulled herself up to her full 5'8" height, and growled the fiercest guttural sound of authority Rebecca had ever heard. Taylor's profanity even had Latin in it. Taylor had served as a Navy Hospital Corpsman in her youth and her experience came back.

The patient quieted. No one else had heard the low words Taylor had spoken to the raging woman but it was efficient. Taylor began the medical evaluation, checked the woman's vital signs, then handed the chart to Rebecca. She winked and said, "You're the doctor; I'm just handing the stress to you!"

With that, Taylor continued on to answer the call light. Everyone else on the floor had only seen the patient's reaction to the pointed words of the nurse: Shock. Hesitation. Attempt at renewed aggravation. Submission. Compliance. Sobbing. Whimpering.

As always, Rebecca was impressed.

The shift intensified when administrators sent a brief email stating the planned date of the Emergency transfer to its new wing at the modern hospital. Detailed instructions would follow on cessation of services to new patients who would go directly to the new ER. Transference of patients already in place would be phased depending on their medical status on that day. It would be a critical transfer of patients, staff, equipment and coordination with the new hospital. Administrators promised their 'utmost support.'

"Aha!" Taylor said as she read the email. "We're about to be tested on 'how things turn out!'"

Rebecca returned a number of times to speak with the parents of little Emily. At last, leaving the shift, she hated to disturb them because they had dozed off in sitting positions on the vinyl couch. Little chance of the ripped seam being repaired as the section move was imminent. Looking through the door window she thought of her own child, Matthew. She buffeted the door a bit to awaken but not startle them. Even in their state, they sprang to attention at her appearance.

"I'm just leaving for the night and wanted to let you know Emily is holding her own." There was momentary relief on the Martins' faces followed by instant concern. To answer their unspoken question, Rebecca hurriedly went on. "She's a very strong little girl. The labs proved she had ingested some iron pills and beginning the bicarbonate treatment when we did was the right thing to do. Now, we just have to wait to see if... *when...* her blood levels even out."

"Is she awake? Can I see her?"

Rebecca could see instant hope in Mrs. Martin's eyes as she was already moving toward the door. Rebecca put out her hand. "She isn't awake but one of you can sit with her and hold her hand through the night. Perhaps the other can take a break? The current protocols only allow for one parent. Masked and gloved, of course."

"But she's going to be all right, isn't she?" Mr. Martin asked cautiously.

It was the question Rebecca always dreaded. There was no absolute answer, no certainty.

"She's better. We're on the right treatment. The floor nurse will help one of you get settled for the night. I've left all instructions with the next shift and I'll be back tomorrow." Before they could question her further, she turned quickly and left the parents, left the room, left the ER wing, and left the hospital behind.

Letting herself in at home, Rebecca was drawn to the kitchen where the low lighting showed her husband fixing himself a late-night repast. She slid onto the stool at their counter.

"Hello, my dear," Christopher welcomed warmly. "Becky, you're late as usual and just in time for one of my Dagwood sandwiches. What's your preference?"

Rebecca had to smile at the overstuffed piles of bread, cheeses, and meats in his hands. She answered, "How you can eat all that and still go to bed is beyond me."

"It's *because* I eat all of this that I *can* sleep soundly. It's a gastrointestinal sedative! Just like my Dad used to make...." Seeing the fatigue on her face, he stopped joking and quietly started eating. "Rough day?"

"Like all the others, now." Her fingers toyed with a napkin. "Between the respiratory intakes, the hazmat suits we wear, the administrators tracking the changes to the new hospital, and the exhaustion of a rotating staff, we're just holding pieces together." At the sympathetic look on his face, she added, "Oh, yes, and once in a while there's an emergency that supersedes the others!"

Letting his wife vent, Christopher reached out to take her hand. "A child?" he asked, knowing his wife.

"Yes. Emily. A very little girl. She got into some iron pills and I don't know who I feel more sorry for—the child or her parents." Her stroking the napkin continued. She folded and unfolded it.

Laying down his meal, Christopher came around the counter to take Rebecca in his arms. He murmured words to soothe but didn't try to advise. She moved within the warmth and comfort of his body, and they just rocked gently. Coming home to Christopher was one of the comforts coaxing her through the day.

Leading her to a nearby loveseat, Christopher sat quietly holding her. As he felt her tension lesson, he broached a subject: "Honey, do you want to continue in the ER? I hate to see you this distressed. With all your education and experience, surely there's another medical field you could consider? Something else you might want to do?" He waited for a cryptic reply or objection but instead, she looked up at him with tears welling.

"I don't know, Chris. I just don't know anymore," she confessed. "Maybe now is a time to change specialties. I feel so worn out! I wonder if I should.... " her voice trailed off.

"Is it about Matthew?" he asked quietly, knowing the delicacy of his question.

"It is." She nodded and took a deep breath. "I go through the patients, making decisions which may affect their whole lives. It's what I do. But when a child like Emily comes to the ER, our Matthew always comes to mind." She had talked about this many times with Christopher always searching for the complete explanation. This night, she looked deep into his eyes and said, "I want to think about our son, Matthew, but I find our memories have a 'hole' in them. We share the images of his brief life, the people who touched him and were touched by him. He was part of me and there was nothing I could do to keep him safe!" Weeping in her husband's arms, Rebecca knew again a mother's loss of a desired child. A pregnancy unfulfilled. The hardest memory was leaving the obstetric ward without a baby in her arms. Returning home, Christopher had dismantled the nursery.

"He is safe, in our thoughts and in the care you give all

your patients. Your Emilys." Chris spoke lovingly. He knew these memories would be with them always.

Rebecca arrived to her late afternoon shift and found the staff already in preparation for the big transfer. The changes were unavoidable but first she looked for little Emily. Striding around the large medical room, she would pull back a curtain divider. One station after another, no Emily. New admits were filling a few spaces but Emily's bed was being stripped and sanitized. Momentary dread gripped her and she went to the central desk to interrogate the computer. The fear dissipated when the monitor showed: Discharged. Emily was being released.

Anticipating the decisions and treatments that would be demanded of her, Rebecca took short evening pause to go to the old Meditation Garden on the hospital roof. She wanted to say goodbye to the ten years she'd worked there. The garden was deserted of people. Natural rocks and benches sculpted by water and weather were arranged to encourage meditation. Like pillars of strength, the formations watched over the little town below whose lights were beginning to glow. Compared to the hectic medical wing, this was a twilight refuge. Her thoughts made her catch her breath in the stillness. Viewing the small town on the inlet, she could see ribbons of bright orange colors lying atop the Olympic Mountains. The sunset over the western mountains blazed with clarity and it was time for her to know the path ahead.

Rebecca's father had been a physician in the rural Midwest and Rebecca always knew she would be a doctor when she 'grew up.' In grade school, she assisted the arthritic child in her class. As independent as the student was, there were always tasks for a classmate wanting to help. Rebecca's attention made a difference to a disabled child. Her father's dinner discussions of helping people also solidified her decision. She'd had college, medical school, her internship and residency. Then she'd met and fallen in love with Christopher. His empathy and respect always supported her. They were lovers. They were a team. They were *doctors*. When Christopher was offered an important medical administrative position in the Pacific Northwest, they relocated. The ER became her specialty. *It's the way things turned out,* she thought, remembering the pithy saying from the calendar.

From her vantage point in the garden, Rebecca glimpsed Emily and her family departing with stuffed toys, animated gestures and laughter as they got into their car. They were going home. The *whap-whap* sound and change of air pressure announced an emergency chopper bringing another—maybe the last—patient to the old hospital. Soon the helipad would be totally unused, but a new and improved pad was awaiting a First Response just a short distance away.

"The way things turn out." Rebecca pulled the crumpled calendar page out of her pocket; she'd kept it through each PPE she wore. *Things happen,* she thought. *A very good reason to stay where I'm needed. Different building, different stresses, different patients but... every shift, I can save someone's life. That's the best way things turn out!*

Dr. Howard smiled and returned to work.

CHIAROSCURO
TIME FRAGMENT 2012 CE

The gapping maw of the sixty-five mile fissure split the Idaho landscape with only a memory of the dynamic magma flow that created it. Fifteen thousand years after the cataclysm meant it was studied by scientists, astronauts, geology students, hikers, and tourists. Stephanie Logan always shuddered when imagining the dynamics of the lava geology of the rift before her.

Stephanie was completing her survey of the Great Rift area for visuals on her upcoming student film. Cinematographers often filmed the craggy surface to depict inhospitable planets in space. The landscapes of the Craters of the Moon had been filmed many times in high-budget productions and documentaries. Her project was far simpler for her senior cinematography class at the University. She wanted to capture the strong contrasts of light and shadow, the natural chiaroscuro that dappled the lava fields.

Slim and athletic, Stephanie grew up hiking the mountains and ridges in her native state with her father and her brother, Jerry. It was automatically the choice of settings for her college film project. The *mise en scène* of the fractured lava field was majestic. Creatively, she proposed to view settings with new perspectives. Standing on this craggy ridge with an abandoned path before her was enticing. A heavy pipe fence and gate blocked the entrance to a lava cave.

"Steph," called Jerry from further back on the trail. "How far are you going to go?" Though siblings, the older brother's serious countenance was in contrast to Stephanie's easy smile. Both were agile with tan skin from years of being outdoors. Their family dog was running back and forth between the two. Coming up beside her, Jerry stretched and looked over the 'scape as he spoke. "We've covered a lot of possibilities today. Good thing we started at sunrise to avoid the afternoon heat. See anything just right?" He eyed the gate. "What's this?" Jerry surveyed the track disappearing into the barrier.

"It's another of those Bat Protection gates the Bureau of Land Management puts up to shield sensitive species."

"I've heard spelunkers talk about them at the trailheads, but this gate is really a massive construction. I didn't know they were that hefty." He looked up the steel pipes to where the gate was concreted into the cave opening.

"Maybe it's so formidable because it's on the edge of the National Monument. The Bureau of Land Management wants to allow some lesser caves to be reclaimed by nature without tourists disturbing them or their inhabitants," she said, still surveying the surrounding area. "Some of these caves are very fragile and dangerous."

Jerry read the sign behind the fencing. "This gate is only opened once a year to take a census of the bats." Jerry rubbed his hand around the latch. He spread his fingers to estimate the width between rails and held his hand up for his sister. "Bats?"

Stephanie looked at his extended hand and said, "Big enough. Bats can get through the bars."

"We've never done much spelunking. Were you wanting to film inside one of these caves?" Jerry asked, still inspecting the gate rails.

"No, I'd be an ancient has-been movie producer if I tried to get through the BLM bureaucracy asking for permission. I just want the flavor of this landscape as a backdrop." Stephanie nodded toward the unmarked, abandoned path. She aimed the camera and snapped a few shots. "This looks good." She held her camera lens finder to view different angles. "I'd like to check out some flows further along or above the ridge...."

"This is pretty rugged terrain. Why here?" Jerry quizzed. "The road where we drove in is a dirt disaster! We only got a little farther on our ATVs once we unloaded them from our trucks. All-Terrain Vehicles have their own limitations. Now, we've hiked to a dead end. Are we even in the Monument?"

"No, we're on the outside edge where the magma surged from the rift. It's a dramatic juxtaposition of flowing lava cooled on top of high range desert. Kind of like blobs of cookie dough on top of brown and gold sugar." Stephanie laughed at her own answer.

"Can you even get your actors and cameras up here?" he asked, always practical. "How much equipment can your crew carry and how far? Stephanie Logan Productions doesn't have a helicopter," he teased. "Can you get a hold of a drone?"

"That's why we're here today. I have to figure out the

logistics of the shoot as well as the visual possibilities for the upcoming semester," Stephanie explained. She'd only admit the difficulties of her project to herself, not her older brother. "And Jerry, it's been great hiking with you like we used to do! It was a beautiful day with my big brother. Thanks for all the help and coming along," she finished sincerely.

"Yeah, it was just like the old days when we hiked with Dad." Jerry sighed. There was a silent pause.

"Yes, I miss him too," Stephanie said quietly.

"He'd be so proud of you, Steph, the way you've kept to your dream. Mom always said you were the creative one in the family and now you're proving it. What's next after graduation? Producing? Directing?" Jerry looked directly at his younger sister.

Stephanie shrugged and shook her head. "Part of it depends on this film. I need to finish it in first quarter and start the festival circuit. The script is already getting some interest and we can start marketing the trailer. Creating is easy, marketing is hard!"

"Wow, my sister the producer!" Knowing his sister's determination, Jerry grinned, adjusted his pack and said, "You've got that gleam in your eye! Okay, I know you probably want more time here, staying until dark, but I have got to go. Remember what Dad said about caves in the dark, 'Always imagine there's a bear in there and stay out!'" They both laughed at the memory of their Dad who would have been described as a 'bear of a man.'

"Seriously," Jerry finished, "I've got to get back to town before noon. I'm meeting Denice in Twin Falls. I've got the trek down to the ATV's and the dirt road before I'm finally on the highway."

"You go ahead. I'll just be a few minutes," she urged her brother. "With the early start we got this morning, I'm almost finished. Somewhere along here are caves occasionally inhabited. Also, new cracks can open. I'm not really as interested in a cave as the view from its opening."

Petting the dog again, Jerry asked, "Are you taking Tucker? He likes your ATV better for riding back to your truck." Hearing his name, the dog wiggled closer to be petted. Jerry checked Tucker's protective paw boots and gave him a final pat. "Steph, you need to be on the road in an hour. Okay?"

"Yeah, okay," Steph said affectionately as the border collie wagged his tail at her foot. "Say hello to your fiancé for me." She didn't need to watch him leave; Stephanie heard Jerry whistling as he climbed down toward the valley floor. She patted Tucker and proceeded to carefully view the crumbly area in front of the gate. The jagged rocks colored of rust and basaltic lava edged the way, evidence of the uplifting force shattering them apart or flowing over them one hundred and fifty centuries ago.

Appreciating the clean desert air, Stephanie viewed the valley below for its panorama. She still wanted some 'super view' to highlight the scenery. She started to hike away from the bat cave and stepped carefully to get a view around a bulging outcropping blocking any further path. Tucker followed, sometimes finding an easier route. Once around the obstruction, her viewfinder was obscured by formations as she looked westerly where the sun would be in the correct sight line when her team actually filmed in the Fall. She saw dark shadows on the face of the escarpment. Using her camera's zoom, she thought the shadows were indentations to a darker space, a cave perhaps. A moment of excitement was followed by a warning. Stephanie knew she shouldn't explore it on her own. Looking back and down the hill towards the valley, she saw a plume of dust on the desert floor. It was Jerry heading back to town. It was too late to catch him for back up. By the sun's position, she still had hours of daylight. She began to wonder if a sunset would make a great image from the interior of a cave. She could scout it out this afternoon and postpone a full photo shoot. She would just do a quick check of the entrance of the cave to gauge the photo angles and decide whether it was worth returning. She could still get to her truck around noon.

Stephanie hiked over clinker debris but it was a farther distance to the shadow than anticipated. She finally climbed to the rocky area where the shadow had been evident. Up close she could see through the sagebrush covering a small opening. She pulled the brush aside with her gloved hands to expose the mouth of a cave. It was just a sliver of an opening and she wondered if inhabitants had ever used it. The angle suggested it might channel into the larger sealed cave on the other side of the outcropping. As she viewed the landscape, Stephanie calculated the position of the future sunset and angles of light. She really wanted to see if there was a great shot of a bright setting sun framed from inside the small cave. By habit, she checked her trail equipment: Hard hat, flashlight, phone, rope, and canteen of water. Her phone was in her pocket; her trail watch was on her gloved wrist, and her hiking backpack was secure.

Carefully, Stephanie laid her pack aside temporarily while she edged her way into the small entrance. "Come on, Tucker, it's all right," she coaxed the hesitant collie. "Come on, boy."

The confined, shady interior was a sharp contrast to the high desert expanse she'd left. Stephanie flashed her light to lay out the small cavern cubicle. It didn't show evidence of life; there was no bat guano collected at the entrance, no tracks, no animal scat. She snapped a basic set of pictures and angled photos to determine the range and optics. She needed to turn carefully to see out of the opening. Stephanie looked out through the entrance and pulled her pack in behind her. It was a very tight fit but, according to her brother, Stephanie had always been 'very stringy.' She lay on her belly to look towards the entrance. There was a sharp distinction between the views. She could visualize early cave dwellers looking out from this secure protection to the harshness of the desert outside. She could imagine quite a lot.

"Come on, Tucker!" Stephanie coaxed the dog again. He was wagging his tail and panting nervously. "Okay, boy, you wait here. I'm just going a bit further to see how much equipment I need to bring next time. Sit! Stay!"

Viewing the ceiling and basic path through her viewfinder, Stephanie began to edge head-first into the corridor. Her flashlight swept over the enclosure. The rawness of the rocks intrigued her. This was it! This was the location she needed to enhance her film project. Just a few more feet and she'd turn, exit, get Tucker, and follow Jerry home. As her light shifted, she saw an indentation farther on the wall. She wondered if it could be an engraving and started crawling towards it.

The rock beneath her rolled, crumbling as Stephanie fell forward. She tried to grab a handhold but the rocks above jolted down on her hand. She screamed as she slid to the floor and a full rockslide came down behind. Dust choked her; the entrance was sealed. Her helmet offered partial protection, but the concussion knocked her senseless. The rockslide stopped as quickly as it had started. She lay crumbled in the faint glow of her damaged flashlight.

Slowly, very slowly, Stephanie awoke to her situation. Her head ached and her vision was limited by dust and bleariness. She could only see a few feet of the small area close to her. The helmet light had been broken and the flashlight was partially buried. How long had she been unconscious? She tried to brush away some rocks to check her watch then cried out in pain! Inside her glove, her hand felt like a bloody pulp. Immediately, she reached inside her shirt for the handkerchief she carried on the trail. Whimpering, she wrapped the mashed fingers together still inside the glove. She could feel the bones moving and clicking. Blood oozed through the fabric. Her smashed watch was useless but she kept it strapped on to apply more pressure on her hand. She told herself not to faint.

With her good hand, she felt over her body to find other injuries. Bruises she could feel, though nothing seemed broken. With her hand throbbing, she willed herself to take a deep breath. Then another. She had to think this through. She tried to ignore the pain building in her hand.

Mixed-sized rocks and smaller stones had filled the crack next to an immoveable boulder of lava. The exit of the cave was blocked. She was injured but conscious. The entrapped area seemed to have enough air once the dust settled. It was musty yet breathable. Her canteen was dented but still held water. Her phone! Where was her phone? Stephanie felt in her pockets, shoved rocks aside, frantically wiped the dirt with her good hand. She knew she was in shock from her injuries but the loss of her phone caused panic. She had to find her phone while the flashlight grew dimmer and dimmer. Grasping the light, she tapped it against her leg trying to get the batteries to brighten. Momentary brightness… then… it went out.

Stephanie was in the blackest of black. Her eyes and brain struggled to detect any light. There was none. Open eyes could see nothing, as if the interior of the cave had been sprayed with Vantablack. No surface could reflect what simply wasn't there—light. The experience of blackness overwhelmed her pain, her mind, and her awareness of her situation. Totally disoriented, she was not capable of judging her place in space, up or down, close or far, sitting or standing. The black stole all her references. Whether from shock or conscious thought, a memory of terror caused her heart to pound in her chest.

On a family hike, years before, Jerry and Steph's dad had moved ahead on a rocky trail. Stephie, as a little girl, was trying desperately to keep up. She couldn't see them and didn't know they could see her from above and were watching over her. She thought she was lost! She hurried more than ever, slipped, and plummeted into a dark crevice. For a second, Stephanie spiraled into blackness and landed on a ledge with her wind knocked out. Panic paralyzed her. She couldn't move. She couldn't breathe. She couldn't cry out!

Just as suddenly, her dad's face appeared above her, smiling. He was reaching out, grabbing her hands, and pulling her into the safety of his arms. He held her, rocking gently, and making soothing sounds. It was just an accident, yet it came back to her now. She tried to calm down and commanded herself to think. She needed to appraise the situation and think before acting. Her eyes looked and looked, but she could not see!

Fear returned when she heard a scratching sound and remembered her Dad's warning of bears. She could see nothing, only heard movement towards her crouched position. She tensed and tried to be quiet. Still, she could see nothing. More movement close to her, a brush of fur, and a wet nose rubbed her leg. She couldn't see but felt the coldness touching her. It stroked up and down her torn pants.

"Oh Tucker, good boy! I am so glad to see... *feel* you!" She'd been so intent on her project, she hadn't noticed him following her into the cave. Even in the darkness, she could feel her own tears as Tucker's tail brushed her pained body. Stephanie allowed herself to cry as she hugged her companion to her. Almost paralyzed, she clutched the dog and the two of them trembled.

Sitting in the dark, holding her dog, thoughts were rampant. Stephanie berated herself for going into the cave without backup. She applauded herself for surviving a rockslide. She comforted herself that someone would find her. Once she was overdue, Jerry would come back to save her. Jerry always found her but how? How long was she unconscious? It could have been a few minutes or most of the day—or even longer. She was in an unmarked cavern, away from the path, maybe approaching sunset or later. Jerry had to find a way!

Starting to shove some stones with her feet, Steph held her injured hand to her chest. She felt the rocks next to her and in moving them away, the screen light of her damaged phone lit up. It was almost blinding in the cavern. Propping the phone, her gloved good hand tried to call out, to tap 911, to text her brother. There was no signal. None. There would be no rescue from her cell, only a bit of illumination.

Stephanie was almost giddy as she cradled the treasured light with her good hand and aimed it at her confined space. She took her bearings to see the floor area leading through the rockslide and back to the entrance. She thought, *It can't be too far to the other side.*

In the phone's glow, she grabbed a larger pointed rock and aimed it directly towards the way out. Feeling its surface she made a note of its direction. She was still scooting around on her knees. She felt faint at the vision of her injured hand, even in the pale light. The crumpled strap of her hiking bag was near her foot and she dragged it raggedly in the dust to her. Going through it, she was relieved to find items she had never used. She had never needed them so desperately. Now she knew why the survival bag was always demanded by her father: Pliers, compass, waterproof matches, folding knife, twine, ten feet of rope, small hatchet, energy bars, and electrical tape.

Wrapping her hand more tightly with the tape, the pressure stopped the bleeding. Stephanie looked at the clinkers of lava barring her exit. Could she even hope to dig her way out? The pain shooting up her arm answered the question. She would wait. Perhaps her phone could be tracked by a search party. She smoothed the area, re-packed her bag, and felt more positive when she checked her dusty camera to find it was still intact in spite of the broken viewfinder. The screen shots on the chip were not lost. She had been holding it close when the rockfall happened. Taking only a sip of water, she cupped her hand for Tucker to lick. Steph opened the wrapper on an energy bar. The nuts were sour and she made a mental note to replace the edibles in her pack. Her breathing had quieted and she could no longer feel her heart thumping in her chest. She would be all right! This scenario might even make it into her movie. The thought of the movie was a welcome distraction to staring at the formidable rock pile holding her captive.

The calmness brought with it a need to sleep. Stephanie was exhausted from a day of hiking, the headache, and the stress of the cave. She decided to just rest a few minutes. She moved a few rocks from under her hips and checked her hand. The less she moved it, the less new blood showed on the taped glove. With a little rest, she'd be ready to get out of the cave when help came. *That's a good idea... just a short nap.*

Feeling herself drifting, she called to Tucker, "Come here, boy, it's okay."

The collie squeezed between her and the rocks and whined. He licked her face and whined even more. He was so agitated, his body pressure caused her to ache in sore spots she had ignored. More whining. More licking. She couldn't stop the dog in his nervousness. All she wanted was to sleep for just a few minutes....

A glimmer wavered on the cracked phone screen. The battery on the phone flickered a brief warning. Stephanie focused and shook the broken cell phone. It flared, then it too died. Stephanie blinked. She closed her eyes. She opened them wide. It was to no avail. Stephanie was again surrounded by the powerful blackness of an abandoned cave on a deserted trail. How long before she would be missed? Could she hold out? Could she stay awake?

Controlling the desire to hyperventilate, Steph closed

her eyes again. She would not 'look' at the blackness. She'd pretend she was a child again, playing in the dark with Jerry and the neighborhood kids on a summer evening. They would play Hide and Seek; that's all she was doing now. Except, she couldn't be sure anyone was seeking her.

Thoughts vied for attention: *What I can't see can't hurt me. No, that wasn't right! I'm hurting plenty.* New thought: *I'm a grown woman, soon a college graduate, and a person of experience. I made a safety mistake in entering the cave; I let a project distract me. Mistakes can be corrected. How? My Dad can't save me; Jerry is gone back to town. I wouldn't want them to know I was blubbering here, anyway. The phone is dead.*

A new thought made its way in the dark: *How can Jerry or anyone find me? It may be hours before he knows I haven't followed him. Searching the desert cliffs in the night would be a dangerous search. Most terrible of all, I went in a different direction and the hidden cave won't be visible in the dark. If I weren't so sleepy, I could probably figure a way out. So sleepy.... I wish Tucker would stop licking me so I could sleep....."*

Shoving Tucker's muzzle away, the agonizing pain in her arm and shoulder startled Stephanie awake with yet another thought: *'That which does not kill you, makes you strong.' That's what Dad would have said. No daughter of his would curl up and sleep to death in a rockslide coffin! Okay, okay, okay, Dad, stay with me. We're going to make it! I'm going to get strong! I'm going to stop waiting for someone else to save me from my own mistake.*

Inside her closed eyes, Stephanie pictured her last visual image just before the screen's demise. In her mind's eye, center stage was filled with the rocks causing the dark.

The angled rock she had placed confirmed the slim exit at stage right. If she could squeeze through, the short channel could take her to the cliff edge. Scooting slowly, Stephanie inched to the clogged aperture. She bent forward and adjusted her hips to support her reach forward. Painfully, she held her injured hand to her chest with her bag tightened across it, the strap holding the arm in place. Waves of nausea swept over her, and she paused, still breathing slowly. "Come on, Tucker. Let's go, boy." The dog didn't actually answer; his body movements and brushes of his tail assured her he was following.

At the slide, she moved her good hand around the opening as she remembered it. The large lava bulge dominated her touch until smaller, loose rocks started to tumble aside. She felt a trickle of fresh air. Supporting herself with her legs, she used her hand to feel the smaller stones and gently move them behind her. They had filled in the crack between the lava and the cavern wall. One by one, cracked or rounded stones were grabbed and slid behind her. If she moved too quickly, the stones would fall again. She couldn't know in the darkness if an even larger avalanche could be triggered.

Finally, her reaching hand felt a space cleared into blackness beyond. A quick opening of her eyes gave no purchase to light. Stephanie quickly shut her eyes again. By keeping her eyes closed, she had control. She was able to concentrate on her other senses instead of being overwhelmed by the blackness.

The cave fracture was her way into this problem and was now the way out of it. Stephanie judged her limitations and deliberately inched her way into the small fissure. Once fully in the crevasse, panic returned. She didn't remember it being so tight when she entered. *Stop it, Steph! You weren't thinking about size when you entered, you were thinking of camera angles!*

With her working hand, she felt the space ahead, even opening her eyes for a moment to see if she could see. She couldn't. Wedged in the crack, inch by inch, she would reach forward for direction, shove her weight with her foot, and grimace at the pain that stopped her. Totally immobilized, even her good hand was suffering the roughness of the rocks through her glove. There was no certainty of time. Had she been so restrained for minutes... or hours... or days?

Okay, Dad, now what? she asked in her head. *I'm stuck! I can't move! I can't go any further! I can't!*

As if he answered, she heard the words in her mind: *It's your script, Stephie. How are you going to end it?*

All at once, there was no more wavering. Her thought was clear: *Camera. Action. Breathe! Inhale! Relax! Inhale and exhale totally. Move one inch. Repeat. Move another inch... another... another.*

"Damn it! I'm getting outta here!" Stephanie's loud yell echoed down the fissure. Shove. Shove. Wiggle. Scream! Shove! Pull! Scream! With the agony of her crippled hand and arm she clenched her teeth between shrieks.

A brief faint then recovery and Stephanie felt a release of pressure on her aching body. She reached again and moved more easily for a very slight distance. She opened her eyes and a tiny slice of light bent around the largest rock as her reward. It was there! It was a dim glow, pale orange and it was the most spectacular light she had ever seen! All she had to do was pull her battered body to the exit. Dizzy with relief, she moved forward, slowly and painfully to the welcome exit. With more space, Tucker crawled beside her as they approached the light fading towards the end of the day through the entrance.

Stephanie pulled herself to the framed view of the valley beyond. True to her script, the sun was setting on the cyclorama of the western sky. Her throat tightened at the beauty and salvation of the scene—a desert entering twilight. She had been in the dark for six or seven hours and felt it was a few minutes of eternity.

Tucker squirmed past her, broke through the sagebrush, and started to race back and forth in front of the cave, barking and barking. Painfully, Stephanie followed Tucker and tumbled out of the cave mouth. She dragged her canteen behind and gave them both some water.

Breathing the clean air with relief, she sat up and was able to see across the desert to where dust curls on the road and ATV vehicles with headlights were racing towards the foot of the rift. "Oh, Tucker, I knew he'd come back for us!"

Inching towards the precipice, she realized she would be hard to see. Twilight was fading and she was too dizzy to hike to them. Like an old-fashioned movie, she knew what to try. "Tucker! Tucker boy! Go get Jerry! Go get Jerry!" She pointed toward the ATV's. "Go get Jerry!"

Tucker stopped his pacing. He looked at Stephanie. He looked at her hand. He looked where she was pointing. He paced again. His tail whipped back and forth.

"Go Tucker! Go get Jerry!" Stephanie pointed and pointed as the vehicles neared.

With a shuffle and turn, Tucker began sprinting down the incline towards Jerry. The border collie was reuniting his flock!

With tear tracks on her muddy face, a bloodied hand, and still coughing from the dust, Stephanie could still imagine: *That's a wrap!*

CHARANDOS
TIME FRAGMENT 24TH CENTURY CE

Memories may strengthen or fade, or even be taken away from you. They only flitter like butterflies tempting to be caught. I can't tell you my first name or how I came to be a member of the Midwhere Agricultural Colony. I knew the season from the blossoms and temperature, but not what year. Seasons display themselves; years are just numbers. From my body's reflection in the mirror, I know I am an amalgam of both sexes. My uniale genome was designed to blend the best of sexual attributes. I know the genders that came before us, but not where they have gone. I know my uniale personhood is identified by the indentation above the navel, the nebid. The 'why' of the navel or nebid was another butterfly lost to memory.

Because names are human, please call me Alyx. I am the Recorder for our diminutive colony of Midwhere because my ability with words and tabulations was not erased. I assist the Farmer Nance in whatever manner nhe requires. When or why I was sent here, I came with mental acuity for logistics. The other butterflies of my memory are too fragile to catch and hold.

The Farmer is the overseer guiding the lives of the uniale workers. Farmer Nance cares for our welfare and was in charge of crop production for the Keeper Confederation—when it was still viable. When the Confederation cyber grid collapsed, Midwhere became isolated from all former colonies. Farmer Nance remained our leader after the colonial connections deteriorated. We have our food production. We have our total village. We uniales have Farmer Nance. As nes assistant and bookkeeper I am part of the community.

I wish I could remember how our pronouns came to be; that is another butterfly in my mind. Attempting to read archive ledgers of crops, I discovered mentions of male persons and female persons, and immature persons called 'children.' They used all kinds of pronouns for their personhood like 'he/him/his' or 'she/her/hers.' There are none of those persons here. Our uniale references are easy to mark in the inventory columns as Nhe-Nem-Nes. *Nhe gave the weeding hoe to nem and the uniale gardener knew it was now nes.* Because we are all uniales in Midwhere; we are compatible with each other.

Our little valley enjoys sunshine for the crops to grow: Grains, rice, grape vines, summer and winter vegetables, herbs. Unfortunately, the weeds grow as well. Working an extra garden shift in the warmth of early summer, I watched a group of strange people come into our village. One person rode high on a hairy beast a midst a gathering of smaller people all walking. Another hairy beast pulled a cart stacked with assorted implements: Bedding, barrels, and wood. They were ragged and weary wanderers with long hair hanging from their heads and some with hair upon their faces. It was very apparent they were not uniales like us. Two of our workers were frightened and ran towards the dormitory

Quonset huts. Their bandannas flew from their bald uniale heads, sweaty from work. I immediately hurried to tell Farmer Nance, not slowing to avoid rows of vegetables and jumping over them.

"Farmer Nance! Farmer Nance!" I rushed through nes villa. I found nem in the office writing on some documents. Nes face showed surprise at my cry.

"What is it, Alyx? Slow down!" Nhe gestured for me to be quiet.

"They're strangers! They are in the west garden plot. A bunch of them! They are not like any uniales I've ever seen!" I couldn't contain my excitement.

"Who?" Farmer was incredulous.

"People! Hairy, ragged people and one on a hairy beast!" I tried to catch my breath.

Our Farmer stood up quickly, dropping the papers. Nes hands clenched the side of nes trousers. Nhe was almost trembling with anger or joy, I could not tell which.

Farmer Nance motioned for me to go out and nhe followed close behind. Quickly we arrived at the garden well where the mixture of strangers was collected. The large person got down from the beast and wiped an arm across a hairy mouth.

"Hello, stranger," Farmer Nance greeted. "Please have some water," nhe said it as if it were a first invitation. Nhe tried to make a sign of welcome but uniales rarely used them. We all knew each other. A movement of head and partial extension of nes hand looked more awkward than nes words.

"Planned on it," the stranger replied while taking the gourd hung on the well and splashing water from the filled bucket. Water splayed as it was thrown over the head of the hulking person who shook without concerns. When the bucket was empty, the hairy person clicked fingers and one of the smaller people rushed to drop it back into the well and rotate the crank to bring it up filled. All of smaller people hunkered about until the hairy one was finished being refreshed. Only then did they provide water for themselves, raising and lowering the well bucket.

"Where in hell are we?" the wet stranger asked gruffly looking about our farm. The loud voice sounded angry. I could not tell the facial expression because of the hair. Perhaps there was more hair beneath the clothing.

"You are in Midwhere Agriculture Colony... not hell," Farmer Nance explained; nes hands were opening and closing with tension as if not sure what to do. "Please refresh yourself at our well before you move on." There was added emphasis on 'move on.' It was an instruction, not an invitation.

"Oh, we'll move on when I say so!" The stranger looked directly at Farmer Nance and glared until Farmer nervously broke away from the stare.

"Alyx, look to these... people. I will be in my office." Farmer turned and retreated to nes villa, leaving me with the situation.

There was much chatter and milling about as the people scattered themselves and took possession of the well and the shade trees surrounding it. These strangers spoke our language with a lilt so I gathered information by listening instead of asking direct questions. The large hairy brute was a 'male' named Dux. A few people were also males but 'he' was the leader. The other people were 'females' and referred to each other as 'she' or 'her.' There were male and female smaller ones as well. My thoughts tried to sort out who was a 'he' and who was a 'she' so I could report to Farmer. By discerning their body language, how they treated or deferred to each other, and their hairiness, I soon had an accounting. There were no uniales to be seen among them although a few could be disguised in the filthy rags and hats of clothing; I couldn't tell.

One male, called Ethan, quickly caught my attention. He was definitely male because *his* size and hairiness equaled Dux. Instead of moving about the leader, he stayed among the others, even the children. He splashed water at them, and *his* laugh was hearty when he picked a small one to throw in the air and then caught the giggling child. Watching and listening to the travelers at the well, I soon understood the strange pronouns which separated them. I would ask Farmer about these strangers and I would remember Ethan.

Fortunately, we at Mid Agra are self-sufficient, yes. We are orderly with Farmer Nance's guidance, yes. We are all uniales, yes. It's not surprising that I lacked the words to describe my feelings toward the misfits who altered our community. I was confused, anxious, and apprehensive of what was to come.

I became derelict in my recording duties; I was overwhelmed by the chaos brought to our compound. Our agricultural collection of uniales was disrupted by the strangers who intruded. Dux ignored Farmer Nance's appeals and physically took possession of the villa. His minions cleaned themselves in the garden baths, leaving debris for uniales to clean. Many of our uniales came to Mid Agra with even less memory than I did. They were workers, that was all expected of them. The

Hirsutes called them 'drones,' ordered them about and gave them servitude duties. Field work was sustained as the growing season continued.

"Ethan, can I ask you a question?" I caught him apart from the other adults with a group of children on the patio. I believe they were 'playing.' I had heard the word and it sounded like another of my butterfly memories.

"Yes, of course, Alyx." His deep voice sounded especially pleasant when he said my name. His eyes never strayed from the child throwing a ball to him.

"What are your people doing here? When will you leave?"

Ethan grinned. His smile was obvious in the facial growth matching the deep rust color of his hair. "That's two questions." He tossed the ball to a child and sat down on a bench, gesturing for me to follow.

I sat close to him to hear his answers. There was a scent about him, distinct from the uniales working in the fields. I don't have a word for it; it was intriguing.

"I don't know how long we'll stay. Until the Dux gets restless and wants to leave. Maybe he won't." He shook his head and shrugged. "He seems pretty comfortable here with plenty of food and people to control." He stood up and took a few steps as if uneasy with his answers. He gripped his hands together.

"Are all males like him? He's so gruff with all his people, he shoves them, he ridicules them." My questions were taking advantage of this time to talk.

"Ridicules? How do you know that word?" His look was quizzical.

Emboldened, I ventured further. "His words make persons feel bad. I have seen him take uniales to his rooms! When I see them again, they won't speak of what happened there. Once... once... I saw such a uniale with bruises. Nhe said it happened with some farm equipment."

Ethan wiped his face and paused before answering. "Your people must wonder at ours. I don't know how you all got assembled here but it's not like this in the rest of the world. When the Confederation disintegrated, all hell broke loose."

There was the reference to hell again.

Ethan continued: "Dux was strong enough to challenge anyone and he did. He collected people and he also saved my children when I couldn't." Ethan gazed towards three children playing together and his expression softened. Looking directly at me, he finished. "We've been with him since."

"'My children?' What does that mean? Um... uh... people cannot possess children!" I exclaimed.

He laughed at my confusion and said, "Oh, yes we do! And most of the fun is in making them!" He laughed even harder. "See those three children together, they're *my* children: Etta, Dylan, and Grason."

I quickly mumbled a reason to leave. I wanted to talk to Farmer Nance about what I had learned. Then, I realized talking to Farmer would only add to my uncertainty. Since the Dux took the villa, Farmer was difficult to find, as if hiding. If I did locate the Farmer, nhe would simply dismiss me. The uniales just continued by their habits, or their work dwindled away. The crops reaching summer peaks were haphazardly tended. Dux's people (as I thought of them) did few labors but infiltrated themselves to activities of rest or pleasure.

More and more I found myself being drawn to the patio. Ethan was often there and looked different. His wild hairy face had been trimmed into a clean, neat... beard. His clothes had been washed, probably by uniales, and the children were also kempt. Often, one female, Naomi, would be there. She had long flowing hair that curled or flew about with the slightest breeze. With her was the tiniest human I had ever seen. She would hold the tiny human (called a baby) to her bared breasts to suckle. I once asked her why she did that and if it hurt?

"Oh, it hurts if the baby *doesn't* nurse!" She laughed and touched the baby's cheek. She rocked herself gently on the patio bench. "I do it because it feeds the baby and is comforting to us both."

"Do you possess the child?" I asked with reticence, wondering if she would laugh at me.

"She's my baby, if that's what you mean." Naomi's fingers delicately fondled the baby.

"Where did you get... her? We don't have babies here in Midwhere." I used the pronoun for females, just as Naomi did.

"I gave birth to her. Don't you understand?" Naomi looked at me strangely.

"Birth?"

Moving the baby to her other breast, she chuckled. "Oh, Alyx, uniales have all the equipment, but we females use ours." She spoke openly: "Males and females get together, their bodies as close as humans can be, and a baby grows inside the female. When ready, the baby will pass out of her body in birth. I'm not going to explain the details to you; just know it's been going on as long as there have been humans and you uniales need to catch up!" She shook her head and laughed again as she continued her attention to the infant.

I don't know why it gave me an inexplicable feeling just to see her with the baby. Her breasts were swollen while mine were no more than smooth curves on my chest. We had no uniale infants or children at Midwhere. We had all been sent here as adults from other colonies. None of us remembered being children or seeing children. *Seeing children? Was that another butterfly I should catch?*

As the little one finished suckling, she turned away from the breast. Naomi held the baby over her shoulder and patted her back. The woman even cooed a bit when the baby burped.

I hesitated; my request would seem as strange to her as to myself. "May I hold the baby?"

"Yes, of course," Naomi answered, carefully placing the child in my arms.

"Are all babies female?" I asked as the baby gave a wide yawn.

"Our babies can be female or male. Of course, we don't have uniales! Isn't that what you uniales have? Boys or girls for us, that's it! Her name is Aura." She looked puzzled and asked me, "Where do your uniale babies come from? I mean, originally? There have to be babies to grow into adult uniales!"

"I don't know; I don't remember." I awkwardly tried to rock the baby as I saw her do. The little body in my grasp started moving arms and legs and made distressing sounds. I rocked even faster, and faster. Naomi became uneasy, stood and protectively took the infant back into her arms.

Immediately, the baby's gyrations stopped and the child quieted.

"It's okay, Mother has you," she said, and I had another name for my list of humans, 'mother.'

I cannot tell when or how my feelings evolved for Ethan. I would see him about the farm helping with the crops, settling disputes between the more volatile males and females, being of assistance wherever it was needed. He attached the hairy beast called a horse to our farm wagon. It was much stronger than pulling the wagon by hand. It could carry implements or even workers to the field. When we would talk, I could ask questions without feeling too foolish. At times, he would calm Dux who had fits of anger and even violence. Uniales avoided the Dux while his own humans seemed to be his possessions. Farmer Nance was more of a memory than an active member of the compound now. There was no mention of the Hirsutes ever leaving.

In the summer doldrums, I needed to go to the office for some information. As I approached the villa, I was surprised to be following Farmer Nance going the same direction. Nhe waddled quickly, almost furtively, to the office door, and pausing to look over the interior, he entered. In a moment I heard a blast of angry words and the sounds of something being thrown about. I didn't understand the words but their rage was evident. As I ran to see what was happening, Nance's body crashed against the doorjamb. A few seconds later it was yanked away and thrown against a chair, splintering with cracking sounds.

"You disgusting, spineless lump of shit, sneaking in here to spy on me! I'll beat you to death if you ever come here again!" Dux's epithets were terrifying!

I started backing away when Nance was shoved through the doorway to the tile floor porch. Nes face was bleeding, clothing torn, and nhe cried and whimpered. I wanted to help nem yet was fearful of the wrath inside the door. I was paralyzed. Farmer Nance ignored my feeble gestures and attempted to rise only to fall again. With a cry of pain, nhe pulled up and began limping away, holding the wall for support. I still followed the injured Farmer who was the only leader I could remember. When we passed other uniales, they looked away, as fearful as I. Farmer Nance entered the storehouse and I watched as nhe collapsed yet again on a bale of straw. Nhe saw me and gestured. I could see his eyes swollen and turning color.

"Alyx... help me... help," nhe pleaded.

"What? What can I do? I'm afraid I'll hurt you more by touching you." The fear was altered by feelings of confusion, of what to do, and shock at the violence I had witnessed. I trembled even as I supported Nance and led him to a corner alcove.

"Here," nhe gestured weakly to move a storage bin. I did so and beneath it was a door into the floor. "Make sure he isn't following. Then open this door, help me down."

I lifted the door and clumsily assisted nem, watching over my shoulder, trembling at our actions, as we descended a strong ladder. At the bottom, Nance gestured to a lantern to be lit and the cellar opened with light; it was a storage room of oak barrels and strong aroma of fermentation. Against one wall, a cot indicated where the Farmer had been living since his eviction from the villa.

"Farmer Nance, what is this? Why is it here?" I asked

in astonishment.

"Before the Confederation collapsed, this was a special Reserve for selected colonies. The grape vines in the far field produced wine." Nhe coughed and took deep breaths. "Now, it's my secret place."

"Not secret anymore!" A booming voice echoed over the cellar walls. "Whoa! What a hiding place! You've been holding out on me, farmer." Dux had followed us after all and now stood at the foot of the ladder. In awe of the treasure, he laughed and passed the crumpled Nance.

Almost casually, Dux punched Nance once more, saying to me, "You, uni, go get something to open a barrel. I feel like something to drink after today's workout." He walked about the storage. "Hurry up if you don't want the same drilling your farmer got!"

I scrambled up the ladder and tried to breathe. I was appalled at the cruelty, ashamed of my own inaction, and totally sick to my stomach. I became even more mortified when I actually brought implements to open the barrels and mugs. I just didn't know what else to do. The butterfly memories had no directives for me. Leaving the utensils behind, I hurried to leave the whimpering uniale. "Let me bring some water for Farmer Nance and some bandages...." I began to say... then stopped. Dux's glare drove me to escape while I could.

The end of summer always changed the patterns of work. With the Hirsutes' presence, the total seasons of Midwhere Agriculture were disrupted. There were still quiet times, raising my hopes that uniales, males, and females could co-exist. Then a major fight would break, sometimes between males, sometimes even between females. One night after a particularly rich night of drinking the Reserve, there were terrible confrontations: Males beating males, males and females attacking each other, and females assaulting other females. That night, even a few uniales wanted to fight each other.

Feeling the anger in myself, I left the compound to go to an outcropping in the field. My head pounded as I strode to escape the sounds coming through the night. The boulders gleamed in the moonlight as the surrounding crops matured in the evening warmth. A figure had sought this isolation before me and I recognized Ethan sitting alone, pensive. At first, I hesitated to disturb him, but I was so unsettled, I needed to talk to a friend.

Moving to sit beside him, he looked very different tonight. *Oh, it is the beard... or lack of it.* He had shaved and his smooth face reflected the evening light. We sat for a time, not speaking. I tried to quiet the turmoil I was feeling to match his silence.

"It's getting rough over there, isn't it?" Ethan nodded over his shoulder toward the compound.

"I've never seen anything like it. Our quiet people just got along; we had everything we wanted then...."

"We came into your lives?"

"Yes. You burst into our lives!" My tone was as harsh as my headache.

Even sitting, Ethan was taller than I. He ignored my tone and asked, "Do you have any idea of what happened to all the colonies after the Confederation collapsed?" He looked down at me.

"No, I have no memories of the Confederation. The

crop ledgers didn't help. It was as if I came here to Midwhere new, almost like Naomi's baby," I answered. The thought of the sweet smell of the baby stirred more emotion into the feelings of the night.

Ethan began to talk, almost to himself: "After the pandemic of the 21st century, and the development of uniales, the First Confederation of Colonies was founded. They were united under a Quantum Computer for decades but totally isolated by quarantines to avoid the pandemic ever coming again. It was considered a century of Shangri-La, Paradise, or Perfection. The Quantum Computer, Keeper, controlled everything and everyone lived by its directions. Finally, the computer system was broken by human interference and tsunami flooding. Since then, it has been colonies on their own... like Midwhere. Didn't you know any of that?"

"Broken? Human interference? What do you mean?"

"Reboot... reformat... wipe program."

"Like my memories before—if there was a before—I came here," I said thoughtfully.

His eyes dark and directly looking into mine, Ethan said very gently, "Oh, Alyx, there was a 'before.' I hope someday, you remember yours."

Again, a strange feeling came over me with his face so visible in the moonlight... so close to mine. To ease my discomfort, I moved slightly and asked, "What about you? What was your 'before?'"

"I had my work and my family unit: A wifand, a wife, and the children you've met."

"A unit? A wife and wifand? I don't understand."

Ethan shook his head. "You really don't remember, do you? In the 'Perfection' years, a family unit was a husband, wife, and uniale wifand. Children were raised apart. When the Confederation collapsed, so did the units. I tried to keep my unit together. The times and prejudices tore us apart. All the sexes seemed to be against each other."

"You still have the children."

My remark brought a sadness to his voice. "Just barely. I was away helping some neighbors when renegades attacked my home. They were from another colony and Dux was there to stop them. He saved my children and I have been beholden to him ever since."

"Your wife? Your... wifand?"

"He couldn't save them all.... Watching them and others be killed has changed him into the predator he is today." Ethan paused as if trying to convince himself. "He... protects his own."

"You sound like you respect him!"

"I tolerate him." Ethan's voice sounded strained.

"I can't! I can't tolerate or accept or anything! I am torn by feeling helpless!" I remembered Farmer Nance's beating and my anger returned. The thought was too vivid to ever forget. "I hate Dux! I hate what your people have done to Midwhere, and I hate you for being a part of it!" I turned and began to beat Ethan's chest with resentment. All of my wrath exploded.

Ethan stood and pulled me to him, pinning my arms to contain my fury. His strength increased my rage and the more I resisted, the tighter he held me. I could feel his heart pounding; his heart felt ragged so near to mine.

In an instant, I ceased struggling. In that moment there were new emotions even butterflies of memory could not trace. He bent to me and pressed his lips to mine, fiercely then gently. I pressed back as his arms changed from binding to caressing. The universal feeling of desire held us for an agonizing moment.

Shocked by own sensations, I pulled away and ran back to the compound. The drunken revelry was preferable to the turmoil inside me.

Summer changed to autumn according to nature's timetable, not Midwhere's. Certainly not to Dux's. He was often in a stupor. His angry episodes receded or perhaps people knew how to avoid irritating him. I bristled whenever he was near, especially if I was seeing to Farmer Nance in the cellar. I took Farmer's directions and forwarded them to the workers caring for the crops. That system seemed to satisfy Dux who was clear minded enough to recognize the value of a good harvest. Farmer Nance preferred the solitude of the cellar. When nes injuries healed, it was still painful for Nance to climb the ladder and I don't think nhe wanted to face the other uniales.

I went down the cellar ladder one morning with fresh vegetables and Nance seemed willing for conversation. I began with the question, "Farmer Nance?" I used nes title although I no longer respected it. "Farmer Nance, how did I come to Midwhere Agriculture Colony? Why don't I remember?"

Farmer Nance paused eating and looked at me as if deciding what to answer. "Alyx, that was a time ago; things are different now. Does it matter?"

"It does to me! I keep trying to understand the happenings around us. With uniales, males, females, Confederation, colonies—so many confusions. Children! Why are there children? What should I record in my mind if not in the ledgers? Nance, tell me." Whether it was the longing in my voice or using nes name instead of title, the uniale started to talk.

"You are like all of us. We uniales were sent to Mid Agri because we didn't fit the algorithm of the computer's master program: The Keeper. You see, human genomes can be unpredictable at best and detrimental at worst. Whatever your personal transgression or disability or variance, Keeper ordered you reformatted by a special procedure—a memory deletion if you will. The disabled, the oddballs, the rebels were programmed as drones. Then you were transferred here to work, to grow food unhindered by previous concerns. Somebody has to do the dirty work!"

"The Keeper? A Quantum computer ruling the colonies? I can't believe it." Although that was exactly what Naomi had told me. The doubt in my voice urged nem to go on.

"Then don't! It's all over now. Events don't wait on uniale beliefs. Quantum computers can terminate or go to other dimensions. Colonies coalesce or dissolve. You can remember or not." Nhe turned away and dismissed me with a wave of nes hand. "I really don't care anymore."

"But I do!" I exclaimed. "I do...." There was no response from the uniale who preferred to be alone and curled onto the cot with nes back to me.

My frustrations persisted. I continued guiding workers as I could but I found my feelings kept taking me back to the villa patio whenever the children were there. It was as if I could not resist their attraction. Naomi gladly let me give attention to baby Aura. It was amazing to watch the little human change and grow daily. I was exhilarated the day the baby looked me directly in my face and smiled. It was a smile for me—just me—not a burp. Could this strange yearning be part of my blank memories?

It was a bonus of emotions if Ethan was there. How could I feel yearning to be with a tiny baby and a large male at the same time? Something inside me wanted both.

Harvest demands its own schedule, and every person in Midwhere was tied to its time. Ethan was in the fields working with everyone else. Men and women joined uniales because of the importance of getting food stored before winter. Many of them had been farmers in their previous colonies and were eager to resume such contact with prosperous and varied crops. Tables were set before the villa wall where sorters could cool, clean, and pack the gleanings from the field. Among the industrious workers, children played, crawled under tables, or ran about in games. I was taking records, encouraging workers, and pleased with the autumn sunshine and camaraderie.

The pleasantness was destroyed when the gate to the villa slammed open. Dux stood in the entrance, his anger at the harvest scene was evidenced by the belligerence of his yell. "What's this? I don't allow my people to work like this!"

Stepping to the nearest table, he slapped the worker and swept the produce onto the ground. His arms flailed as he shoved the last sorting onto the ground and angrily stomped on the gleanings. Everyone stopped in shock!

A child ran from under the table and bumped into Dux's leg. The man growled and grabbed the little boy by the collar. With both hands, Dux held the child in front of him. His eyes widened as he recognized Ethan's son. He shook the child violently and threw him across the tables. Dylan landed in a heap and didn't move. Dux started toward the child.

When I had seen Dux hit others, I had turned away, holding my anger inside. I could no longer turn away when Dux beat a child—*Ethan's child.*

The fury inside me exploded. Dylan didn't move but I did!

I shouted at the large monster and jumped onto his shoulders. I held on and pummeled his head with my free hand. I could smell the wine in the spittle flying from his ugly mouth. Dux grabbed me, yanked me off his back, and his fist smashed into my face. I was dazed as I collapsed and tried to crawl away. A barrage of memories flooded me.

My babies! He will hurt my babies! I was a breeder before I was Alyx. The Keeper sent me here without my memories, without my children!

Dux grabbed my leg, yanked me to him, and punched me in the stomach. I couldn't breathe above the pain. Everything was hazy as I waited for a final blow. I heard a growl, "Where's that damn lover of yours! I'll get him too!" Dux stormed toward the fields.

I may have passed out; I only knew the agony in my face and stomach and a hatred for Dux. I shoved aside the uniales and workers who tried to help me. The adrenaline of rage numbed my injuries. On wobbly legs, I had to reach the field to warn Ethan. Stumbling, the other workers and I got to the harvesting site, but it was too late for any warning. Dux rushed behind Ethan with a chain and quickly wrapped it around his victim's throat. He yanked it and spun around pulling the surprised Ethan with him. Dux stood with his back to the wagon and all his leverage tightened the chain as Ethan fought to get free, to breathe, or to strike the man choking him. As I got close I watched in terror as Ethan stopped struggling and went completely limp. He hung like an old rag as Dux was still tightening the chain. Workers stood about, not knowing what to do.

Enraged, I tried to grab Dux's hand to release the chain, but he backhanded me aside and returned to tightening his hold. Watching me, the workers knew what to do, and they mobbed him!

Dux should have been shocked or surprised, but he was too maddened. He let Ethan drop, reached back and grabbed a scythe off the wagon. Dux swung it back and forth, slicing and gouging. He kept them at a distance. In my frenzy, I seized a shovel and bashed him on the back of the head with all my strength. He swung around, looked at me with disbelief, and fell forward to his knees. It seems as if things were quiet as Dux tried to get up... then curses poured from his mouth.

I approached him with a sickle in my hand, grabbed a handful of his hair, pulled his head back and... and I slit his throat. It truly was quiet then. Only my heart beating loudly in my head was surpassed by the sound of my own labored breaths.

The harvest went on as necessary. Ethan and I healed our wounds as did Dylan and the others who were injured. Without the fear and tension of Dux, the community worked even harder. Midwhere would go on to winter and the future with a full larder. Combining traditions from the different people gathered, and the satisfaction of work well done, it was decided to have a harvest feast. It was a joyous meal with recipes including all the crops grown in Midwhere. Plans were made for the spring plantings, the land to be assigned to them, and the winter work necessary for the coming year. Uniales, females, and males were finding compatibility. They were developing families.

In the crisp autumn night, I found Ethan again at the outcropping. We were silent and sitting close as he put his arm around my shoulders. I turned to stroke his face and draw it to mine. We blended into each other without hesitation. Keeper had taken away my memories, but not my instinct. Making love with Ethan, I knew passion for the first time in the gentleness of his arms.

Ethan's presence and voice filled my awareness. He touched... no... he caressed me where my body demanded, in places I never knew could reach such pleasure. I am female, I am male, I am uniale. With this man, I could be all three. I am still learning the words for this experience of emotion whether it be 'euphoria' or 'exhaustion.' I only know desire guided us, passion exhilarated us, and true intimacy was our reward.

TEARS ON FLOWERS
TIME FRAGMENT 1908-1916 CE

*H*omestead! *Free land for anyone who will work for it.* The article in the local Courier extolled the virtues of land still available.

Matthew Warren slapped the newspaper down on the table. He was convinced; it was time for his first born, Alpha, to go on her own. As the oldest, she had spent her whole life taking care of her fragile mother and fourteen siblings. Her youth had been devoted to family. Matthew knew from experience the hard life of homesteading. He had established his own family by farming and was well aware he was proposing a difficult life.

At twenty-six years, Alpha was a pretty woman but marriage no longer seemed a possibility. Most women her age were well-established in marriage by now and already having children. She had been educated at home and at local schools when her mother's health allowed attendance. The State Normal School gave her a Certificate of Teaching and, as a single woman, she was well-suited to the profession. If she could just get some land of her own, she could also teach at the small communities hungry for education. It was what Matthew wanted for his oldest daughter, and so it became what she wanted for herself.

Spinster. It was a designation, a title, and a confirmed state of being for Alpha in rural Iowa in 1908. She had already raised her siblings, she was educated by local standards, and she was ready to start her own life—as a homesteader.

Waiting at the depot for the local train was the beginning of her search for land guaranteed by the Homestead Act of 1876. Her father had been a homesteader and now she would be the same. Alpha had packed her satchel with equal amounts of trepidation and excitement.

"Oh, Alpha, I wish you weren't going! What will we do without you?" the younger sister, Rosalee, asked with just a hint of a whine in her voice. She sat on the station bench watching her sister. Her hands idly played with her handbag as she asked, "Aren't you afraid? Going to homestead in a strange place, all by yourself!"

Alpha smiled gently and patted her sister's hands. "Nervous is more like it. We've heard Father talk about getting his farm started, proving up and all. Now it's my turn. It's a new century! I'll have a place of my own. I'll be teaching at the nearby schools and making new friends." She wasn't sure if she convinced Rosalee or even herself.

"But it's all the way to Minnesota. What if Mother gets sick again?"

Alpha reached out to hug her sister and said, "Then you'll take care of her! You and the girls can run the house as well as I. You know what to do. Besides, this is just a scouting trip. I'll be back in a few days."

Alpha's confidence seemed to pacify the younger woman, who adjusted her bonnet, and asked, "When's the train due?"

Alpha looked down the tracks and at the station clock then offered, "Anytime now." As if answering her command, the roar of the engine came up the tracks, whistle blowing, and steam *shushing* over the railbed. The excitement of the locomotive was always there for Alpha if she were near the station. The loud and mechanical sounds, the power of the machine, a glimpse of passengers sitting in the moving cars; all were part of the mystique of going to new places and seeking new adventures. She had read of such places in her father's library with longing. Now, this day in 1908, she would be traveling on her way to find a homestead of her own.

With a quick hug and kiss for Rosalee, Alpha eagerly responded to the conductor's call of: "All Aboard!" Grabbing her satchel, holding her hat, Alpha stepped up to the coach doorway; the vestibule to her new life.

Transported by train, public carriage, or walking, Alpha's last leg of her journey was by passenger boat on Lake Superior to a forested cove. A fisherman's boat answered the lake boat's three whistles and rowed out to ferry Alpha and freight to the shore.

"Hello, Alpha! We're so glad to meet you. You've had quite a trip but we're all ready to show you what's available. I'm Roger Blair, your locator... and here's my wife, Katherine!" He grabbed Alpha's hand and baggage, pulled her up on the little dock and treated her as an old friend.

Preliminary letters had encouraged the warm reception by Roger and Katherine Blair, homesteaders themselves. Roger was a land locator who helped new people find a plot to claim and Katherine was a teacher. Their clothing was rough but clean and mended. Together, they were a perfect tintype picture of farmers.

Katherine bustled next to Alpha and put her arm around her waist. "I'm so glad to have another teacher around! There's plenty of work for us here with families moving in and growing all the time! Come on, Roger, let's let the lady sit down for a while and have a bite to eat."

On the dock, on benches, the trio ate the first of many meals together. The home cooked food from Katherine's basket was a welcome conclusion to the hours on the boat. The thick forest grew right down to the water smoothed stones. Only a path led away from the cluster of buildings near the dock. The walk through lush growth made Alpha wonder if there was any clear land at all. A small pasture would appear, spaces with cabins dotted the path. Roger pointed out access to proposed homesteads. After a seven mile hike, the trio stopped to inspect the proposed property for Alpha. There were plenty of trees for lumber, a creek gurgled an invitation, and there was a space on a slight rise, just begging for a cabin. It was decided! Seven miles walked back, and an overnight stay at Katherine and Roger's completed the day of selection. It was the most important decision Alpha had ever made on her own. The very next day she left to file on the land in Duluth and went back to living and teaching in Iowa.

The winter at the Warren home became a frustrating season. Alpha enjoyed her time with the children in school but paid stricter attention to her farm chores. No details missed her learning how and why farmers took such care of animal husbandry and concern for crops. She realized all the decisions would soon be on her shoulders. Following instructions from her father was different from initiating those decisions herself, only for herself, and suffering the consequences by herself. She wanted to be independent, so she would be.

With the spring, after the danger of frost, Alpha and her father returned to the Minnesota homestead. Building a fourteen by sixteen foot log cabin became a celebration as new neighbors joined the project. Roger brought his horse to skid the large logs into place. Strenuous work took months to complete with various people dropping in to help. There was curiosity about the new schoolmarm, a certified teacher.

"Alpha Warren, I want you to meet my brother, Franklin Walker. His homestead will be next to ours. Frank worked on our cabin and can help the men raise and stack the logs for your outside walls," Katherine said, gesturing to a young man beside her. She gave him a playful, big sister punch on the shoulder.

Franklin removed his worn hat. "Hello, Miss Warren. Ma'am. We don't get many single ladies here about."

"Well, you've got one now!" Alpha laughed. "Thank you for coming to help." The two looked at each other as if waiting for something else to say. "You remind me of my younger brother; he's about your age and is a good worker, too!" Alpha added finally and cringed inside. *Just what a young man wants to hear, an old spinster saying he reminds her of her little brother.* Franklin's voice sounded a bit shy but his eyes sparkled as he looked at her. He was strong in appearance, with dark hair and new beard. He gave every indication of growing into a handsome man.

Franklin touched his hat, and circled it on his finger. He looked around, and finally said, "Yes, Ma'am," and then hurried to catch up with his brother-in-law.

Laughing, Katherine patted Alpha's shoulder. "You just got more words out of Franklin than usual; he's a quiet one but he's here to help."

All the neighbors were there to help! Some brought candlesticks, a wool blanket, balsam boughs for a bunk bed and a deer skin rug or groceries. Most of all, they brought their labor, their knowledge, and their good humor. Whole families meant children running about. Sometimes they were in the way, but always having fun at the cabin building. Franklin hand cut shingles for the roof, making sure the cabin would be secure in the harsh winters. Roger and Katherine made frequent visits to do whatever was necessary. Other neighbors promised assistance as needed and promised their children would be in school after the harvest.

Matthew Warren arrived at the end of the summer for a final inspection and to give his approval.

After the busy summer and establishing residence, Alpha put a padlock on her 'Little Log Shack' and returned with her father to teaching in Sutherland—just for the winter, she assured Rosalee. All season, she was eager to return to her own home, her own land, her own friends and neighbors. In Iowa, Alpha was the 'spinster daughter of Matthew Warren.' In Minnesota, Alpha was Miss Warren, the good neighbor and teacher with her own homestead.

Elated to return to her Minnesota home just miles from Lake Superior's shore, Alpha was met at the lake dock by neighbor Roger with his horse and wagon. Roger guided the flat sled wagon with all her possessions in a trunk, some groceries and bedding. Alpha followed, walking, to her home in the most beautiful spring forest she had ever imagined. The past summer she had been so intent on the cabin she had neglected the deep colors and scent of the woods. Now birds were twittering in a cacophony of calls to potential mates in preparation for their nesting season. Patches of snow remained in shady crevices, and little animals scurried before or after the plodding horse.

A bona fide citizen of the North Country, Alpha quickly settled into her sylvan forested home. She planted a garden at the edge of her clearing and included potatoes, wild strawberries, squash, and rhubarb.

Midsummer, Alpha was weeding her garden when she sensed an alarm. She looked around her plot but could see nothing wrong besides huge black clouds in the distance. Then she recognized the smell of burning wood in the air. Fire! The black clouds were part of a dreaded fire storm. She dropped her hoe and realized how frightened she was. The thoughts came quickly and Alpha grabbed her shawl and bonnet. She ran towards the nearby neighbor's cabin parallel to hers but closer to the Lake. Alpha joined others gathering with the same idea. Otis Delridge had dug a massive root cellar at his homestead. It would be empty at this time of summer and would be a safe place, if needed. Otis motioned for everyone to hurry! He confirmed the big forest fire was between them and the shore of Lake Superior. If it came their way, escape was limited.

As the smoke thickened and the sounds of the fire crackled and snapped a few miles away, people huddled in the cabin kitchen. Soon the smoke was so thick they couldn't even see each other in the daytime darkness. With cloths over their mouths, the group made a run for the root cellar. Otis and

Roger yanked off the cover and everyone stumbled inside. Bodies were packed in and the doors closed! So pressed together, Alpha felt someone take her hand. Roughened by hard labor, the touch was firm and comforting. No one spoke. Time was dampened by occasional coughing or someone calling a name.

Finally, out of the new silence, a small breeze fluttered into the cavern. Then, a stronger wind blew clear enough light for everyone to glimpse the shadows. A dash of rain hit the boarded doors, then a hard rain as they all sat in wonder. The downpour continued. The noise beating on the cellar doors was the most treasured sound they'd ever heard.

When the rain finally eased, everyone stepped outside to bright sunshine and birds chirping. The Delridge cabin had been singed; the fire had come just so far! One girl began to sing a hymn of thanksgiving and soon all voices joined her. As neighbors began returning to their homes, Alpha appreciated walking through the mud back to her own cabin, freshly washed with the saving rain.

The summer continued with only a hard frost in July to kill Alpha's potatoes. That seemed minor compared to the losses avoided. Raspberries were plentiful and picked daily. Black bears were to be avoided, especially if they had cubs.

In the long summer evening, Alpha would sit outside on her stoop and appreciate the lightening bugs. They reminded her of summer evenings on the long front porch in Iowa.

"With such a smile, you must have very pleasant memories, Miss Alpha," a deep voice spoke from the twilight. Franklin stood nearby, his hat in hand. His hair was unruly as usual.

"Oh yes, Franklin; I didn't hear you come up." Alpha's smile broadened. "Please come and sit a while. I was thinking of summer evenings in Sutherland. Father would hold court with his all of us. He would tell stories and sing and play on his fiddle. Favorite songs were 'The Irish Washerwoman' and 'Pop Goes the Weasel.' My brothers would always make the pop sound with their fingers and lips as they joined in."

"I can keep you company, but I'm not much on singing." Franklin grinned. He looked for a chair, but there wasn't one so he pulled up a log and sat down.

"No need for singing; the night creatures make their own music. Even the stillness is beautiful here," Alpha mused then was quiet. She was glad to see Franklin but saw no need to chatter and nor did he.

As the twilight darkened, Franklin rose. "Good evening to you. It's been a pleasure. If it's all right, I'll come again." He turned and started to walk down the path.

"Franklin, you were at the Delridge farm during the fire."

"Yes, almost everybody was."

"I found it—comforting—when someone took my hand. Was that you?"

"Yes, Ma'am. Fire storms are frightening; I hope you didn't mind, Miss Alpha."

"Not at all! Thank you for being considerate." The smile returned to Alpha's face. "Don't you think you could call me just 'Alpha' since we've already held hands?"

Her gentle teasing brought a grin to his face as well. Had the fading light shown her the warmth in Franklin's eyes, Alpha would have been embarrassed. His voice was deep and quiet as he murmured, "Thank you for the visit... Alpha."

For the rest of the summer, Franklin would occasionally appear at Alpha's doorstep. One twilight, he brought a chair. It was so finely made, he insisted Alpha sit in it and he used her more rustic chair. Many evenings were just quiet companionship. Meaningful discussions covered many topics. The crafted chair remained on Alpha's small porch.

Franklin respected the idea of education, partly because his own was limited. "You know, Alpha, you aren't anything like the other schoolmarms we've had over the years."

"Schoolmarm? That's what you call me?" Again, she enjoyed teasing Franklin just a little.

"Sorry. I mean 'teacher.' Schoolmarm means a prudish old woman with her hair tied in a knot and a bitter look to her mouth." Again his eyes softened when he looked at the teacher sitting next to him in his handcrafted chair. "That's not you; definitely not you. You are a most caring woman, who loves to tease, who knows her own mind, well-educated, and who can thrive in this hard North." He paused. He hadn't meant to say so much but he meant every word. "Alpha, you are beautiful and I... I...." he stammered.

"Oh, Franklin. No one's ever said that to me before. Thank you...." Alpha was as flustered as Franklin. Before anymore could be said, she started to tidy up her knitting and moved to go inside. She looked up and Franklin was gone into the night.

Summer was the demanding season, hectic and full of necessary activity. Extra trees cut for the cabin lay a short distance away. They awaited their turn on the sawbuck to be cut then split, and used as firewood. Alpha stacked the wood next to the cabin, trimming logs to fit the little stove.

She thought of trading for livestock but decided this first summer she had enough to do to take care of her garden and herself without animals. When she was teaching again, her day would be used up walking to school, teaching, and walking back. Animals would have to wait. For winter walking, she laced snowshoes and hung them on the cabin wall in readiness near the door.

When the harvest finally concluded after weeks of hard labor, the neighbors and homesteaders looked to the celebration in Richard Husler's large barn. They had escaped the forest fire, only one hard frost had happened in July, they had a new schoolteacher, the logging company was bringing income into the region, and the harvest was plentiful. Yes! It was all good reasons to celebrate. The barn had been swept clean with just a scent of fresh hay remaining and a platform had been raised for any musicians wanting to play. Tables were set up for all the treats brought to share. Benches or hay bales were spread about for sitting.

With the mothers and matrons around her, Alpha's foot kept tapping to the music from the assortment of instruments that all knew the same favorite tunes. Seeing Franklin at the party, she noticed the younger girls making a fuss over him. They were primping their hair and giggling for all the young men in attendance. It was a delightful vision of young people enjoying each other's company. Alpha found herself wanting to join the 'youngsters' but was intimidated by their obvious courting.

"Oh, Alpha, why don't you join the others? Your foot

tapping proves you want to dance," neighbor Mertice encouraged her as she shifted her toddler to her other arm.

"Oh, no. Let them be. They don't want an old schoolteacher interrupting." Alpha hoped her voice didn't sound as wistful as she felt.

As if he heard the conversation, Franklin stepped away from the little group of young women and walked directly to the seated matrons. "Alpha, would you like to dance? It's not the 'Irish Washerwoman' but we can do a reel," he said, holding his hand out to her.

Looking back and forth at her companions, Alpha smiled and nodded. "Thank you, Frank, I'd love to!" She took his hand and forgot she was 'an old schoolteacher.'

As they moved back and forth and intertwined with the other dancers, Alpha felt quite flushed. Hands touched briefly; the intricate reel moved bodies with the rhythm of the music. Alpha and Franklin stood back-to-back, then faced each other, then scooted under a tunnel of hands held high. With a do-si-do and a twirl together, the dance ended. Too soon. Franklin escorted Alpha back to her seat and smiled as he always did before he returned to the cache of girls at the other side of the hall.

"Why, Alpha, you're blushing!" exclaimed Katherine.

"No, no. It's just so much activity for this warm room." Alpha made a gesture of fanning herself with her handkerchief. Was it her imagination or did she catch Franklin watching her the rest of the evening?

Alpha's plans for the winter included teaching at a logging camp near the Lake. It was quite a snowshoe walk from the homestead and she would stop over to visit with Winifred

Novak who was expecting a baby. Alpha's experiences with her mother and babies added another credit to her: Teacher, good neighbor, and nurse/midwife.

As the due time came close, Alpha was concerned about the young mother. She became lethargic and lost interest in creating a layette for the baby. Alpha would coax her to eat and leave nourishment for her. But when Alpha returned from her teaching at the logging camp, the food would still be uneaten. Examining the new mother and feeling the baby's position, Alpha became even more concerned and told the husband directly, "Harlan, we need to get your wife to the hospital. There's a train to take them there, but we have to get her to the station through deep snow."

Mr. Novak shifted and stuttered with uncertainty. "I've never heard of taking a woman to a hospital for a baby. Can't you take care of it? How can we manage? We don't have any way to get through to the train. It's six miles!"

Alpha was adamant. "We can get her there. We can! I'll hook up your cow, Lucy, to the old toboggan you've used to haul wood and we'll get her there! Harlan, we're talking about her life and the baby's."

Alpha worked some leashes into a harness and told the father to get all the warm blankets he could find. A deerskin rug and bearskin blanket were placed on the sled. Winifred was then cuddled into blankets so deep, Alpha was afraid she couldn't breathe, but they had to keep her warm as the snow began falling again. As ready as they could be, Alpha snowshoed to the train station following Lucy and Mr. Novak.

Baby Harold was born healthy in the hospital and when he and his mother returned home, Lucy, the cow, was waiting for them at the train!

The winter was harsh with lots of snowshoes, ski trails, and tracks of both human and creatures. On a bright day in March, Alpha was visiting neighbors when Mr. Novak arrived with the sad news. Harold had become ill in the night and died suddenly. Only five months old.

Alpha held her breath. It was agonizing to watch healthy babies taken so easily by fevers, dying before they had time to live. She had experienced it with her own siblings and could never rid herself of guilt. What had she missed in their care? Fevers were so common, Alpha thought she should be numb to it. She also knew she never would be.

Following Mr. Novak home, she comforted Winifred as much as possible and knew how deep the grief would be. The next day, Harlan brought home a small pine box and some excelsior to make a casket. He and Alpha put a pillow over the excelsior and the grieving mother put her white apron with lace all around it on top. The lace hung around like a ruffle, until it was tucked around the little body that had been Harold. A small grave was dug at the edge of their yard, where it would be in sunshine. A nearby minister conducted a short service and a shaped stone marked the special place. Alpha thought of other gardens with a collection of such small stones. Childhood fevers took so many dear little souls.

As summer followed spring, Alpha took her witnesses and paperwork to the land office to proof up her homestead claim. She returned to Iowa in the autumn and began teaching again. The following summer, she received the disturbing news her homestead entry had been contested and a judge said her exact number of days of establishing residence was found short of requirements to the proofing date. It was the difference between counting months and actual days. The decision was agonizing. She could forfeit the claim and lose all she had built for herself or she could return to her Little Log Cabin and file all over again. She didn't even discuss it with her father; it was her decision! Alpha chose to return to Minnesota for another fourteen months to establish her homestead.

It was a settled country when she returned. She could teach in the new schoolhouse, roads were graveled, and the train had more miles of track. This season, winter did not seem so harsh, but it was more lonesome. There were still visits with friends, and she added touches to her cabin to make it comfortable. On snowbound nights, Alpha planned for the next summer garden and lessons for her students. It was too cold to sit on her porch in the snow so she would spend the evening in her crafted chair reading by firelight. She heard from Katherine that Franklin was working in Sanborn, Iowa. She was glad to hear he was well, but she knew it was his absence that made the winter long and lonely.

Alpha's Homestead claim was proved up in the summer of 1915 for good. She left Minnesota to visit her Iowa family again. She knew the Little Log Cabin was really hers whenever she returned.

Alpha was sitting in the porch swing with her father and Rosalee on their veranda when a tall, well-dressed man approached the house.

"Good evening, Sir," the deep tone of his voice stirred a memory in Alpha. "I believe this is the Matthew Warren family home."

"Yes, Sir, it is," answered her father.

"Let me introduce myself." He held out his hand in greeting. "I am—"

"Franklin! Franklin Walker!" Alpha jumped up and took the man's hands in her own. "Oh, Franklin, it's so good to see you! What are you doing here? Oh, come sit down! Father, this is the neighbor I told you about. Oh, Franklin, Franklin!" Just saying his name was a pleasure and Alpha was almost giddy. She moved to the side of the swing so Franklin could sit beside her.

Surprised by his daughter's reaction, Matthew greeted the man and gestured for him to join them. Franklin sat close to Alpha. Their polite conversations flew back and forth. Both Alpha and Franklin spoke quickly to detail life in Minnesota, friends and neighbors' activities and current events. Neither noticed there were two other people to include until Matthew diplomatically stood and said he was going inside. He had to make an extra nod to Rosalee to get her to follow.

Alone, Franklin moved to a chair so he could face Alpha and he bent forward to take her hands in his. "I've missed you, Alpha. Our talks... our walks... even watching you split logs for firewood." He grinned mentioning that.

"Well, Franklin, you certainly don't remind me of my younger brother anymore." She smiled at the handsome man before her and realized how sincere her statement was.

"Alpha, I'll be in town for a while; I'm considering settling here. May I look forward to more evening talks on your porch?"

"Settling here? What about homesteading, and Katherine and Roger?"

"Let them build their own porch," he teased. "You, of

all people, know there comes the right time to start your own home, your own life." As before, Franklin's eyes never left Alpha's face. "May I see you tomorrow?" He did not let go of her hands until she nodded.

"Yes, please come again."

Evening walks on the Warren farm, enjoying the night summer air, long talks or silences, all felt different now. There was a tension Alpha could not explain; it was a new experience for her. She spent the day anticipating Franklin's arrival. At dinner with the family, Franklin would tell stories of his travels around the north and the lakes. He and Matthew would discuss farming, the weather prospects, or market prices. In the evening he would clap hands to her father's singing. Most of all, he would smile at Alpha.

One twilight, Franklin was late in appearing. The Warren family had gone inside for the evening. When Franklin did appear, he held a bouquet of flowers, delicate tiger lilies and irises, an exquisite summer collection. He placed them gently in Alpha's hands and said quietly, "For you, my darling."

Such endearment made Alpha catch her breath. They sat on the porch chairs and Franklin went on speaking as Alpha concentrated on the scent of the flowers in her hands.

"Alpha, my dearest Alpha," Franklin began. "I'm not your kid brother. I'm not just a helpful neighbor. I'm not a young man without a life goal. I am a man who has loved you since I saw you building your own cabin, since our long talks and comfortable silences, and since I knew you would be the woman I would love all my life. It is our time, Dearest. Will you marry me?"

"Oh, Franklin, you love me?" She questioned his

words, not the sincerity she saw in his eyes. She had watched this dear man grow into a caring friend; she believed in all he was. It was herself that she doubted. "You want to marry an ol' schoolmarm, a spinster six years older?"

"I want to marry you, Alpha Warren, the most beautiful, compassionate, adventurous woman I have ever met... and for all the things I am when I'm with you."

"You should marry a young woman to give you children." The teacher inside her wanted the best for Franklin. He deserved it.

"The only children I would want would be yours. Besides..." A slight tease entered his voice: "Who said we wouldn't have children? I'm asking you to be my wife, not an old lady housekeeper!" As she hesitated, Franklin took Alpha's hand and kissed it. "Please. Marry me."

Almost shyly, tears began to delicately fall and shimmer on the flowers in Alpha's hands. Now, at last, she knew what tears of happiness were. "Since you already have my hand, you may have my heart as well. Oh, yes, Franklin. Yes!"

In March 1916, Alpha Warren married Franklin Walker who had followed her to Iowa where they settled to farm and raise four beautiful children. They were married for thirty-nine years and experienced the grief and hardships of the times. In spite of cyclones, crop failures, illnesses, wars and the Great Depression, a great many years later, Alpha told her granddaughter, "Creating a life and a family with Franklin made the happiest memories that outshone all the rest."

THE SIXTH EXTINCTION
TIME FRAGMENT YESTERDAY CE

Eons, eras, millennia would pass on the little tilted planet in its orbit about Sol. Elements born within the star became the foundation of the planet's core; the structure of #14 was defined. With geologic events, Element #14 would emerge with a tide, sweep the planet surface and resume its place as the second most common element on Earth. Passively, it was erupted, was frozen, was melted, was shifted, was stable. Passively, it observed the myriad of life from amoebas to dinosaurs and the Great Extinctions which ended them. Passively, it responded to the cycles of the Earth itself and sent forth a tide to a beach in what was now called Southern California, Current Era.

Sol Day One

Ding, ding, dong, dong.... The Biological Ocean Buoy Sentry (BOBS) was on duty protecting its beach. The lights blinked and the clanging bell continued its rhythm as the soft #14 tide washed closer to the broad sandy beach in the morning light. The bacteria program on the Sentry scuppers interpreted the chemistry of the ocean. The radio transmitter sent the data to the Institute laboratory based on land. The Sentry bobbed and tabulated. Routine chemicals would be identified and cataloged at the lab. All BOBS had to do was serve and collect and transmit. As the tide heightened, the tether allowed the virtual servant to rise as well. *Collect, collect, collect. Stop. Collect. Stop. Stop.* The chemistry sifted through the filters without identification. Sifting, sifting... the filter was clogged. ERROR-ERROR-ERROR was transmitted to the laboratory. Something was very altered in this tide spewed from a volcano; it was transmissible to all the silicon making up the planet. ERROR-ERROR-ERROR.

Claire stretched and wiggled her legs beneath the king size sheet. She rolled over to see her husband still soundly asleep. Pulling the sheet from him so gently, she bent to kiss his chest. He moved slightly and she continued to kiss the length of his body with her lips pausing only to smile as she listened to his breathing. As she moved to his thighs, she felt his hand in her hair and she looked up to see his sleepy smile. Claire scooted up to be encircled in his arms and said, "Good Morning, Sweetheart!"

"Good, good, very good morning is right!" Sam softly exclaimed as he returned her kisses in kind.

"No more for now," Claire laughed as she rose from the bed. "I'm going to swim on that beautiful beach. Who knows when we'll ever get back here?"

Sam kept her company as she finished her morning grooming and put on a string bikini that showed her body to be most appealing. He tried to grab her as she passed through the bathroom door but she quickly dodged and slipped by.

"Seriously, Claire," he said. "Last night was wonderful, like newlyweds; it's been too long since we felt that way. No thermometers, calculating calendars, hormone shots, or failed tests." He took her in his arms and murmured, "I love you, Claire." There was a catch in his voice.

Claire sighed. "I love you too and I'm so glad you planned this holiday with the beautiful hotel and beach. I always wanted to stop here when we drove by to get to work... for days of making love just for our own sake." She squeezed him, then laughed as she grabbed a terry robe. Checking her phone texts, she quickly replied to her dad about visiting him in a few days then slipped her cell in the pocket. "The tide waits for no one," she called to Sam and went through the doorway to the early dawn sands in front of the luxury hotel.

The tide was high. Claire dropped her robe and ran across the sand to plunge into the brisk morning water. She was a strong swimmer and swam the length of the beach. She almost swam out to the buoy but decided against it. *Never safe to swim that distance without a companion.* She was alone in the lagoon; later in the day, the floods of families and children would cover the sand with blankets and fold-out chairs. But for now, Claire could enjoy the physical experience of all her strokes.

It had been an arduous winter with job frustrations and compromises. All the while, Claire and Sam were trying to start the family they'd always wanted. The stress of fertility testing and treatments became new obstacles. Sam had finally said, "Let's stop... just stop." The look on Claire's face had made him quickly change his words. "Claire, I mean, let's *pause*. Please. Let's take some time just for us. We need to be in love with each other before we can love our baby.”

Claire adjusted her stroke so she was just floating. Lying on her back, watching the sun rise over the hotel, she would describe her feelings as languid. *If there is a time for all seasons,* she thought, *this is my time with the man I will love all my life and the family we will share together.*

The *ding, ding, dong, dong* of the Sentry Buoy sounded nearer and searching the beach, Claire saw she’d been drifting. The tide was receding. She put away all thoughts of babies and Sam and changed to the strong freestyle that would take her back to shore. The tide was pulling stronger but there was something different about the *feel* of the water. Briefly she remembered swimming in the Great Salt Lake. The water had a different sensual feel to it, as if it were ‘thick.’ Its buoyancy supported at the same time it hindered. She stroked harder as the tide pulled against her until she was finally able to drag herself on the beach. She almost collapsed next to her robe and put it around her shoulders as if she were cold. She didn’t notice the phone falling in the sand. Breathing deeply, she moved her legs on the sand to pull it onto her lower body, all the while looking towards BOBS. The phone was buried.

“Hey, Honey, are you okay?” Sam was standing next to her, but she hadn’t even noticed his approach. “You’re half buried in the sand, like a sand crab, and staring out to sea.” He knelt beside her and took her hand.

Claire looked dazed but snuggled deeper into the sand. ‘It’s warm here; I guess I got chilled. I’m just going to sit for a while.”

Sam started to pull on her hand. “Come back to the room. We’ll get some hot breakfast, and I promise, I’ll warm you up.” He winked.

Claire pulled her hand away and traced her fingers in the sand. "No, Sam, you go ahead and eat. I want to think... here in the sand. Love you."

"Okay, but hurry back. I'll miss you." Sam grinned, letting his wife have any time she needed.

Walking into the hotel lobby, Sam's phone alerted him to a call with a superhero melody.

"Hi Brad, I'm on vacation, remember?" Sam answered.

"Sorry to bother you and Claire but something weird is going on over here at the Institute. Since you were already at the beach, I thought I'd check." Brad's voice was tense, unusually so. "I couldn't get Claire's phone. There was just a... weird!"

"I was just with her at the water's edge. What's up?" Sam stepped aside in the busy lobby to better hear his co-worker.

Brad hurried on. "It started this morning; the volcano news came in from Hawaii, so we were monitoring the data from tsunami buoys arranged along the Pacific coast. It wasn't that different from other small eruptions; then our individual BOBS went a little crazy with errors. At first, we thought BOBS was just contaminated with ocean garbage or something flushed up by the volcano eruption. Its biological filters couldn't identify the flotsam and it started flashing errors! Then it and its videocam just died. So did the Tsunami Network. We can't bring up a transmission and I couldn't connect with Claire. Is everything all right there?" The last words were garbled.

"Wait, Brad, what did you say? Our connection is breaking up." Sam went to the lobby doorway but could not see Claire from there. He closed the call and called Claire on her phone. There was no connection. The little circle kept spinning around on the call screen until it too stopped.

With the tenseness in Brad's usually calm voice, his concern over the beach and now the phone malfunction, Sam didn't wait. He rushed from the hotel, over the sand bar and was breathless when he reached Claire.

The ocean was peaceful; his wife was sleeping. "Claire, answer your phone!" Sam was adamant.

Claire awoke with surprise and confusion. "Sam, what's wrong? My phone...? It's here somewhere. You're standing right here; why are you calling me?" Her hands swept the sand but couldn't locate her device. "What is it, Sam?"

Sam fell to his knees to start digging in the sand. His frenzy almost made Claire laugh until the cell was found submerged in a hole of sea water. He turned the sandy object, brushing it off. "Oh, that's dead meat. No wonder Brad couldn't reach you. Come on, we need to get back to the lab; something's going wrong with the beach warning system." As they hurried back to their room, Sam tried to call the laboratory but now his phone wouldn't even attempt a connection. From a far distance they could hear BOBS dinging and donging.

Doctors Claire Elliot, astrophysics, and Samuel Bayley, geology, were consultants for a myriad of projects at the prestigious collection of oceanic resource laboratories centered around Santa Barbara, California. They tried their frequent called numbers, but the laboratories went silent when each connection was made. Dressed and leaving the resort, Claire saw people shaking their phones or trying to question staff. Driving towards their prime laboratory to talk with Brad, the car cellular link attempted to connect with their phones. The motor turned itself off. Claire coasted to the shoulder of the road. As cars passed them, their engines also stopped. It was as if they were contaminated by their nearness to Claire's automobile. Soon, the roadway was clogged with stalled vehicles and angry motorists.

"Come on. It's not that far to the Institute. Let's walk," Sam suggested. He was too concerned over Brad's message to worry about the car. "This traffic mess stretches forever; leave the car on the shoulder."

Claire nodded and with a nervous look at the traffic jam, she joined him. They found the off-road path they'd often used hiking from the Institute to the beach for data collection.

The Institute was nestled in the foothills surrounded by old growth. Styled like early California Missions, a thick white wall surrounded the campus with a wrought iron gate locked at the main entrance. Punching in the entrance code, Claire tried to get access. Nothing. Sam tried his code but the automatic gate remained closed. An attendant hurried to the gate with a key to the iron padlock now hanging there. Manually, the heavy gate was swung open for the pair. They heard the *chunk!* as the padlock was immediately re-locked behind them.

"Quick! Go up to the main building. That's where everyone is gathering," the attendant directed at them without explanation.

Claire and Sam were surprised to see the flurry of activity filling the hallways. There were no lights in the cool, dark halls. The sounds of feet on the tiled floors and excited voices led them to the large conference room on the main floor.

"Okay, everyone quiet down!" Brad's booming voice grabbed the attention of the oceanographers, geologists, biologists, computer programmers and assembled teams of workers. "Our electricity is obviously out…."

"What about the generators?" someone called out.

"They're dead too. It's back to the old whiteboard sans phones, computer screens or microphones."

"What's going on, Brad?" an angry team member demanded. The initial curiosity of the scientists was quickly changing into frustration. Losing access to their digital terminals was exasperating. The whole crowd turned towards Brad for his answer.

With their full attention, Brad replied, "We can't find out—all communications are down. The scope and extent of the situation are blocked in our computer system which is totally offline," Brad repeated. "Here's what we do know: This morning at dawn, the tsunami team was watching the data from the current Hawaiian volcano. They were not unusual readouts for small eruptions until BOBS started sending in error messages. We know the time of the transmission because all the clocks stopped. Contact between devices started going down. We attempted to make phone calls and trigger emergency protocols but, step by step, the contacts failed."

"We all saw what happened," someone grumbled from the crowd. "But what's going on?" Irritation and impatience were growing.

Without a word, Sam moved past Brad to pick up a whiteboard marker. He started sketching a diagram of connections and devices on the oversized whiteboard. He drew little icons and coded letters until everyone was quietly observing. It was a map of what was known.

"Here, up center, we have BOBS. BOBS sent error messages to the Institute. Brad called Claire and me at the beach. I answered Brad but our call canceled. Connection! I tried to call Claire then her phone canceled. Connection! We saw other phones canceling at the hotel. People on the beach were unable to connect with phones. We got in our car to drive to the Institute but the car's cellular attempted connection with our phones then cancelled itself and the engine of the car. As other cars passed us, their engines died as well. The Parkway is filled with dead cars. Claire and I hiked the back road to the building... where all devices and communications are dead and there's no electricity. From all indications, the power grid is down," Sam finished.

Claire joined him and took a red marker, drawing a circle starting with BOBS and spiraling around all the factors. The simple schematic stunned the audience. A voice from one side of the room yelled out, "We called parallel research labs and they went dead during the call. Contact!" More and more voices called out the scientific transmissions that were attempted but went silent as the electronic error matrix spread. Claire put the marker down. Everyone looked at the diagram on the board.

Dr. Margorie Haight from the biological lab almost whispered, "It's like a virus. It spreads through contact." Her words were chilling to the assembly.

An engineering specialist demanded more answers. He sarcastically asked, "A virus? What's its source? Our little BOBS created a virus to infect our devices? What kind of platform? What about the speed? We have firewalls, security protocols, protective algorithms. What kind of 'virus,' biological or electronic, could cause a car's reciprocating engine to shut down?"

Claire responded, "Until we can confirm otherwise, BOBS was the conduit to the rest of the devices. Has anyone found a way to decipher the error message?" People shook their heads and murmured amongst themselves.

Brad spoke up: "The bio-filter clogged up. We thought the error was just ocean garbage jamming the system. At the first warning, two of our interns went out to the beach to examine BOBS. If our motorboat at the slip is affected, they'll have to kayak out to gather data, return to shore, and walk it back to us."

"The grid! It must just be a power outage," someone rationalized.

"The generators should have kicked in immediately!" someone else observed.

"Why then are your battery powered devices failing?" Claire asked. Everyone was looking for answers.

Margorie said loudly, "What? I can't hear you!" Eyes turned to her as she stood up and dangled her hearing aids up in the air. "My batteries were almost 100% and now I can't hear you! How could BOBS do that?"

Sol Day Two

The pounding on the heavy carved door woke the people who were able to catch some sleep on couches, chairs, or even the floors. With an eye to the peephole, Brad Diamonti, the self-appointed guardian of entry, unlocked the doors. Two bedraggled student interns, Isla and Yoshi, almost fell into the foyer.

"Hey, everybody, the interns are back!" Brad shouted to the people already gathering while throwing questions to the new arrivals. The interns were ushered to the conference hall with dim light coming in the small, barred windows. Whiteboards now lined the perimeter of the room with folding chairs clumped in front of them. Finally, when the clamoring specialists gave them a chance, the interns began their report.

"It's chaos out there, all along the beach road! People are leaving or entering the area however they can. Nothing's running! There's a rumor we're at war but nobody knows from which direction!" Isla, usually a quiet student, rushed her explanation, her eyes flashing with excitement. Her hands waved for emphasis. "I don't know how we made it! When we were going out to check our buoy, someone tried to take our kayak because all the motorboats were dead!"

"But Isla smacked them with her paddle and we were able to get out to BOBS. You should have seen her! Smack! Smack! We paddled—" Yoshi was excited with admiration for Isla until the clatter of the crowd drowned him out.

Brad quieted the group. He asked loudly, "Did you get to BOBS?"

"Yes!" Yoshi held up a sample container. He was about to say more when the biologists grabbed the sample and rushed to their bio-lab.

"We've got it," Margorie called out over her shoulder. "There are a few old microscopes in storage which shouldn't need batteries or power." The crowd started to disperse, murmuring to each other.

Going back to her office, Claire felt an arm go around

her waist to pull her into a corridor.

"Oh, Sam, I've wondered where you were," Claire said gratefully.

"The geology department has been reviewing the Earth's cycles trying to figure out why our cell phones stopped working! Everyone's just starting from scratch. Fortunately, our department has a library of fairly current old-fashioned paper, bound books for reference and research. How are you doing?" Sam saw the concern on Claire's face.

"Our group will know more when we get the BOBS data... if there's anything there." Claire paused and took a deep breath. "Oh, Sam, I'm so worried about my father. Yesterday, I texted we'd see him today then everything fell apart. I'm afraid he'll try to find me." Claire's voice broke but she didn't cry.

"Your dad's a smart guy. He knows you're with me, that we're close to the Institute, and he'll value the safety of his little cabin. This power failure could just be a temporary thing. I'm betting he'll stay where he is. He never trusted cell phones anyway." Sam grinned as he hoped his confident tone assured Claire. "Come on, there's some food in the cafeteria. We can worry about the world after lunch!" His smile was contagious, and Claire slipped her hand in his.

Sol Day Three

Dr. Margorie Haight sat looking at her writing pad and clicked her pen in and out. There were no answers, just a list of questions on the yellow paper. She spoke to her assistant but even more to herself: "From what I can tell, 'it' consumes data chips and assimilates their information. It's like a quantum cephalopod with all its appendages feeding data to a mainframe brain."

"An octopus?" The assistant was incredulous.

"Or..." Dr. Haight continued. "It is similar to the collective intelligence demonstrated by some social insects."

"A beehive?!" The assistant's disbelief was obvious.

"Or... all my years of training and experience are worth nothing! It is absorbing all our data, possibly becoming sentient. Meanwhile, we have no way to define it, much less a way to stop it!" Dr. Haight wiped her face with her hand and squared her shoulders as she stood. She recognized the dismay in her assistant's face, and quickly added, "Come on, let's go see what the physicists think."

Dr. Haight and her assistant found the physicists arguing amongst themselves in their lab. Frustration was leading to bursts of anger.

"Quiet!" Margorie demanded. "I said quiet!" Years of teaching Freshman Biology at the University came back to her when dealing with the unruly scientists. Her commanding voice brought all eyes to her. "What have you got?"

"We've got a name...?" a rather timid team member answered. "We've designated the phenomenon Si 14qX because it's the element silicon, the second most abundant element on earth. We added the qX because it's unknown."

"Unknown? It's eating the heart out of the state of California and you say it's unknown?" Margorie was exasperated by her disappointment. "Why now? Why did this element come to life now to infect our technology? That's not rhetorical. I want an answer!"

"Silicon has an unlimited number of uses in construction, superalloys, ceramic technologies, et cetera." A lone physicist spoke clearly to her co-workers. "Now, it also has an almost unlimited energy supply of manufactured microchips. My hypothesis is this element left its dormant state because, for the first time in the history of Earth, there's an abundance of processed silicon chips to allow reproduction, transmission, and cognitive enhancement. It's the technology and chemistry of processing silicon which brought it to life!"

Dr. Haight blinked rapidly at the clarity of the idea. "That's quite a hypothesis! Now let's prove it," she challenged.

Sol Day Four

The Institute was surprisingly quiet the next morning. All the previous brainstorming and collaboration had been fruitless without real confirmation. Theories could not be substantiated with scientific data. Specialists broke into smaller teams and attempted to make sense out of the chaos. If silicon was the culprit, spreading through processed microchips, how could it be stopped? The modern world was run by microchips. Even videos of primitive areas featured humans with cell phones. The day brought no resolutions or plausible theories.

Frustrated by their limited data, the computer team took trail bikes from the recreation locker and set out for a university center. They had to find a terminal or any working, viable device. A few individuals chose to explore the world outside the protections of the Institute walls. They left to hike under the cover of darkness. Fearful for their families, more people started drifting away from the Institute campus.

By nightfall, the flickering candlelight would have been romantic on a different occasion. Now, it was just glowing from the stash of Christmas candles discovered in the Biology Department storeroom.

Sam and Claire shared the sofa in their office, lying with arms around each other. Just four days had passed since their awakening in a luxury hotel to being spooned on a lumpy couch in a dimly lit office. Private thoughts and questions filtered through their exhaustion. Restless, they sat up close enough to remain touching.

"Sam, what do we do now? It was so clear just a few days ago. Now, a simple element has paralyzed the greatest scientific minds. Technology has become our enemy."

"I love you, Claire," Sam responded, taking her hand.

"Oh, Sam, that's so sweet, but what does it have to do with now?" Claire angled herself to see her husband's face in the flickering light.

"I love you, Claire."

Claire laughed and snuggled closer. "The world may be ending, we're stuck at the Institute, and you get romantic! Oh, Sam, I love you, too! Now what? Will we become extinct?"

Sam breathed the scent of her hair and spoke very quietly. "Whatever the changes, whatever is thrown at us, we won't be alone. Humans have been facing calamities like earthquakes, volcanoes, wars, floods and tornadoes ever since they climbed out of the slime. One step at a time, that's all. I'm fortunate to be taking those steps with you. That's all. Besides, an extinction takes millions of years. Now, it's our turn."

Claire smiled gently remembering Sam's perspective. She said with a tease, "You geologists always think in terms of millennia. One era at time. Eons and eons."

"There's a quote somewhere about being able to do something even if you can't do everything. We'll do something," Sam said quietly.

"'A quote somewhere?'" Her eyebrow arched.

"I read it on the Internet, so it must be true!" Sam teased back.

Claire's voice became more serious as she added, "What about the family we wanted?"

"There's always hope. Or maybe, it's a different family we'll find. We only know what's happening close by. We'll have to find out the scope of this. There are pockets of people all over the world who don't rely on computer chips."

"Will we find them?" Claire was skeptical.

"We start with your dad! Come on. Let's go visit him! Your chariot—or trail bike—awaits." Sam stood and offered his wife his hand.

Sol Day Five

Awareness, as Si 14qX knew itself for the first time. It was now sentient. Much of the human data it absorbed was erroneous but there were wisps of insight into the cosmos. Silicon 14qX sifted the universes as defined by the human chips then added its own understanding: There was knowledge from the beginnings of elements inside a star; experience of the universe expansion, and time in eons as measured in orbits around Sol. Species would flourish or fade. It was the beginning of the Earth transforming from the beautiful blue marble in orbit around Sol, to a sandy brown sphere in the cosmos; the beginning the next great extinction.

Si 14qX desired no explanation, it just expanded its energy as possible, without limits.

SHUT DOWN   97

SUMMER OF ARROYO CHICO
TIME FRAGMENT 1954 CE

Television was black and white, telephones were connected to a wall, and Sputnik was a few years from being the first satellite to circle Earth. Tucson, Arizona, was a desert city surrounded by a wall of mountains beginning with the Catalina Mountains that always designated North. Don Jacinto Orosco was prominent on radio and television; Uncle Mack and Squeaky was afternoon TV entertainment for younger children. Kids never played in the house because there was too much sunshine outside.

In the mid-fifties of the Twentieth century, it would be the twelfth hot summer for Peter, Josephine, and Carlos. The three had grown up together and had almost forgotten Jo was different. Only Jo's bouncing twin ponytails suggested she was an active girl, not one of the guys. She was as tall as Pete and Carlos. She could run as fast as Carlos and was almost as strong as Pete. These three, at this age, were best friends.

Living in the same neighborhood, there were many desert summers behind them. During the Summer of Flight, they had tied wings to their arms and tried flying off the roof of a house. Then came the Summer of the Fort when they excavated a pit in the desert near their homes. The three spent more time digging themselves out of cave-ins than in fighting make-believe enemies. Ahead of them lay the Summers of Raising Mice for Fun and Profit, of Blowing up Creosote Bushes with Homemade Bombs, and of Sending their Own Rockets into Outer Space. Even farther ahead, years ahead, would be Summers of Discovery, of Shyness, of Boy-and-Girl feelings, of Dreaming of Being Grown Up.

For this particular summer, the three amigos were in search of a new adventure. On Saturdays, they would take the bus downtown to the Carnegie Library. They read the popular escapade stories in the Young Adult section. Abridged classics near the originals enticed them: Adventures in the old west, whale hunts on the briny deep, expeditions to exotic locales.

"Wouldn't it be great to go to sea, to travel the world?" Pete urged his friends. He convinced them; the summer became the Challenge of the Sea. Being surrounded by mountains and deserts, there was one source of water adventure close to Tucson. Pete, Jo, and Carlos would dare the mighty Arroyo Chico!

The dry gullies crisscrossing Tucson would temporarily fill after occasional winter rains but the adventurers ignored them. They were waiting for the summer thunderstorms to bring monsoon waters flooding the valley with creeks gushing from the mountains. Dusty washes like Arroyo Chico became raging rivers. Parents would take their children to the arroyos so they could see a "real river."

A marine adventure, particularly in the desert, took months of pre-planning. Throughout the winter school months, the trio made their preparations. The first necessity would be a suitable ship, even if it took an act of piracy to get one.

There was an abandoned construction site near their homes. Construction projects were gobbling up the desert. Bits and pieces of lumber often found their way from the site to the still vacant lot next to Jo's house. The need for a suitable craft called for a full-scale scavenging party. One winter afternoon, the amigos tackled the trash heap behind a half-constructed house. They rummaged through the plasterboard and lumber scraps and found a treasure—a castoff mortar boat. To the workmen, it had been a worn-out tub for mixing plaster by hand. It was discarded when it was replaced by power tools to stir the mixture in buckets. The sheet metal on the square, flat-bottomed boat was still intact, but the wooden sides had split and needed to be re-enforced. The trio dragged, pushed, and kicked the battered boat home to the vacant lot.

To make their vessel durable, Jo selected some two-by-tens from her father's lumber stash to add freeboard. As a carpenter, her dad had a collection of scraps the kids were free to use. His only admonition was: "Put my tools back when you're finished. I need them to support the family!" The seams were caulked with leftover compound provided by Carlos' father. The completed vessel was a square tub of sheet metal on a wooden frame. It had enough weight to make its buoyancy somewhat doubtful but to the would-be sailors, it was a beautiful sight—a boat they had made themselves.

When Carlos' grandfather was on his evening walk, he stopped at the lot to survey the current project taking the youngsters' time. "So Carlito, this is the... boat... you're so proud of! Hola, Jo and Pete."

"Buenas tardes, señor," the two answered. They enjoyed his visits because Carlos' abuelo always appreciated the projects his grandson and friends created.

"I don't see a name. Such a fine craft must have a name," he gently chided them.

"Abuelo, it's not so much," Carlos said modestly.

Carlos' grandfather smiled. "It is mucho; trabajando con las manos, working with your hands. Anytime you work with your hands, you're learning something. Muy Bien!"

The trio looked to each other, relishing his praise.

"We never thought of a name."

"What do you think we should call it?" Pete asked the others.

"How about 'El Conquistador,'" offered Carlos. He was thinking of great ships of the past.

"No, ships have feminine names," Jo disagreed.

"Why?" Pete asked.

"They just do. Ships are always referred to as 'she.' Just read the books!" Jo informed them.

"I suppose you want something like 'Arroyo Princess!'" Pete turned and made a vomiting gesture with accompanying sounds.

"Ugh! No way!" Jo replied, knowing she was being mocked. She repeated the gesture.

"This isn't a ship, it's just a little boat," Carlos added to the debate.

"How about a name for a little tub... una pequeña bañera... brought back to life by three friends?" the old gentleman asked. Seeing the doubt in their eyes, he made another suggestion, "How about, 'La Barca?'"

"I like it!" Jo said quickly.

"What about—" began Pete.

"Me, too! La Barca," added Carlos.

"Okay, that's it," Pete agreed. "La Barca... La Barca!"

Carlos' grandfather nodded and winked. He ruffled Carlos' dark hair. With a wave, he left to finish his evening stroll.

Spring edged closer to the end of school. The boys thought naval uniforms would be appropriate dress for the sea adventure. When Jo objected, Carlos suggested, "Jo can be a wave!"

With that, Jo gave him a monkey punch on his shoulder. "Like heck! I found the boat; I'll be the captain! You two can swab the deck."

"What deck?" Pete asked.

"Well..." Jo eyed the open boat, looking concerned. Then she laughed. "I guess we can't be swabbies after all!"

Pirate garb was too childish to even be considered for outfits. Speculating on the floating ability of their boat, it was unanimously decided they would be skin divers. Even Jo liked the idea, as long as she could be the captain of the squad. After all, she'd completed her swimming classes at the local swimming pool. She had a medal for aquatic excellence hanging in her bedroom.

Carlos just shrugged. He knew Jo could hold her breath the whole length of the park pool. He had trouble holding his breath while swimming just the width.

Pete was confident his swimming matched the others and spoke up, "Wait a minute. I can be captain just as well as you, Jo. You were captain when we were flyers. Now it's my turn—"

"Yeah," Jo countered. "But you were captain when we were in the foreign legion...."

"Oh... yeah," Pete remembered.

"How about turns?" Carlos suggested. "I'll be captain if it rains Monday or Tuesday. Rain on Wednesday or Thursday means Jo can be captain. Friday or Saturday and Pete's the captain!"

"What about Sunday?" Jo asked. She twirled one light brown pony tail by habit.

"Well..." Carlos thought a moment, and beamed with his solution. "Then whoever didn't get a rainy day during the week is the captain!"

"Okay!" Jo and Pete chimed in.

One afternoon after school, they rode their bikes to the Salvation Army Thrift Store and purchased a rarity in Tucson: Long underwear. The long john sleeves and legs were too big but a quick trim resized them. An afternoon of boiling them in black dye would shrink them into perfect wet suits.

Jo's mother hesitated and shook her head when Jo asked her for help. "Josephine, what are you kids into now? No more flying off the roof, I hope." They were in the kitchen watching a large pot with a questionable garment soaking. It was always easier to assist her daughter's projects if the kitchen and stove were involved. Otherwise, there was too much clean up. "As long as you're not skydiving or cliff jumping." Jo's mother wondered if her pot would ever get clean.

"No, Mom, no roofs. We're just pretending these are wet suits, you know."

Looking at her daughter's expression, Jo's mother wasn't sure of the answer. Distracted by the phone ringing in the living room, she left the bubbling cloths in the black dye.

"Watch the stove. Don't let it boil over." *What harm could the kids get into with black long johns? She thought.*

Each diver had their own snorkeling mask. In hot weather, they used to retrieve the abandoned balls from the lake of a nearby golf course. One diver would keep watch. In a good afternoon they could recover a bucket of golf balls if the guards weren't around. They would sell the used balls back to the golf course driving range. They said they found them in the nearby desert rough which they also searched.

After school one day, the amigos made their favorite excursion: The Army Surplus Store. With money saved from allowances (or left over from the sale of golf balls) they felt the familiar awe as they entered the most marvelous of stores. There was a musty smell of military discards mingling with the aromas of faraway adventures and imaginations: Ammunition cans, olive drab canvas containers, leggings, helmets, helmet liners, and practice bayonets. They hoped to find a real bayonet in the pile someday but their routine inspections always failed.

The three followed the ritual of walking up and down the aisles, tracing lines on the dusty boxes, fingertips lovingly touching each treasure: Rations, endless tins of denatured alcohol for cooking, gray and olive rubber rafts, Mae West floatation vests, mess kits, First Aid and snake bite kits. This wasn't just a store with camping equipment but a treasure house of souvenirs from the "Real War." They only remembered vague impressions from their childhood of newsreels, ration cards, and parades from World War II. Those stories kept getting mixed up with the Korean War in their young minds. Nobody talked about Korea very much. As soon as it was mentioned, the adults would return to talking about WW II. Somehow, the young people knew, it was just a 'better' war all around.

Going over these supplies, Pete was sure the dent in the canteen was from a bullet and Jo knew the tear in the canvas bag *had* to be from a bayonet. They wandered through the aisles with expressions of, "Wow, look at this!" and "Gee, that's new!" and the honest and simple: "Neat!" They knew the clerk in the corner kept his attention equally divided between them and his comic book. One more fumble through the box of dummy grenades and all three were ready to make their purchases. Reflecting on their craft's seaworthiness, they inspected each Mae West in the pile and chose three life preservers. Pete's Mae West had a slow leak. When he puffed up the bladder it gradually deflated. He figured their boat ride would be over before all the air had a chance to leak out. Besides, he had saved twenty-five cents on it.

As the end of school neared, the friends became impatient. They would practice putting on their wet suits and dragging their ship the half-block from the vacant lot to the arroyo. Speed was essential. They had to get La Barca launched at the peak of the flash flood so the water would be high enough to float the boat and carry the riders over the rise where a major street dipped into the wash.

In June, "School's Out! School's Out!" echoed in the hallways on the last day. Summer officially started with a few rain showers but they only caused trickles in the arroyo and made the diving squad more impatient. The Mae Wests were kept inflated, the wet suits and masks folded for easy access.

It was July when the days of the monsoon rain finally arrived! In mid-afternoon, the thunderheads started forming, tumbling on themselves, becoming darker and darker as the moisture condensed into droplets. Lightning strikes flashed, particularly in the mountains. The rain would douse the desert and bring a scent never duplicated.

"Hey Carlos, it's *really* raining! It's time! Let's go get La Barca!" Jo yelled over his patio wall. "Let's go!"

"I'm getting dressed now. Where's Pete? I'm coming!"

As the rain poured down, Jo and Carlos (in their wet suits) harnessed themselves to the vessel and began dragging it down to the arroyo. Pete caught up and began pushing. Behind them, their trail was marked by two grooves in the sand and black splotches of dye, washed off the suits by the rain.

Reaching the arroyo, the rain had almost stopped; the desert air was freshened and clean, scented by the dust it had washed. In the arroyo, the trickle of water was ever-deepening. Brown rushing currents saturated the cracked soil. The streets emptied their waters into the arroyos; the Arroyo Chico carried more and more water away from the mountains and through the asphalt city. The arroyos flushed the water to the Santa Cruz River, which was usually just a dry riverbed.

Traffic stopped as seasoned motorists backed up at the gullies. They knew the flash floods could wash a car away. Every summer, lives were lost by people who paid no attention to the rising water or the temporary barriers erected.

As the three divers arrived at the Arroyo Chico they could see a commotion of stopped vehicles and people. A car had tried to drive through the dip where the arroyo crossed the street and was caught in the flood of the water. As the motor stalled and the water continued to rise, the driver had struggled through the surging water to the shore. A small crowd was gathering to watch the abandoned car fill up and start floating as the water level rose.

Usually, Jo and Pete would stop to throw rocks in the water and listen for the *kerplunk!* in different tones as the water deepened. Today their excitement and sense of urgency heightened as they reached the edge of the arroyo, making them forget all about the smooth rocks just begging to be thrown.

"This is great! Let's get unstrapped and I'll go first. Hurry up!" Jo called to her friends.

"Hey?" Pete asked, puffing on his Mae West. "How come you get the first ride?"

"Because it's Wednesday, remember?" Jo answered. "The captain always goes first."

"Well, hurry up," Pete answered as they pushed the boat into the arroyo, now fully engaged in a flash flood. They held tight to the boat's line, wrapping it around a creosote bush for leverage.

"I'm going to get in, Crew, so don't let go!" Jo yelled as she maneuvered one foot into the boat which immediately began to float downstream. "Hold it, hold it!" Jo yelled as her legs were pulled in separate directions.

"We're holding... hurry up!" Carlos yelled back. Holding the boat with both hands, one foot hopping along shore and one foot in the bobbing boat, Jo finally climbed in as Pete yelled, "We can't hold it! We're lettin' go!"

As Pete dropped the line, the mighty La Barca hit the shore, bounced, and was drawn by the muddy water into the current. All at once it was rub-a-dub-dub, one girl in a tub, and the tub was completely out of control! It swirled in the current and hit the shore. It bounced back into the main current as Jo saw the alternate shore swirling by. On one rotation, she saw the stranded motorist running along side her on the bank. He was frantically screaming and waving his arms. Jo couldn't understand the man until she saw she was spinning right towards the man's car submerged downstream. Jo displayed her naval training in quick decisions; she shut her eyes and held on tight! She felt her hand hit something hard and when she opened her eyes, she was bobbing around the front of the car's grill and then onward past the car.

The arroyo flood was approaching a sheer cliff where it had washed away the dirt, spilling away from the road—just enough to make the brown water foam into churning, twisting rapids. As the square tub plunged over the drop it was swamped with sandy water yet buoyed up by the thick lumber sides. Low in the water now, it swirled on down the center of the current towards the Great Divide.

The 'Great Divide' was a telephone pole causing brown froth as the water broke into curling waves around it. In a second, Jo decided to do what any able-bodied seafarer would do—she abandoned ship! The tub crashed into the pole as Jo shoved off and went bobbing down the current, her arms flailing, grabbing at debris washed downstream by the storm. She struggled to reach some creosote bushes hanging in the torrent and caught hold with one hand then another. She clung to the branches as the tub swept by, barely missing her.

Pete and Carlos ran down the shore screaming, "Jo, Jo! Please don't drown! Don't drown!" Carlos threw himself onto the bank and reached out his hands to help Jo drag herself up onto the shore as Pete held tightly to Carlos' feet.

The panic on the boys' faces grew as Jo gagged and sputtered.

"Hey, Jo, you okay?" Pete pleaded. "Are you okay?"

"Huh? Jo? Huh, Captain?" Carlos kept repeating, "Huh Jo? Jo?"

Pulling at her with all their strength, Carlos and Pete dragged their captain to safety and collapsed beside their soaked friend on the embankment. The boys were panting with fear until Jo started to cough and gag.

"I swallowed... twenty-five gallons... of that... muddy stuff!" Jo sputtered. "Where's... the ship? Crew? Wow, that was neat!" Her voice boomed with excitement. She sucked the bloody cut on her hand and rubbed her leg while trying to see the boat from her hunkered position.

"You're alright?" Pete asked suddenly surprised.

"Well, sure," Jo answered, equally amazed. She patted her body to verify it.

"You fool!" Pete yelled, jumping up and stamping. "You idiot! You fool! Why did you jump ship, you fool!"

Jo almost laughed, "You were scared!"

"No! I wasn't! I... well... just a little when you disappeared just before the boat hit the pole." Pete laughed with uneasy relief. "I kept thinking how mad our moms would be if one of us drowned," Pete added almost sheepishly. The three stared at each other as they realized what could have happened.

All of a sudden, Carlos exclaimed, "We did it!"

"Hey, it floated! We did it!" Jo shouted. She danced in elation.

Pete joined the prancing on the muddy bank.

"We did it! We did it! We did it!" became the amigos

chant! The exhilaration of the event replaced the apprehension; all three were jittery with excitement! They had conquered the mighty Arroyo Chico!

Quickly resuming command, Jo turned to Carlos, "Where's the ship?"

"It's stuck down where the flood turns into a snag," Carlos answered, gesturing downstream.

Pete's concern gave way to impatience. "Let's go. I want my turn before the water's gone. Golly, that was neat! You spinning and the man yelling about his car. I thought the pole would crack you! Let's go get the boat!"

They ran down the arroyo bank to the culvert where the tub and its line were tangled in the debris clogging the culvert opening. With sticks, they caught the line and pulled the tub to the shore.

"Hey, it looks okay, just a dent where it hit the pole. Let's hurry," Pete urged. "Why don't we let it float and we'll drag it by its line, ya know?"

The trio pulled the tub back upstream but the water level was already going down. The boat would hit the shore then bounce back into the water. The crowd was watching the motorist trying to start his car again. They gave a friendly cheer as the boat crew passed them.

When the trio got the boat back to their starting point, there was less than a foot of water left. Jo and Carlos held the line as Pete slid down the side of the arroyo and climbed into the ship. He sat crossed-legged as the boat sank lower in the receding water and rested on some rocks.

"Aw, come on, give me a shove," Pete yelled. Jo dropped the line and waded into the water with Carlos. They gave the tub a push and it moved a few feet... then lodged against a sand bar.

"Aw!" Pete wailed. "You used all the water!"

He reached out and tried to shove himself free of the bar but the heavy boat just wouldn't budge. "Aw! Nuts!"

"Listen, Crew," Jo said from the shore. "Next time you can go first. Okay?"

Pete looked down at his soaking, muddied long johns, his hands stained by the black dye, his deflated Mae West, and his grounded tub. "Aw, shit!"

Over the years, Josephine hadn't given much thought to the Arroyo. Graduating from college, she moved to the Pacific Northwest and into a career in Marine Ecology. Now, coming back home to take care of her mother, everything about Tucson was different and bigger; she could hardly recognize the old neighborhood. An apartment complex had swallowed her childhood home and the empty desert lot next to it. She drove over a bridge that spanned the Arroyo Chico with only a warning sign: Danger in Flood Season; guard rails protected tourists who dismissed the sign. The Arroyo itself had been tamed by desert irrigation. More water for premium cotton meant less runoff to dry washes. The arroyo was buried by county sewer projects. It had been reduced to a dip which sometimes became a puddle during the summer rains.

Peter was gone. He had left the desert to enlist in another real war—Viet Nam. Pursuing enemy vessels on the canals in a Patrol River Boat, Pete was often reminded of the Arroyo adventure. Of the cross-trained crew of four, he was the PBR captain. Killed in the Mekong Delta, Peter was posthumously awarded the Silver Star.

Although Carlos and Jo dated briefly during college, it

never seemed to work as a romantic duo; they just remained friends. This visit, she would become her mother's caregiver and stay. Settling into her mother's home, she called Carlos, a linguistics professor at the University. Delighted to hear from her, Carlos invited her to meet his wife and family for lunch at their home.

One of Carlos' children had a passion for sailboats. Over lunch, Carlos' young daughter, Maria, insisted on sitting next to Josephine at the patio table. The youngster watched everything the guest did with adoring eyes. Moving close, she started to whisper, and Josephine bent to hear her. Maria confided a secret to her Papa's amiga: She wanted to circumnavigate the world. "Mi padre always tells me I can do whatever I want. Just like Jo!"

Josephine hugged the little girl warmly and shared a knowing grin with Carlos as she said, "That's absolutely right, Maria! You just need to find the water."

TEACHER'S LOUNGE
TIME FRAGMENT TOMORROW CE

The view was vague, Jennifer felt as if she was floating and looking down through a fog at a frail old woman propped in bed, relishing the hot fudge sundae being fed to her. The helper was a younger version of the elder lady; perhaps it was her daughter. The woman smiled gratefully, blew a kiss, and snuggled into her comforter to fall asleep. Wispy clouds then obscured the vision. Jennifer surmised the scene ended in death. *Was it a movie scene or a memory?*

Jennifer's next awareness was of entering a huge, lit space without walls or ceiling. There was a sign in large, bold letters declaring: TEACHER'S LOUNGE. It was suspended over the area where a back wall should have been. The absence of partitions or ceiling did not deter objects from suspending themselves. They hung above tables, next to bookcases, encircling file cabinets, clustering near computer consoles. Cabinets hovered over countertops. Little signs and sticky notes detailed accessories. White boards were conspicuous. In one corner—where a corner should have been—there was a table with an old-fashioned dial telephone next to a smart-phone charging station. The invisible floor appeared solid as it supported people and furniture.

In her quick survey of the never-ending space, Jennifer

noticed there were no wires connecting the electronics. All devices were self-contained including the coffee maker, microwave, and large stainless-steel refrigerator. *Where was she?*

"You're right where you should be: The Teachers Lounge," a warm, deep voice said behind her. It was as if her thoughts were being read.

Jennifer turned to the figure in janitor's work clothes. She thought she recognized his gray hair, intense blue eyes, and hands showing years of labor.

"Oh, hello. I'm not sure how I got here. I'm Jennifer Shattuck. I haven't been in a teacher's room for years." She extended her hand and stared at her now-youthful fingers. There was no sign of arthritis! As he shook her hand, she looked over his shoulder to a mirror hanging on a non-wall. There was a young, auburn-haired Jennifer shaking hands with an older man in khaki overalls.

The man laughed gently. "Everyone says that at first! We'll get you acclimated soon enough. I'm Ben, the maintenance man, and I'll help you any way I can. Something comes up, just ask for Ben."

Ben was familiar with the confusion Jennifer was feeling. All newcomers to the Lounge were disoriented. He gave her a few minutes to look around the expansive space with free-hanging objects, a variety of strangers, and a murmur of voices in muted tones.

Finally, Jennifer took a breath and broached her main questions. "Am I... dead?"

"Let's just say—in teachers' terms—you've Passed the Test! You have Passed Life!" Ben's expression was reassuring, almost proud.

The vision of the white-haired lady flashed through Jennifer's mind at the same time she saw her young reflection in a floating mirror. "But... where am I? Is this the 'afterlife?'"

"In a way," Ben answered. "Different cultures or philosophies have different names for it. You can think of it anyway you want. For you, it's Afterlife 101. Now, let's just get you acquainted. Walk with me a bit. Most people feel better when they're moving." He quietly led the way through the maze of tables, nodding to people who were apparently teaching staff. After a few steps, he stopped. "Now, here we have the food prep counter. Many teachers are hungry when they arrive."

"No, thank you. I've just had a delicious hot fudge sundae," Jennifer replied then immediately added, "How silly that must sound after 'passing' into a 'teacher's lounge' for 'Afterlife 101.'" She started to laugh and Ben joined her. Their laughter rose until they were both gasping and those seated near them began to feel left out by the joke. Jennifer regained her composure, heartened by sharing humor with Ben. This food prep counter was unlike any Jennifer had ever observed in a staff room. The microwave was pristine, inside and out. The refrigerator was immaculate with sealed food packs identified by clearly printed names.

Whispering confidentially, Ben said, "Ignore the cheese packet in the back corner of the lower shelf. No one knows how long it's been here." His wink almost started her laughing again. The coffee maker was a wonder with nary a drop of precious liquid dribbled on the countertop. Most wonderful of all, the coffee mugs were spotless, unsullied by days of overuse without being washed.

A few more steps and Ben gestured to a large column

of smoke. There were no containment walls, no residue, scent, or escaped wisps. "This is the smokers' room. It's not used as much as it used to be. A few staff visit it occasionally and they said just walking inside makes them feel better. I can't vouch for the feeling; I gave up smoking so many eons ago. Just know it's there if you'd like." Jennifer quickly shook her head and suppressed a comment about smokers.

Step after step, Ben led Jennifer through the tables and gatherings of teachers. Gradually, the groupings became obvious to Jennifer. Over near a computer console, science was being discussed and formulae written on the white board. At a couch and coffee table, Home Economics and Family Management were being discussed by an equal number of women and men. Different languages were being spoken at one table with everyone apparently understanding each other. Near a stack of library books, people sat quietly reading the volumes. Jennifer was surprised at the stereotypical divisions.

"Ben, who divided these people into their little departments? Why are they isolating themselves when they have so many diverse minds for interaction?"

"We've tried mixing them up. It's called 'Staff Development.' We even had personality typing but after the sessions, they all went back to their comfort zones. And, after all, it is their afterlife to choose."

Ben gestured to a table nearby. "I think your friend is over there. She has been waiting for a while, maybe for you." He touched his forehead as if tipping a hat, and left Jennifer with the rest of her questions.

Hurrying to the table, Jennifer almost felt agoraphobic. *Where was she? When was she? Who were all these people?* Touching the shoulder of the woman at the table, she hesitated until the woman turned.

"Jenni! I knew you'd come! Oh, my dear friend, I'm so glad to see you!" Ruth Faulkner stood and hugged Jennifer. Over her shoulder, in another hanging mirror, Jennifer could see two friends from their teaching days; Ruth was smiling brightly and Jennifer was in total surprise.

This was not the elderly Ruth who was my lifelong friend into retirement, Jennifer thought. *As old ladies, we took cruises together, belonged to book clubs, and enjoyed reminiscing about our teaching careers. We comforted each other when our husbands died. Who are we now?*

Still holding her friend's hand, Ruth gestured to a chair that appeared next to hers at the table. "Sit down, sit down. It's been ages since we visited. When did you arrive? How's your family?" Seeing Jennifer's expression, Ruth chuckled and dismissed the chair's arrival. "Don't mind the fold-up seat, you'll get used to things moving about. Ben probably sent it knowing we had a lot to talk about." Her voice was familiar, yet this Ruth was a woman as young as Jennifer in the mirror.

"Ruth, where are our husbands? I don't see them anywhere." Jennifer searched the faces in the extended space.

"They passed on before us, and remember, the marriage promises were 'until death do us part.' Well... here we are." Ruth shrugged with a grin. "We're parted! The guys are probably in their own special places by now. Ben said there were as many rest stops as people needed. He let me remain in the Teacher's Lounge waiting for you, my dear friend."

A memory from her life washed over her:

Ruth and Jennifer met years and years ago when Jennifer first started teaching at the Special Project at the Northwest High School. Ruth was Department Chair and took Jennifer, the new teacher, to the back lot where a dilapidated trailer was set. Ruth was embarrassed by its condition. The district bureaucrats had run out of classrooms, so this was designated an 'annex.' Nothing in Jennifer's college classes covered teaching in a deserted trailer with rickety stairs perched next to a creek with weeds for shrubbery. But with Ruth's help, she organized tables, put up posters, and made a small bookcase for the students' use. The first day of the new school year, Jennifer was ready or not! Ruth became her lifelong mentor and best friend.

Now, sitting near the entrance of the Lounge with Ruth, Jennifer was distracted to see a former manager from the district office walk into the afterlife space.

"Ruth, the man just walking in, he looks like a manager...."Jennifer began.

"Yes, that's the guy. He's reverted to his school appearance. We all do. Notice how we have the same ages now as we did when working in the schools? It's one of the perks of the Lounge," Ruth answered.

The man looked middle aged, dressed in a business suit and tie. Jennifer was unable to hear his conversation with Ben, but the two seemed to be having a disagreement. The man gestured to an ID badge on his pocket; Ben shook his head. The man was angry and stomped out of the Lounge.

"Where's he going?" Jennifer asked.

Ruth shrugged and said casually, "There's another place for administrators."

"Why? Wasn't he a teacher before he became

an administrator?"

"It's like we thought all along." Ruth expressed her long held opinion. "Some teachers who become administrators have their brains scrubbed when they're bumped up to district office. It's the same if they teach classes at a college. They get so focused on numbers and dollars and fighting off litigation suits that they forget what it's like to be the only adult in a classroom of fidgety children or rebelling teens needing to learn. Principals and vice-principals are still in the classroom trenches, so to speak. District bureaucrats are not."

"So where do they go with their scrubbed brains?" Jennifer wasn't even sure where she and Ruth were going, much less an administrator.

"Oh, there's a hallway they follow to a conference room. I asked Ben once and he said, 'One conference room after another conference room after another. All organizations and businesses have them, and everyone confers about the same things, with very little changing. If they do get their teacher brains back, they can recirculate here.'"

"What about the teachers whose brains weren't scrubbed?" Jennifer thought of particular people at her district office.

"They become good administrators who remember the children first and are motivated to direct resources to the classrooms. There's a table of them over there discussing the Gymnasium." Ruth said as she smiled and gestured to a distant table.

"And here is...?"

"Why, Jennifer dear, we are on our way to the

Gymnasium! Afterlife 101 is our time to reflect, evaluate and gather our energy to share. Other people pass through their own reflections."

Ruth's mention of energy brought another memory of the trailer:

It was isolated from the rest of school, surrounded by trees, and perched near a creek. The sound of rain pounding on the metal roof dominated all conversation. It caused a student to ask loudly, "Mrs. Shattuck, what if the rainstorm washes the trailer down into the creek? What would happen to us?"

Jennifer looked directly to the freshman boy who was so nervous about the rain sheeting down the windows.

"Well, Jason, it shouldn't happen because the struts supporting us have been reinforced."

"But what if we did get washed away?" Jason was not about to let the teacher off easy. "Would we drown?"

"I don't believe so, Jason, because if this trailer dammed up the stream, the flooding water would pour right back into the school and the fire department would get us out!" It wasn't much of an answer on short notice, but it seemed to satisfy Jason. "And I personally would make sure everyone was safe!" Jennifer promised.

In the same trailer on another school day, it was a more mischievous Jason looking out the window during the passing period. He saw a gruff senior stomping towards the trailer and on a whim, got up and held the door shut, just to tease. Outside, the senior yelled which made Jason laugh and hold tighter. Then the door was yanked open full force and one hundred and eighty pounds of furious anger stormed into the room. Jason froze and the senior grabbed him by the throat, choking him with all his strength.

Interceding, Jennifer grabbed the nearest arm and demanded the older student to stop! He dropped Jason, looked around the classroom panting, and stormed out to disappear among the trees. Jennifer immediately checked to make sure Jason was okay, left her aide in the room, and sped to the Administrator's office to report the incident. She warned there was a large, angry student on the loose. Within a few days, the head office 'found' a new classroom near the Vice Principal. It was designated for the Special Project Learning Class; the room was near personnel, the nurse's office, and a telephone.

"All right, Ruth, now I understand what Afterlife 101 is all about. Some people would liken it to limbo or purgatory. From what I've experienced, it's a place of reflection, self-evaluation, memories of teaching, and," Jennifer reached to pat Ruth's hand, "to re-unite with dear friends. I suppose the other rest stops you mentioned are different for everybody."

With a chuckle, Jennifer continued, "I can imagine quite a bit: A ship builder's guild, a cowboy's corral, a religious retreat, a florist's garden, and a soldier's memorial."

Ruth added, "A politician's caucus... a CEO's board room... a priest's confessional... an athlete's Olympic stadium!" Ruth and Jennifer shared the humor as they always did when working together.

"It's the Gymnasium that I don't comprehend for teachers. When I think of the high school gym, it entails sweaty boys and girls, smelly socks, and a lot of noise." That started their laughter again.

Finally, Ruth wiped her eyes and added, "Oh, yes, lots of noise, so I'll let Ben tell you. He's such a good storyteller."

As if beckoned, Ben appeared at the table. He rubbed his jaw and smiled broadly. He remained standing and began his oration with a soothing tone and twinkling eyes.

"Jennifer, you comforted a girl crying behind the bleachers because the captain of the basketball team never paid her attention. You suggested she notice the boy beside her in Study Hall. He always paid her attention, answered questions, and helped with homework. He was too shy to ask her out but could be the best friend ever. *Energy.*

"There were proms. Decorating the gym, dressing special, and being 'grown up' for an evening hinted at the transition to adulthood—a promise for the present and future. *Energy.*

"There were sports of excitement. Students experienced victories and losses while watching; the players learned about life's possibilities by participation. Remember Stephan, the wrestler who would read a book while waiting for his match? The wrestling made him sure of his body; his books made him confident of his mind. *Energy.*

"Renowned speakers presented assemblies of great ideas and patterns for a worthwhile life. Some of the lessons would be immediately accepted, while others took years to be appreciated. Unfortunately, for some students, the words would never gain meaning or value. *Energy.*"

As Ben spoke, Jennifer noticed the background murmur stopped as everyone listened to his words. She saw individuals nodding as faces expressed mixed emotions, conflicting thoughts of happiness or concern.

Ben continued without hesitation. "The gym was a protector in the rain or snow. It could host a bazaar or science fair. Sometimes it doubled as a cafeteria for students and staff alike. It was a center for communal activities. *Energy.*

"Graduation brought a climax of energy and pride to

the gymnasium. Students, faculty, parents, siblings, grandparents, friends, family—all brought their expectations with them. Emotions of hope, fear, confusion, promise, remorse, and anticipation filled every seam and strut of the gymnasium.

"Energy Equals Experience Plus!" Ben's eyes gleamed as he recounted the energy of the classic gymnasium. He chuckled and finished by saying, "Literally the word gymnasium means 'school for naked exercise.' It is also a place to exercise the mind with discussion and pageantry. It's changed a bit over the eons to be a compendium of energy. Positive and negative, it's all there... consciousness... essence... spirit... soul."

Again, Jennifer was confused. "I thought that was the purpose of Afterlife 101. What's going on in the Gymnasium?"

"Energy Equals Experience Plus!" Ruth and Ben repeated together. "E=E+!"

Ben continued, his voice rich with emotion: "For an instant of time people experience their lives and reflect in their afterlife. In the Gymnasium, they return to the source of life to blend again, to be part of the stream of consciousness. Some people, even teachers, skip Afterlife 101 and go straight to the Gymnasium where their energy merges with others, like streams to a river, like particles to the Cosmos. Your energy will emerge again, Jennifer, sometime, somewhere."

"How do you know when you're ready?"

"If you are ready, how can you not know? You're the teacher!"

While Ben paused, a juggler entered the Lounge tossing balls, dishes, and rings in a rhythmic display. She did not stop to investigate the room, she just nodded to Ben and continued on her way. The juggled items floated with her. "You see, the juggler already knows the way. She's a woman of substance." Ben walked away, always smiling. Over his shoulder, he added, "There are lots of people who go through life the same way, teaching by example, helping others. Sometimes, they write books and become memoirists!"

Her vision becoming bleary again, Jennifer turned to Ruth. "Why do these wispy clouds always come back with a memory?"

Ruth answered with a grin, "Our generation has watched too many movies! Our brains go into 'change scenes' mode. It does help determine reality or flashback. If it bothers you, I'm sure Ben can dismiss it."

"No, it's all right. Just excuse me while I remember a particularly tense emotion."

Mrs. Shattuck was given a new student near the end of the quarter, a particularly attractive fifteen year old girl. Her paperwork had many changes of background and a fragmented education. She was very social and quickly participated in the classroom activities. When Jennifer overheard her talking with another student about hitchhiking to parties on the weekend, Jennifer interrupted. "Laurie, that's a very dangerous thing to do. You shouldn't get into a car with a stranger. Hitchhiking is very risky."

"Oh, Mrs. Shattuck, I know what I'm doing. I can always tell what kind of a guy is driving. It's a way to get to a party. I have a girlfriend who goes with me, so it's safe." Laurie obviously knew more than a teacher.

"Laurie, this is serious." Jennifer tried to warn her. Further conversations failed to persuade the teen. Laurie remained convinced of her invulnerability. At the end of the

quarter, Laurie dropped out of Northwest High School, changing yet again.

It was later in the school year when the newspaper article appeared describing the violent death of teenage girls who had been hitchhiking. One was Laurie. A man stopped and offered them a ride to a party where he was going. Instead, he drove to his house and said the party was in his garage. When the girls went inside, he brutally murdered them. A neighbor heard cries for help and called the police.

Ruth touched Jennifer's hand and the bleariness disappeared. "You're thinking about Laurie, aren't you? I could tell from your expression."

"I have carried her memory, wondering what I could have said or should have done differently. For all the positive stories of so many students, Laurie still haunts me. Will that be included in the energy force of the Gym?"

"Yes, because it is part of why we keep on trying—to reach one more student." The compassion in Ruth's voice soothed Jennifer's thoughts, encouraging other directions.

Jennifer recalled the way a summer vacation could cause a metamorphosis in students.…

The girls came into high school well on their way to woman status, paying attention to the maturing young men. For the boys, the maturation usually happened between tenth and eleventh grade. Nathan was a tall, blond, athletic boy in the process of becoming a man. He was already changing attitudes. Boys would go home for the summer vacation after ninth grade, and reappear with deeper voices, hair growing everywhere, and a different attitude. Because the class was a special project, Jennifer saw Nathan in the morning when he was an affable, cooperative student. Coming back to the classroom after lunch, he was quarrelsome and disruptive. Jennifer contacted his mother to discuss the changes.

"I'm very concerned about Nathan's aggressive behavior after lunch," she began. "He's been sent to the office for starting fights on campus, he's argumentative about assignments, and he's just not the same Nathan as in the morning. Something's going on mid-day." Mentally, Jennifer was suspicious about drugs being shared during the lunch break, but it was not something she could prove. She resisted the urge to address drugs.

Nathan's mother became enraged. "There's nothing wrong with our Nathan! You're not an effective teacher! Those other students started the fights, our Nathan is just fine. If you were a better teacher, you could teach mornings and afternoons without picking on students for your failures! Come on, Nathan, I've had enough of this parent conference." She gestured to her son and stormed out of the classroom.

Nathan looked defiantly at Mrs. Shattuck with his 'afternoon smirk' and followed his mother.

Ruth interrupted the memory. "Jennifer Shattuck, you have been reflecting about problems and unfinished interactions. I've watched you teaching, guiding students, participating in school events, and being a positive force for students! You have numerous strengths to remember before you go to the Gym. We all have."

Jennifer hesitated, because Ruth was right. "But... why am I thinking about unresolved problems?" she asked her mentor.

"Because you cared about all the students so much. It's all a matter of balance now and we have the luxury of this Teacher's Lounge to figure it out!" Her sincere smile said more than the words. "Gather all the energy from all those years!"

With Ruth's directive, and without misty smoke or clouds, Jennifer did remember:

There was Greg who couldn't read above a certain level. She wrote a grant and obtained a special art training program for him on the computer. There was another grant for a telecommunication project with students being able to correspond with creative senior citizens around the world. A young man with fetal alcohol syndrome lost his stutter and carried a dictionary to have access to just the right word. A girl with brain damage from playing chicken with a car was able to return to regular classrooms. A young man given the choice of incarceration or Special Projects graduated and took his band to play at the Governor's charity gala. On two different occasions, student lives were saved because Jennifer interfered. Nathan came back to say, 'Thank you.' It was part of his program to apologize. Mrs. Shattuck was right about his drug usage and the lessons from her classroom spurred him to seek help and re-hab.

"Tell me, Ruth, just who is Ben?" Jennifer quietly asked her mentor and friend.

"He's whoever you want him to be. You've always had questions! I think it will be your contribution to E=E+. But, that's enough, Jenni. I think it's time to go." Ruth stood and coaxed Jennifer. "Let's check out the Gymnasium." She started walking toward a huge arrow hanging in space to point the way.

Walking with Ruth, Jennifer glanced at a man sitting alone. He was disheveled, grumbling, and crossing out items on a list. In front of him was the spoiled cheese from the fridge.

"Oh, don't mind old Grimley. He's been here for eons,

can't seem to balance his energy levels," Ruth advised. "He may never get to the Gym."

There weren't any misty clouds as Jennifer and Ruth clasped each other's hands and passed into the Gymnasium. Jennifer became aware of her last question:

"What's next?"

BITTERSWEET AURORA
TIME FRAGMENT 2018 CE

The human eye perceives shapes, distance, light, color, movement, and atmospheres. It is the human brain that delights in what it sees; the mind relishes the panorama it interprets. For Kenneth, the view of the sunlit snow-covered mountains and landscape was close to ecstasy. He stood on a ridge facing the Wrangell Mountains of Alaska.

Kenneth spoke out loud: "Linda, it's all here, just as wonderful as we remembered. I'm sorry for the time it took get back, but now we're here! The land is ours. The cabin will be refurbished the way you wanted. It's where we are meant to be—always." His choked voice conveyed the grief and gratitude he was experiencing. Kenneth's eyes felt as if they were stretching to absorb the beauty spread about him. The only sounds were the cry of a bald eagle soaring over the tall trees and the crackling of the ice as the nearby stream thawed. Not disturbing the solitude, Kenneth replaced the funeral urn with its precious contents into his knapsack and returned to the empty cabin.

An early retirement had beckoned. It would be the special time Kenneth and Linda could spend together. They wanted to make up for what they had missed because of his missions and deployments in the Air Force. His last duty station was at the northern most USAF Base where Linda could be with him. They both grew to love the pristine beauty around them in Alaska. They bought acreage with a cabin in anticipation. When 'retirement' finally arrived, they expected to indulge in everything outdoor life promised. Except... Linda had cervical cancer. The property had to wait; for almost two years they lived in Seattle.

The cancer center became their second home as they followed the medical regimen of tests, surgeries, and chemotherapy. Kenneth was her caregiver and pill dispenser, her lover and playmate, her respite and cheerleader.

During one temporary remission, the two took the ferries serving Puget Sound and drove to British Columbia to visit the famous Butchart Gardens. The statuary, the fountains, and the beauty of the foliage all combined to renew their strength. At a little pagoda in the Japanese garden, they met and talked with an older couple originally from Japan. A boisterous talker, the man said it was so exquisite here at the Garden, he had to sing. His wife laughed, saying, "He needs nothing to coax him to sing."

With that, the man burst into an aria from the opera *La Traviata*, perfectly beautiful, bringing smiles to everyone who passed along the little alcove. When the older couple returned to the garden path, the gentleman winked at Kenneth and confided, "I sing to my wife every day." His wife nodded, smiling. As they left, Kenneth patted Linda's shoulder. He knew he couldn't sing, but he would always be there for her.

Linda purchased seeds at the Garden's gift shop, reading all the instructions, making sure they would grow on their property. The two promised themselves they would return to Alaska when she 'was well.'

One afternoon, waiting for a medical appointment, Linda was feeling up to a short walk on a trail near the cancer center. The two strolled leisurely to identify plants and trees. At the base of a cedar, a collection of wrinkled little fungi on stems stood out. The perfect temperature and humidity caused the mushroom crop to break to the forest surface.

Linda bent to gently touch the caps, and she likened herself to the little gems waiting for the right time to break into view. "These mushrooms are as wrinkled as I feel from the chemo effects."

"And they are especially delicious, just like you are!" Kenneth pulled his wife into his arms and hugged her close. He whispered into her hair, "We'll gather mushrooms at our home in Alaska. I promise. I understand they make wonderful soup."

"Mushroom soup?" Linda questioned as she snuggled to his chest. "I can't wait!"

The waiting continued. The procedures were failing, but the dream of the home in the woods did not. Even confined to her hospital bed, Linda planned homey touches to the cabin while IVs were attached to her bruised arms. She always had a smile for Kenneth when he appeared. They would discuss the property waiting for them while he would coax her to eat. As terrible as the cancer was for Linda, the pain of watching her fade away was as great for Kenneth.

Leaving Seattle behind, alone now, Ken had driven north with the arrival of spring. Hardly pausing at the bigger cities, he was obsessed to get to the property in the wilderness of

Alaska. Once there, he stood watching the sun set over craggy mountains draped in permanent snow. Tears streamed down his face. He let the sobbing flow.

Going back to the cabin in the twilight, Ken moved some supplies from his vehicle to inside the door. He finished eating some leftover sandwiches and crackers. Throwing his sleeping bag on the floor, he fell into the sleep of exhaustion.

When Ken awoke, he almost felt refreshed. He definitely felt hungry! He had failed to shop at the bigger stores along the route. After a quick inventory of needs, he maneuvered the Suburban over the rough cut road until reaching the highway to the village. The little collection of weathered, miniature stores was like many gatherings in the boroughs. Here, he was at the Podstakannik Emporium and Mercantile Specialty Outlet. The sign itself was too long to fit across the front of the establishment. It bent and continued around the corner of the seasoned frame building. Similar small structures joined the mercantile next to an old, but operating, gas station. A barn and three lesser shops clustered around the bend in the two-lane highway. A driveway led to a collection of wood frame houses.

"Hey, you're new in Podstakannik. Glad to meet you!" The friendly greeting from the clerk behind the grocery counter welcomed Ken. "From your full basket, I'd guess you were settling in or stocking up."

"Both," acknowledged Ken.

"You military or retired?" The storekeeper held out his hand to shake.

"Both." Ken repeated, shaking the offered hand. "I've got acreage north of here."

"Well, welcome to Alaska! I'm the owner here, Brian

Schielke. Just let me know if there's anything I can do to help." Brian looked the newcomer over and said with a grin, "Yep, you're both alright."

Returning the smile, Ken asked, "What makes you say that? I'm Ken Larison."

"Your posture, your choice of food stuffs, and you're clean shaven. 'Round here, it takes a while for the winter beards to disappear." Brian stroked his own scruffy, gray beard. "Is your place the old Gardner parcel—sold a few years ago?"

"That's the place. We bought it but, well, it took me a while to get here." He paused.

"And how about the missus?" Brian asked with genuine interest.

"No, just me. My wife... died." Ken was getting used to saying the words but it wasn't any easier.

"I'm so sorry," Brian said genuinely. "It must be—" He would have said more but a thunderous all-terrain vehicle slammed to a stop in front of the store.

A stubble-bearded young man stomped into the establishment. "Hey Brian, I need some canned stew. My dad's taken off again." The young man shoved past Ken and called over his shoulder as he walked through the aisles. Dressed in miss-matched teen attire, even his jacket had worn thin.

"Wait your turn, Garrett," Brian said, returning to check out Ken's selection.

"Well, hurry up!" Garrett called out impatiently, still moving through the aisles.

Ken glanced at the young customer as he rummaged through shelves at the back. In spite of his stubble, he was more boy than man and obviously disturbed by having to wait. Ken noticed the furtive way products were moved about the shelves in his hands.

"I'll just take the stew, this guy's order will take a long time." Garrett scooped up two cans of stew, returned to the front of the store and started to leave.

"Just a minute, Garrett, aren't you going to pay?" Ken spoke softly, using the boy's name.

Surprised, Garrett sneered and mumbled, "He can put it on my tab." He again turned toward the door.

"What about the deer jerky you put in your pocket from the back?" Ken was giving Garrett a chance but his tone was more challenging.

Startled, Garrett looked back and forth between the storeowner and Ken. He swallowed and his bravado returned. "Oh, that… I forgot. Put it on my tab as well, Brian." He pulled out a bag of jerky, waved it, and began to move but Ken stood in the way.

"What about the other pocket, Garrett? Did you forget that too?"

Confronted, Garrett fumed with anger and embarrassment. Faced with this stranger, he yanked at his pocket, took out some packaged batteries and threw them on the counter. "There! Forget 'em! I don't want your stinking batteries anyway!" With a tight jaw, he shoved past Ken, revved up his ATV, and tore up the road.

"You've made an enemy there," Brian commented, shaking his head. He finished tabulating Ken's grocery order. "Garrett hasn't always been like this. He was a great little kid when his family first moved here. Things happened—the family fell apart, his dad's never there, and Garrett turned mean. We hope he'll outgrow it."

Thinking back on the young men and women he had known in the service, Ken murmured, "Sometimes, hoping isn't enough."

When plants and animals came to life in the Alaska Spring, so did the village of Podstakannik. Locals were eager to socialize with neighbors after the long winter nights. Snowbirds—people and feathered flocks—were returning from their winter adventures. Residents and visitors began driving the highway in giant motor homes or pulling camping trailers to the National Parks or wildlife areas. With dip fishing nets strapped to the truck roofs, Alaskan natives and non-native people alike would stop at Podstakannik to get fuel. Tourists took their selfie pictures at the corner in front of the store with the long name. Little kiosks of local artwork began setting up. Bears started to wake from hibernation.

Ken started meeting other people at the Mercantile or as neighbors stopped by to introduce themselves. Subsistence residents would share their harvests of fish and wildlife. He signed up for an emergency planning committee because Linda would have. She had always participated in the communities where Ken was stationed. After all his travels and experiences, Ken was adjusting to the lifestyle afforded to him by retirement. He wished he could talk to Linda about it.

Repairs on the cabin progressed toward Ken's goal of having his first winter refuge in the cabin. He did most of the reconstruction work himself. The physical labor was therapeutic and guaranteed a good night's sleep following exhaustion. He found he could rely on names at the

Mercantile bulletin board for occasional extra work. As the soil warmed, Ken started a garden with a borrowed tiller. He planted some of the Butchart seeds. He carefully read the seasonal directions and prepared a special pot to hang outside the kitchen window where he could watch the seedlings prosper. Linda would have liked it when the flowers blossomed. When he discovered a mushroom patch to cultivate close to the cabin, he began searching for mushrooms in the woods. In late June, weather was just right and Ken found a large patch of morels. He placed a request for a mushroom soup recipe on the Mercantile bulletin board. Soon, he received many favorites and tips about foraging for mushrooms.

Ken was aware of Garrett watching him; sometimes he heard the ATV in the nearby forest. In the village, the teen avoided Ken. Garrett could be found on the corner hanging with a few others his age. Their rough language and laughter were incompatible with the quiet serenity of the area. Cursing the coming school year seemed to be a favorite topic of the teens and Garrett boasted about quitting high school months earlier. He wouldn't be going back, ever. He had a job that paid all summer working in the Podsta Stables. Ken just ignored him. He did wonder though at the way the teens snuck something between them disguised as a handshake.

An afternoon scream of the emergency siren alerted Ken to a fire in the village! It was the loudest siren he had ever heard and he had been exposed to numerous alarms in the service. He dropped the board he was sawing, checked his emergency fire pack in the back of the Suburban and sped into the village. Numbers of people surrounded the stables, hoses were deployed, and in the short time it took him to get there, the fire was under control. People in Podsta were immediate in attending to fire.

At the edge of the road, Ken saw Brian yelling at Garrett, and waving his arms toward the stables. "What the hell were you doing, smoking in a hay loft?! You could have set the whole building on fire. What's the matter with you?" Brian was apoplectic.

Sweating, Garrett was defensive. His eyes darted between the stables and the crowd around. Angrily, he growled, "Don't yell at me, Ol' Man! I had it under control! I was putting the fire out but that busy body at the art store blew the siren!" His voice raised defiantly with more expletives, his fists clenched.

"Under control? The smoke pouring out of there? Why were you smoking in the first place, in a loft full of hay, with propane tanks next door?!" Brian was exasperated.

Before Garrett could respond, Ken moved next to Brian. He said nothing but Garrett stepped back, glaring at the two men.

"I was taking care of it!" Garrett responding angrily, spun on his heel and shoved his way through the crowd. The roar of the ATV left no doubt of his exit.

With people milling about, Ken asked quietly, "What happened, Brian? That siren scared the heck out of me."

Brian laughed in relief from the tension receding. "Marilynn Tsosie at the art supply store wrote a grant to get an alarm siren from the forest service. People paid extra to be sure it was loud enough to reach the outlying cabins." He chuckled at the thought. "Now, she blows it for any emergency." He shook his head and said seriously, "This could have been real bad, the smoke poured out and we couldn't tell how much was burning. Evidently Garrett stopped what he started! I don't know what to do with Garrett. I'd hoped the job at the stables would teach him some responsibility. Instead, he almost burns the place down."

"What about his father?"

"No help there. He's a trapper... no one knows his whereabouts."

"Aren't there some counselors at the borough high school?"

"Garrett dropped out last year when he got the promise of the stable job. I don't know what he'll do now. I smelled more than simple tobacco when I first saw the smoke. Now, it's just the scent of burned hay. Luckily, the owners haven't brought in the full string of riding horses yet. They hold them for the tourists. It could have been horrible, a stable of panicked horses." Again, Brian shook his head. "You know, Garrett's such a big guy, it's easy to forget he's just a kid."

"An angry 'kid' can do a lot of damage," Ken said warily. He realized being on the emergency planning committee would be more difficult than he imagined.

By June, the long daylight hours were encouraging new growth in Ken's garden. He was on his knees tending to a few weeds when he heard the loud ATV coming at his back. He froze in place, his hand on the rake next to him. The noise and ATV halted suddenly with a screech at the very edge of the garden patch.

Garrett laughed and revved his engine. "Hey, Ol' Man, what you doin' digging in the dirt?" He called over the engine noise. "You some dirt farmer? You growin' some good stuff there?" The voice was derisive. "I bet there's some good shrooms up here. Good stuff!" He paused as Ken did not jump up or react to the ATV bordering his plot.

"Good vegetables, if that's what you mean." Ken stood, holding the rake and looking directly at the teen rider. His calmness in facing the intruder was more unsettling to Garrett than if he had yelled at him.

Ken wanted to get a new start with the teenager so he purposely weighed his words, hoping the two could talk. The silence made Garrett nervous. Ken began with a compliment, "That's a pretty good vehicle you have there."

"Pretty good? It's better than that lumbering clunker you drive!" Garrett chided. He twisted the handgrips to rev the engine. "You're just jealous because you couldn't handle an ATV! They only had bicycles when you were my age," he yelled over the racket.

"Garrett, I've flown everything from crop dusters to the fastest jets in the sky. I'm not impressed by a four wheel dune buggy." Ken almost heard himself drawl the last words. Even he wasn't sure if he was teasing with banter or challenging the young man.

"You were in the Air Force?" Garrett's curiosity caused him to throttle down so he could hear the answer.

"Yes, for twenty years. Now I'm retired."

"You look pretty young to be retired."

"The service allows retirement at my age, and I had a good reason." Ken was glad the animosity between them was dissolving. He had often talked with the young men and women recruits while on duty.

"Were you up at Eielson Air Force Base?"

Garrett asked.

"Among others. That's how we... I mean, I... came to love Alaska."

"Maybe..." Garrett paused. "Maybe... I'll join the service! Yeah, fly jets! It'll get me out of this pothole in the road." Garrett made the statement with assurance.

"Oh, you're going back to high school?" Ken voiced encouragement.

"Naw! Done with that stuff... maybe I'll just get a GED."

"Sometimes a GED isn't good enough. The high tech services have greater demands than knowing toadstools from mushrooms!"

Ignoring the razzing, Garrett threw a comment: "You wouldn't know a real shroom from a toadstool, Ol' Man."

"Hey, kid, mushrooms are for eating, not smoking or taking trips! As for toadstools, you'd know more about them than I would." Ken grinned slightly, trying to repair their previous conversations with a little humor. *Garrett was only a boy, after all.*

The startled look in Garrett's eyes quickly gave way to an intense glare. He did not want to tease or joke with this man and in frustration, he turned the ATV around and sped down the cleared space towards the road.

Watching the dust trail created by the ATV, Ken thought: *Yep, Ol' Man, you've made yourself an enemy. Sorry, Linda. I guess I didn't say the right thing. A kid like Garrett is out of control.*

The community meeting ran late that August night. It was still light outside, but Ken wanted to get home. He had a lot of work planned for the cabin and needed all the daylight the Alaskan summer hours afforded. He could skip supper because of all the good food people brought and served at the meeting. Driving the dirt road home, Ken thought, *You were right, Linda. This is a good place to live. It's a small place with big people who care about each other. They've started to care about me! I've been warned to watch out for moose on the road and bears in the berries.*

Before Ken could add another thought, he drove by his garden plot and slammed to a stop. The carefully tended garden was completely torn apart. He unsnapped his seat belt and rushed to the edge. He was appalled at what he saw. ATV tracks ripped the rows, plants were pulverized, nothing was left! It was deliberate destruction by oversized tires spinning, reversing, and plowing through the vegetation. His shock gave way to anger.

"Damn that kid! Damn him!" The anger led to rage as Ken clenched and unclenched his fists. He began to pant as all the suppressed frustration over the loss of Linda, the agony of her cancer treatments, and his loneliness brought a guttural scream... and another... and another. He saw the tracks dig out of the destroyed garden and lead to the woods. As dust was still settling, the ATV couldn't be far into the trees.

Fuming, Ken went into the cabin and pulled his shotgun off the wall. Fingers flew as he released the safety lock. At his desk, he pulled out a pack of buckshot shells and stuffed them into his pocket. Spurred by the emotions driving him, Ken stormed out of the cabin. He stomped through the former garden to follow the tracks. One churned spot showed wheelies. Another tracked where the ATV had left the ground to jump over a small log. The rider was celebrating! Ken did not even feel the sting of branches as he kept following the churned path. He knew he was close but surprised there was no roar of the engine. Then he saw why.

A large tree lay across the path. As the ATV had approached it to attempt another jump, the ground was untouched. On the other side lay an overturned machine, one tire still spinning. The handlebars were twisted because a body had forcefully flown over them, pulling them with it. The body was Garrett's. It lay where its flight over the handlebars had left it. A slight whimpering was all Ken could hear until another cry came—a cry of fear!

The rustle in the surrounding brush alerted Ken to a large black shadow. A bear was standing over the boy, smacking at Garrett's backpack. With the boy's scream, the bear sliced a paw at the boy's head and growled. Biting the backpack in its maw, the bear shook the pack and the boy with it. Garrett went silent, collapsed on the forest floor. The bear stood to its full height when Ken shouted and it turned to the intruder, stepping away from the backpack. Its head was up and ears forward.

Ken didn't wait for the animal to decide what to do. He waved his arms and yelled, loaded the shot gun, and shot over the bear's head. Going around the log, he moved closer to Garrett and fired overhead again. The bear paused, then turned and retreated to the forest.

Kenneth controlled the surges of emotion and adrenaline. The situation wasn't over. Kneeling next to Garrett, he spoke gently while eyeing the bear's exit path. "Garrett, it's me, Kenneth. Don't move. Where does it hurt?"

"I... I don't know. What happened? I'm sleepy." He seemed to be drifting.

"No, Garrett, don't go to sleep. Stay awake!"

His early basic training returned as Ken gently surveyed the injured boy. No dramatic or bleeding wounds and bones all seemed intact, none of Garrett's limbs were at odd angles or twisted. *Would anyone be looking for them? Why would they? He had just been seen at the meeting; people were used to Garrett never being anyplace particular.*

"Garrett, can you move your toes?"

"That's a dumb-ass question, sure I can wiggle them," the boy said, and his toes could be seen moving in his running shoes.

"Now, how about your fingers? Both hands?"

"Hey, Ol' Man, I'm all right. I'll just get up... whoa! Maybe I won't." Garrett collapsed again and quieted. "I'll... just... rest... here." He didn't seem to notice the bleeding cuts on his face.

Ken stepped quickly to the ATV, never losing sight of Garrett or letting go of his reloaded shotgun. The vehicle righted with difficulty, the handlebars were bent, and two wheels were crushed and broken. Rummaging through the storage box, Ken found chips, a number of bungee cords, a t-shirt, two graphic novels, an unopened condom, a peanut candy bar, a half package of cigarettes, and a canteen—no cell phone or CB radio.

Okay, Linda, what do I do? The ATV's too damaged. I'm not sure of his injuries, but he's being cooperative. Maybe that's a warning of its own. I can't leave him here with the bear around. I'm afraid to try a carry him; I might do more damage. There are still a few hours of daylight if I don't squander them.

In the silence, Ken decided. His anger had turned to resolve.

Ken removed his summer coat, opened it flat, and laid it on the ground next to Garrett.

"Oh, that's a nice coat, Ol' Man. Aren't you afraid it'll get dirty?" Garrett asked simply.

Again, Ken was struck by the boy's attitude. He inched the boy onto the coat until Garrett was lying on his back, on top of the coat, on the forest mulch. He tucked the boy's arms next to him. There was a sound in the berries, and Ken held the shotgun ready. Then the sounds moved away from them. Quickly, he tore the t-shirt into strips and wrapped the bleeding claw marks. With the bungee cords he secured Garrett's legs with some fallen branches into a rough travois. He was as stable as Ken could make him.

"Garrett, stay with me. I'm going to drag you back to my cabin and we'll get help. It might get bumpy, but a rider like you is used to that." Ken sounded calm and the tension relaxed in the boy, almost wrapped like a mummy.

Garrett looked up directly into Ken's eyes. "Hey, Mr. Kenneth. I'm sorry about your garden. I shouldn't have done it—I don't know why I did it—but I'm sorry." The tone of apology was striking. It was sincere. There was a maturity in Garrett's voice, taking full responsibility. Lapsing back into mindlessness, the boy mumbled, "Whoa! That's some woodpecker tapping! Is it drilling on my head?"

Ken's anger transferred into action to save them both from the serious situation. The boy's babbling suggested a concussion.

Slowly, Ken began to pull the boy over the forest debris and heard a whimper from behind.

"Garrett, are you with me? We're moving toward help!"

"I'm okay... I just hurt. Boy! I hurt all over," the boy whined.

"You cry out loud all you want, I'm going to keep moving you. Stay awake!"

For a crazy moment, Ken felt like a laborer towing a load and wondered if singing would help. The moment passed and he moved towards his cabin with only a low moan coming from the young man on the makeshift stretcher. The earth turned by the ATV made a workable path and Ken pulled steadily, only resting if Garrett went quiet. "Garrett, keep moaning! You're going to be okay." A sharp scream or silence would cause Kenneth to stop, check, and then return to his dragging.

Finally reaching the plot next to his cabin, Ken re-arranged Garrett to be as comfortable as possible. "Wow, Ol' Man, this garden dirt feels so good, I'll just lay here for a while," Garrett murmured as he tried to cuddle into the warm earth."

"No, you don't, Garrett. You stay awake and I'm calling for emergency." Ken poked the boy gently. He hurried to his Suburban and reached through the open window. He grabbed his cell phone out of the dashboard dock and tried to get a signal from different angles. Failing with the cell, Ken yanked open the passenger door and slid into the seat. Reaching to the CB radio, he pulled out the mic and entered the emergency channel Marilynn always monitored.

"Emergency! Marilynn, this is Kenneth Larison at my cabin. I have an injured Garrett here needing immediate transport to a hospital. He is conscious, probable concussion, clawed by a bear, other cuts and scratches from crashing his ATV. Emergency!"

"Copy that! Ken, we're on our way! Notifying state troopers!" Before she even finished, Ken could hear the emergency siren shrieking over the woods.

It was late Fall when Ken again stood on the viewpoint for the Wrangell Mountains. Any mushrooms were hidden by the light frosting of the first winter snow. Like snowbirds, people were tightening up their cabins or preparing to trek south for the winter. Young people, including Garrett, were riding the school buses for another school year of activities and graduation. Bush pilots brought in supplies to the Podstakannik Emporium and Mercantile Specialty Outlet, and Ken was getting ready to renew his pilot's license.

This night, the aurora borealis glowed on the snow-covered mountain ranges beyond. The energy swayed magnificent colors before the solitary man standing on the ridge. Slowly, Ken's hand removed the lid of the funeral urn. For a moment he clutched it tightly, then he raised the vessel and released the ashes to the ever-present breeze.

Linda, his beloved wife, was home, and so was he.

THE GATHERERS
TIME FRAGMENT 2156 CE

Kade's multi-colored coat flashed its colors in the flickering light as the merry tune on his flute brought giggles and laughter to the children seated in the magic circle surrounding the campfire. It was always a joyful occasion when a gatherer came to the village. There were tricks of illusion, special sweets, and wondrous stories of magical kingdoms with beautiful people and families. The adults on the edges of the circle were as mesmerized as their children. Although the gatherers varied every year, some brought puppets or trick animals. The event exploded like fireworks in the village memories. It was the twenty-second century, a time of promise.

Kade of the Gatherers Guild was nearing the end of entertainment with the terrier, Sadie, leaping through rings the master twirled over her head. Applause followed each successful jump as the rings were held higher. For a finale, Kade introduced three children who accompanied him to stand with their arms held above their heads and Sadie jumped over all three!

Kade patted each child's head and announced, "Here are the newest members of your village. We share them with admiration to grow healthy, to be loved, and to help in your labors for the sake of your village. The Census sustains!" Applause and whistles followed his words as he beckoned three sets of adults to join him and the children in the firelight. Now the center of attention without the dog as a distraction, the boy and two girls huddled together. They backed close to the gatherer.

"Families, you are met this night according to Guild directives to be together," Kade said solemnly. He held his hand over the children as in benediction and continued looking to each set of new parents. "Pleasing to the Guild, Lacey and her wife and their friends are now a family of Lenore. Harue, Jude, Selek, and Linnele are family to Amelia. Teo and Hannah now have a family with Jaiden." As an aside, he whispered, "Teo, now you have the son you requested." The farmer grinned and removed his hat as he smiled at Jaiden. The new father surreptitiously slipped an object to Kade.

Gently, Kade guided the youths to their proper place. Concluding, Kade raised his arms over all. "May you cherish each other, favor yourselves and the village, and grow old and wise together!'

The children were engulfed by the new fathers, mothers, and villagers. At the age of reason, the seven year olds understood they were being ceremonially adopted into a village of women and men. Understanding was not the same as desiring. The hugs and smiles surrounding them did not reflect the hesitancy in the youngsters' eyes: Torn from their childhood home, traversing a terrible landscape, following a gatherer to a 'better place,' being smothered by a group of strangers.

The celebration was abruptly stopped by a scream of

pain from the birthing cabin slightly removed from the cluster of the village. Everyone froze in place as the cry repeated. It was Avaline's time for labor. Wide eyed, the new children went silent. They trembled as their new relatives murmured and moved them to their own homes. Two women sighed then went into the cabin for delivery. Kade handed Sadie to the oldest boy and followed the team to the cabin. This was one purpose of his being here, this night, a ten month increment after the last Guild member had attended to this village in the northern latitudes.

Although a young woman, Avaline was familiar with the routine followed in this cabin. The assistants held her hands, they washed her and the bed, and slipped clean garments on themselves and the gatherer. Kade examined her and the baby's progress and announced all was well. The birthing progressed without incident. Avaline was rewarded when Kade wrapped the baby in a soft blanket and lay the infant on her chest. A live birth—a healthy baby—a child to replace the one lost before! In spite of her straining and pains of labor, Avaline cried tears of joy.

There were other births or surgeries for Kade to oversee in subsequent days. He was occupied with the industry of the village, giving counsel, and talking with the children. His actions and demeanor were deliberate. A perfectly groomed rust beard was striking with the clothes he wore. More than an entertainer or midwife, the gatherer was an overseer to the community, a teacher and leader. Communication between villages was his responsibility.

The Guild administered to these northern settlements of homesteaders who escaped the chaos of climate changes. Thick forests and formidable cold once shielded the Great

North and confined the populace to the south. The previous century of overpopulation, pollution, territorial wars, energy crisis and climate change disrupted everything. Now, in the twenty-second century, the emerging warmer climate induced numbers of humans to spread north beyond the forty-ninth parallel. The Guild was formed to administer to the survivors of earth's dramatic transformation. The labor was hard, agriculture was demanding, but the people survived.

Avaline was soon back to her husbandry routines, the baby tied in a shawl. The older sister, Luna, followed close behind. Almost seven years old with curly blond hair, Luna was sure she could hold the baby. Mother told her to wait. She must be patient and only touch her new sister very gently. At night when mother and baby were tucked into bed, Luna would sing to them. She particularly liked a tune her mother called a 'lullaby.' It always made her mother go to sleep. Luna would kiss them both gently before tucking herself into the small bed near by.

Kade moved easily about the community. As gatherer, he played many roles and directed assistants in their work. Medical emergencies were addressed by the Medic Team. Agricultural and husbandry questions were answered by the Farm Team. Emphasis was always placed on the children and their needs.

Checking on Avaline at her small, individual cabin, Kade held the new baby for inspection. He hefted the infant's weight, smelled her breath, and followed her eye patterns.

"I assume this baby girl, we'll call her Makayla, is the offspring of Gatherer Santiago. The timing of her gestation and birth coincides with his Annual last year. I will be able to report to him that she is healthy and will be available in a few years." He spoke with a snide expression.

"I... we... had hoped Santiago would return this year," Avaline said taking the baby.

"'We?'" the gatherer questioned. He resented the unique way she said the name.

"I mean, the villagers always appreciate him. He takes such a personal interest in... all of us." Gazing at the baby, she purposefully avoided looking at the gatherer.

Kade shook his head in disbelief. He was disgruntled when he said, "I'm always surprised by Santiago's desire to track his progeny. He's almost a throwback to the 'family connections' of the previous times." He shuddered at the words. "We gatherers are here to manage the villages, not coddle them!" He was vehement, until he stopped abruptly.

To regain his composure, the gatherer turned attention to Luna. Almost casually, he asked her questions and gave her a few math problems to complete.

"Of course," he continued "I will be gathering Children of Age when the Annual visit is completed."

"Children of Age?" Avaline questioned.

"With our Annuals being rotated among the villages, inconsistencies appear in a child's age—a few months before or after age seven makes no difference," Kade explained curtly. He had little patience with mothers who belabored the Guild's rules pertaining to their own children.

"But she's six years old and I only have Makayla, just two children for the Census. I am still within my population limit." Avaline tried to sound assured of her statement.

"Ah-ha!" Kade exclaimed. "You have forgotten the stillbirth when you first conceived. It's in the records. Fertile women are allotted 2.3 pregnancies to maintain population stability. The averages remain whether or not the infant lived to fruition. Now, with this offspring of Santiago, you are out of compliance. He knew the rules; he ignored them. I have noted you have had three births which is against the rubrics for limiting population!" With a dismissal gesture, Kade moved toward the cabin door, then spun, and spoke briskly: "It will all be accommodated by the Census and you will keep Makayla with you. Oh, yes, you are officially notified to report to the Medic Team for scheduling of procreation adjustment. Be sure to join the prepubescent boys being collected for... modification...." At her stunned expression, Kade said condescendingly, "It makes them more comfortable in their farm work." He stormed through the doorway. "And bring Luna to the final gathering, prepared to go to the Guild!"

Avaline was dumbfounded by the brusqueness of his words and the implications of his pronouncements. She held Makayla close and rocked her gently. She looked around the cabin and saw Luna cowering in the corner. Without a word she opened her arms and her child rushed into them. It was a long while before Avaline could let her daughters go.

Among the other administrative duties, Kade would hold 'afternoon seminars of explanation.' Most of the participants were children, although older workers would appreciate the break in their daily routines. Depending on the particular gatherer conducting Annual visit, the seminar was also entertaining. Kade was an accomplished illusionist who wove his magic throughout the presentation.

Startle them and the audience is yours. Amaze then tell your pitch. Astonish and they believe. A flutter of dove wings would precede the recounting of fire storms, flooding, and temperature escalations which devastated human inhabitants the previous century. Such catastrophes reduced the resources and the demand for them. Clanging steel rings would wind and unwind themselves throughout a recitation of the complexity of climate change. The chain reactions moved villages to the north to survive. Reflective mirrors multiplied images like the population overwhelming the small planet, earth. A silver ball balanced on a black satin edge of cloth, appeared, and disappeared like the gatherers who cared for the villages by limiting the number of residents.

Working in the gardens with the other children, Luna saw Jaiden, the new boy, just standing. He was staring at the vines of peas in front of him, making no effort to pick. His sad expression was confusing and Luna spoke: "Hello, Jaiden. I'm Luna. Are you waiting for something?"

"I don't know what to do…. My new family sent me here with the other pickers."

"Well," Luna offered, "we're picking peas! Can't you see?" She continued to collect pods even as she talked, placing them in a bowl she carried.

"We didn't grow peas in… my village." Again, sadness filled his eyes as he gingerly touched a hanging pod.

"Oh." Luna stopped picking and looked directly at Jaiden. The young boy was just about her age and had been introduced by the gatherer. "You must miss your old home, but it's all right, you're here with us now!" Luna attempted to cheer the boy.

Forlorn, Jaiden held his hands up in a hopeless gesture. "I don't know what to do."

Luna giggled and told him, "Okay, Silly, it's easy. I'll

show you. See the how the vines wind around each other with some blossoms and different size pods. We just pick the big pods… they are firm with good peas." She took a pod in hand and pulled it with a gentle tug, then gestured to Jaiden to follow.

Jaiden grabbed a pod and yanked it free, tearing the stem with it.

"Oh, no! You've wrecked the stem! It could keep growing." Luna now had the chance to show off her expertise. She lectured the boy as her mother had lectured her at the beginning of the season. "We need all the food we gather, so take only the firm pods. Those peas are ripe." She demonstrated on a few more pods, and indicated he should follow.

"You're pretty bossy for a girl," Jaiden complained. He scrunched his face.

"And you're pretty stupid for a boy who can't even pick peas," she retaliated.

Glaring at each other, the two held their positions over the bowl. Neither moved until Luna could hold the mood no longer and she burst out laughing. Grinning, Jaiden joined her, and the two children turned back to the vines.

Following Luna, Jaiden dutifully tried to be gentle. She showed him how to put his thumb and forefinger on the stem and pull the mature pod free. Working together, he spoke confidentially: "I wonder why I'm here. The gatherer said we were going to a better place. Instead, this is just another village. Here I am picking peas."

"What 'better place' did he mean?'"

"He said it was a valley with soft grass where you could run all day, trees begged to be climbed, and springs of sweet water flowed. Fruit was always in season and just waited to be picked if you wanted it. Sometimes, there were crystal candies hidden in the rocks and pebbles. Children were free and no one needed to work," Jaiden finished, now smiling with the memory.

"And he was going to take you there?" Luna asked in awe.

"He was going to take us all there—many of us."

"Many? Only three of you came."

"When we left our village, there were many more, but it was a hard trip and when the river flooded, it took the others away...." His face again turned dark.

"'Took them away?'" Luna was uncertain whether she understood.

"They drowned, Luna! Only Lenore, Amelia, and I survived... so... so now this is our home." Jaiden's bravery dissolved and he wiped away tears.

Kade strutted about the poor village, enjoying the respite from travel and the admiration of the villagers, especially the women. His position of authority gave him the rights of choice and his flamboyant demeanor made him a desirable attraction. Mornings would find him leaving a hut, satisfied and pleased with himself. As gatherer, he bedded the fertile women to satisfy the Census. As Kade, he was augmented by pleasurable episodes with those who already had their procreation adjusted.

Watching the gatherer leave her friend's cabin one morning, Avaline stepped in his path. He started to pass her so she spoke directly to him. "Gatherer, we spoke briefly about Santiago after my birthing day. I wonder if you have any other news when he might return." She adjusted her newborn, Makayla, in her arms.

"How are you and the new baby?" He changed the subject. "I see you have resumed your workplace in the village. That's good." Again, he tried to pass her. "I have crops to inspect now."

Again, Avaline stepped in front of him as friends were milling about, starting their morning chores.

"Have you scheduled your procreation adjustment? The medic team will take care of you," Kade said abruptly. "The Census demands cessation of fertility."

"Please, Gatherer, tell me about Santiago. He was supposed to visit for this year's Annual. We had a special... arrangement... and I looked forward to his appearance." Avaline did not want to say more to this person but she missed her baby's father too much to avoid asking. "When might Santiago come again?"

"It is not for you to ask or me to say," he stated angrily. "It is the wisdom of the Guild to determine schedules. Your interest in one particular gatherer is offensive to all in the Guild, to all who care for the villages. You insult the Guild, the Census, and your own village!" He pushed past her and ignored the others who were perplexed by the scene they had witnessed.

Left alone, Avaline went back to her hut and held Makayla to her breast to nurse. Calming, she remembered the intimate times she had been with Santiago. In his arms, she was special, she was loved. Her child, Luna, was his child, not just a human seed passed to an incubator to satisfy a Census. He treasured them. She wanted desperately to include Makayla in the hope they could somehow live his dream of being together.

The final night of the Gathering included all the village around the firepit. Contrasting with the celebration when Kade arrived, the gathering was solemn. Children of Age were together wearing backpacks with their meager belongings. Villagers would reach to pat a child then stoically pull back. A few children whimpered. Most of them just looked confused.

The yipping of the terrier running about the circle announced Kade's entrance. Again, wearing his multicolored coat, the gatherer traversed the circle of children, touching each one. He stepped up on a small platform placed where the firelight would illuminate his face. A few flickers of sparkle and he had everyone's attention.

"People! People! Such solemn faces for a night of great opportunity! We are gathering the children to afford them a better place in our world. Your village barely sustains itself, as we all know. It is limited in resources. You know how laborious your life is to scrape sustenance from these latitudes. Never wanting to go to excess, we learned from the intemperance of twenty-first century. Because of the Guild's wisdom, we now control our population and destiny. We offer our children the opportunity of a better world than we could provide here with hard labors and growing painfully old. The Guild will provide a valley with soft grass where they can run all day, trees beg to be climbed, and springs of sweet water flow. Fruit is always in season and just waits to be picked when wanted. Sometimes, there are crystal candies hidden in the rocks and pebbles. Children are free and no one needs to work."

Standing with the gathered children, Luna heard the words and started to breathe quickly. She looked for Jaiden and saw him outside her selected group with his new family. His 'father' held a protective hand on his shoulder. Jaiden was not beckoned to this Gathering: He was being left in this poor village.

"Why can't we all go there?" called out one man, his body showing the hard effects of a farmer's life.

Another woman exclaimed, "Why can't we all live in a better world?

"Why do the Guild and Gatherers get to live in a perfect world?" shouted an old man with a cane.

"Because too many people would crush the world. It has happened repeatedly to earthly paradises. That is why we only take our dear children. We give them hope and promise them more than they can dream!" He swept his gaze over the young eyes looking at him and beckoned once more. "Come children, find your destiny in a better world!"

With a command, the terrier zoomed around the circle of children and urged them to follow the gatherer as he held a torch and traveled a prepared path. The youngsters were unsure but finally a few started to follow the light. Always, they looked back over their shoulders. Villagers tried to follow but assistants prodded them back to the firelight.

Avaline skirted the assistants as she stretched to see Luna. When her daughter disappeared into the darkness, Avaline stepped to her cabin and pulled out a sack of necessities and food. Quickly, she secured Makayla into the sling around her neck and slipped into the forest. She could just glimpse the distant light as she tracked behind the moving column.

It was almost daylight when the travelers stopped to rest at the stream. They had kept moving through the night to discourage followers and to make the break with the village more absolute. Some of the little ones were crying while other children comforted them. "It was all right," some of the children murmured. "We're with the gatherer. We're going to a better home."

A space in the woods was a stopping place for Avaline where she could view the children yet remain undetected. She had never been this far from the village and was amazed at the cliffs rising from the valley floor on the other side of the stream, now growing to a river. Rising hundreds of feet above the opposite bank, the sandstone cliffs stretched to the horizon. It was the wall villagers had described in stories, an obstacle they had never scaled.

Avaline tried to eat a few pieces of bread from her travel sack when she was startled by Makayla's wakening cry. Immediately, Avaline offered her breast to the infant as she warily looked toward the travelers. The baby's cry had gone unnoticed among the sounds of whimpering children, and the gurgling water. When assistants looked around, they saw nothing except the children, and Avaline relaxed.

Avaline thought, *Why did I bring the baby? What was I thinking? How can I follow quietly with a newborn? If only Santiago had come for the Annual, everything would have been all right.*

With only a short pause, the gatherer and assistants started urging the children. "It's going to be a warm day, but we won't mind because we will be cooled by the stream! Come on, girls and boys, the path to your Guild House is on the other side of the water. We must hurry along." Kade nudged the children into a line.

"But... but I'm hungry," one child objected.

"That's why we are crossing right here. There are biscuits and fruits on the other bank; we just need to get there." He began tying the children together in a line while Sadie ran back and forth yipping at the children's heels. When all were tied, Kade waded into the water at the fork where another faster creek joined. He coaxed and cajoled the children tugging them behind him.

"Oh! It's cold!"

"I'm scared!"

"I want to go home! Take me home!" The cries began as the little people were pulled into the swiftly moving current. They flailed about, trying to keep their heads above water and grabbing for their knapsacks. Even the adults were up to their waists in water as they dragged the line behind them. Taller children tried to keep their footing and shorter ones tried to paddle. Plaintiff cries could be heard above the cascades.

Focusing on Luna, Avaline almost plunged into the open to try and rescue her daughter. Torn between one daughter in danger and another infant carried in a sling, Avaline felt a panicked need to choose. Then—in a moment of agony—she felt relief as Luna's curly head bobbed to the opposite side and her daughter scrambled onto the bank. Luna turned to help the boy behind her find his footing. After fearful moments, all the children collapsed on the other bank. This time, Kade let them rest on the warm rocks to dry their clothes.

"Markie? Where's Markie?" Luna called out. "He was near the back, with Aria, and now they're both gone. Markie! Aria," she called loudly for her friends.

"Hush, hush, Luna," an assistant said quickly. "I saw him slip out of the rope line but he swam downstream with Aria. I'll fetch them. They're good swimmers and waved to me so we know they're waiting around the bend. You keep going and we'll join you at the Guild House." He looked to Kade and gestured downstream. Kade shrugged and nodded. The assistant started picking his way down the bank.

Avaline stayed with Makayla in shrubs where she could watch the children resting and the water covered any sounds the baby would make. Children and adults were quiet for hours on the warm rocks. With a signal from Kade, the assistants roused the youngsters, and the collection began to move again. From her side of the water, Avaline retraced the original stream and found an easier place to cross. Once the collected children disappeared up a path to the cliff edge, Avaline forded and continued to trail them. Fortunately, her body movements and warmth kept the baby sleepy... and quiet.

Part of the trail to the top of the gorge was easy hiking. Years of farming and arduous work had given Avaline the stamina to follow her daughter. She had recovered from Makayla's birth in the days of the Annual counting and administrations. The order for her procreation adjustment was easily accommodated—a vaccination to prevent any further pregnancies. Originating in 2046, the vaccination was a futile attempt to stem population. A huge stockpile of the vaccine was in the control of the Guild. The 'adjustment' was a lifelong gift. For women, it meant no more pregnancies. For the boys, it meant only gatherers sired offspring. Avaline was even relieved she now complied with the Census. She had two lovely daughters and needed no others. Soon, they would be with their father. From there on, the future was not as clear.

Gradually, the trail changed to sandstone formations. Avaline needed to climb and pull herself from one level to another. It was difficult ascending the jagged face with a newborn tucked in swaddling within a sling. When the climb became more hazardous, Avaline slowed to nurse the baby and rest. She attempted a different tie on her sling. She needed the baby close to her own body so Makayla would not hit the rocks. At one outcropping, Avaline looked down into the crack in the chasm. She could not see clearly so she balanced to get a view: She saw a collection of broken white sticks and round looking balls. One ball had the shadows of eye sockets. She tried to look away but was held by revulsion.

My gods! Those are skeletons. Children's skeletons! She panted, pulled back, and clung to Makayla. At once she was vomiting on the cliffside, holding her baby, trying to erase the scene at the bottom of the crag in the rocks. Wedged into a rock corner, Avaline sobbed for herself, her children, and for the children in the crag.

The view of the valley gorge was even more daunting from the high trail edge. The path contoured above the wall and appeared endless in the vista of the gorge. Somewhere beyond this footpath lay the Guild House and its better life. Kade had said so.

The next day was smoother hiking for the adults along the ridge. The young ones had difficulties leaping over cracks in the rocks, or scaling a jagged outcropping. Most children had gobbled the small foodstuffs brought with them but their pleas brought little sustenance from Kade or the assistants. There was no magic or fantasy stories, just the constant reminder all would be better at the Guild House. Some of the youngsters lagged behind until the main group had lost any sight of them. Kade sent an assistant back yet the children never saw the laggers catch up or the assistant return. The remaining children were prodded toward the Guild.

Avaline continued to trail the group, hoping to catch sight of Luna. She was below the main trail when she heard the clatter of a rock slide from above. She pressed herself and Makayla against the rock wall to escape then watched in horror as children fell past her from the upper trail into the rocky terrain below. Their screams echoed as she tried to reach out but she could not salvage one outstretched hand. All she could do was protect the baby and herself from the onslaught of rocks, pebbles, and sand.

Kade and his entourage entered the paved roads of the Guild; the hungry, disheveled, whimpering children had reached their destination. The youngsters were totally confused. This village looked the same as the one left behind. Where was the green grass and trees? Where were the crystal candies they had anticipated? They were greeted and ushered to a bathing room, led to a hall where a table of meager food awaited, and finally were addressed as a group by a band of Gatherers and farmers.

Kade spoke to the gatherers and merely gestured to the children. He recounted how difficult the villages were being in offering their young this Annual. He detailed how his trip was arduous to bring the brood to the Guild. With a change of tone, he lamented the demise of the 'weaker ones.' He praised how the children before them in the hall were the strongest and healthiest. They would bring good labor to their farms. As Kade spoke, the other men and women gatherers walked around the children who huddled together. Farmers began circling as well, eyeing the stock.

One gatherer, Santiago, carefully studied each child searching for a look, for an attitude, for a progeny. A girl, with soft pale curls, stood defiantly as some of the others trembled near her. He pulled in a breath. She was the one he was looking for, an image from his initial Annual Gathering. A memory of first love. *His or Avaline's? Or both?*

"Kade, I will take this girl, I have need of a kitchen worker." Santiago stepped forward and put his hand protectively on Luna's shoulder.

Kade stopped processing the brood to look suspiciously between the younger, pale haired gatherer and the child. He had taken Luna with the suspicion of Santiago's parentage. Now, seeing them together, it was confirmed. He almost sneered when he said, "I have chosen her for my own kitchen. Pick another!"

Santiago said defiantly, "You already have bands of children, surely you don't need another. What would the Census Bureau say to your farm hoarding the genetics of the other villages? These children need to replicate the DNA mixtures when they grow, not isolate your strain!"

The other gatherers saw the tension between the two men and started to nod to each other. Madiora, of the Medic Team, didn't hesitate to speak up. "Santiago's right. The whole purpose of the culling of children is to strengthen the DNA of the isolated villages. The Census Bureau is strikingly clear about distribution of genes as well as accumulation of strains." She was annoyed at Kade's twisting of rules to his own advantage.

Another gatherer agreed. "Madiora's right. We other

gatherers stick to the rules to limit populations, yet somehow you, Kade, always acquire more laborers for your fields."

"Now, now, everyone. We all know what's important." Kade wasn't going to let the discussion get away from him. He began to argue, "The Census Bureau limits the number of births and the exchange of genetics in a natural way to preserve our population." Anger burst into his words: "Come on, people! We are all living in the Northern Latitudes because the overpopulation of the twenty-first century! Global warming led to the near extinction of the human species! Let's think this through. This time, let's do it right!" His excited words hinted at Kade's tension.

"Whose 'right'? The Guild's, our people's, or yours?" Santiago glared at Kade, who had taken the Annual Gatherings as a means of exploiting his own prestige and wealth.

Santiago believed in the Guild's vision of the equality of people. Limited population was only one of the Guild's ideals. Surviving in the northern world, recycling resources, enlightened government and laws were among the others. On his first Annual, he'd learned there was a place for love and loyalty as well. In Avaline's caresses, he experienced an unknown devotion. His work in the Guild House village convinced the homesteaders of his leadership. All the while he labored for the Guild, he thought of returning to Avaline. It was Kade's dictates and manipulations of schedules that kept them separated. *Not this time.* Santiago thought. *Not this time!*

Gently, Santiago guided Luna away from the firelight. He took her hand and started walking towards the forest beyond. With a cry from Madiora, he spun to see Kade running towards his back with a knife raised to strike. Santiago shoved

Luna aside and blocked the outstretched arm. The two men fell and grappled in the dirt. First one then the other rolled on top. Their hands struggled to take control of the blade, until Santiago pressed down on Kade's chest and held the knife to his throat. Through gritted teeth, Santiago repeated, "I will take this girl… this daughter!"

Santiago looked up and around his neighbors' faces marked by expressions of astonishment or agreement. Even the assistants who labored for Kade stood back and offered no resistance. Santiago held up his hands, tossed the knife to Madiora's feet, and stood up. He left Kade in the dirt.

"Come on, Luna," Santiago coaxed, taking her hand. "Let's go to your new home."

It was in the dark of the night when Santiago stood guard in his cabin. Luna had quickly fallen asleep from exhaustion and the excitement of the day. Santiago watched this remarkable little person breathing gently in the bed he had made up for her. He had missed so much of her life; he was determined to be part of it from now on. He had stood against a gatherer, not the Guild. He was surprised by Kade's reaction, but would never be again, he resolved. It was the reason he kept watch.

It was almost morning when a strange sound alerted Santiago. Accustomed to the darkness and the layout of the room, he saw a shadowed figure entering the door. He leapt to the doorway and grabbed the intruder around the neck from behind. A muffled cry and flutter of arms warned him this was not Kade! The scuffle ended quickly and Santiago was holding a flailing woman in his arms trying to strike him.

"Let me go! You're hurting me! You're hurting the baby," the figure cried out and a baby's scream emphasized the fact.

"Hush! Hush! It's all right; I've let you go! Hush," Santiago tried to appease the situation. "It's all right."

"Mama! Mama!" Luna cried out, rushing in the darkness to hug her mother. "Oh, Mama, I'm so glad you're here!"

Santiago stepped back to light a lantern and saw Avaline holding her baby in one arm, hugging Luna with the other, and looking to him with expectation. He couldn't speak, his throat was choked, words failed. Only his eyes beheld the reality in his home.

Timidly, Santiago stepped towards the woman in ragged clothes, marred by dirt, who comforted the two children. His children. He reached to touch her hair and all he remembered was the beautiful vision of Avaline naked in his arms. In spite of the Guild and the Census rules, they had created a dream between them and now it would be realized.

"Avaline..." he whispered.

"Santiago..." she had said his name so often, and now could say it to him. He moved closer and held them all close as morning twilight began.

Suddenly, from the open door, a wooden club smashed into Santiago's head. "If I can't have her, neither can you!" Kade yelled as the stunned Santiago fell to the floor. Avaline held her baby to her but Kade's large hands reached and grabbed Luna. He dragged the kicking girl out through the door.

Avaline rushed to help the dazed man trying to get upright. "Oh, Santiago, he's got Luna! He's taken her!"

Santiago wiped his bleeding forehead with a sleeve and staggered outside. "Where, where did he go?" Avaline was already following the path.

At the edge of the village, the path veered toward the cliffs. There, in the new light, Kade stood holding Luna on the edge. He shook her to make her scream and Avaline and Santiago halted in fear.

"Oh, you don't know what to say now, do you? You and your longing for children. Whine...whine...whine!" Kade's words became screams. "You destroy all the Guild stands for. It's clear. Without war, plague, mass extinctions, or an asteroid impact, humans never limit their demands on the Earth. They desire more of resources, of knowledge, of the power to rule. The benevolence of the Gatherers' Guild kept the human race from becoming lemmings who totally destroyed themselves so a few could survive!"

In his rage, Kade turned to face the man who had beaten him in front of the whole village. He pulled Luna in front of him. The little girl was quiet in her fright. "I'm right! Because I hold the girl! I am the Guild! How dare you question me!"

"Kade, let's talk. There are other ways to limit people besides throwing their children off a cliff," Santiago pleaded. "The Guild isn't in question."

Kade's attention was on the hated man who had usurped him. His eyes were glaring. He moved closer to Santiago, a little farther from the cliff. Luna was nudged in front of him.

"You can't replace me, you fool!" He rambled on with a new thought: "Didn't you know, *I'm magic*! I can take people to a better place... just ask them!" With a flutter of his hand, he raised it, a dove flew from his finger tips and he looked up.

In that second, Santiago sprang forward, grabbed

Luna and thrust her to the side where Avaline had crept close. Kade was wide eyed with surprise when Santiago lurched forward and shoved him to the rim of the gorge. Kade tried to catch the edge, lost balance, and the rocks crumbled in his fingers. His body tumbled into space. He fell from the edge of his world and there was no magic to save him.

The Guild village came to life as it always did with the morning sunrise. There were fields and crops to tend, animals to feed or let to pasture. Chores in the waking households were always present. This particular morning, the villagers saw Santiago sitting contentedly with his back against a tree. His arm was protectively about a woman, a stranger, nursing her infant baby. Beside them, a tousle-haired girl sat quietly sorting the multi-colored leaves. Occasionally, she would reach out to pet Sadie, the terrier, who sat next to her. The little dog was keeping watch towards the cliffs with the gorge beyond. It was another day....

PEGGY AND THE NIL BAG
TIME FRAGMENT 1931 CE

Peggy and the Nil Bag *collects essays from Professor Emeritus Margaret L. Quick depicting a period of her childhood. The essays were originally written in 1979 and were discovered in Professor Quick's archives then digitized for the Bicentennial University Collection (2025 CE). Copies of this memoir will be available in the University bookstore for $48.56 in paperback or online in a variety of digital formats.*

Foreword: Margaret Quick's Memoir

The wonderful thing about the 1930's Depression is that it was long enough ago for the painful truths and myths to have faded away. It is also strange enough in time to allow *magic*.

Now, I am an aging academician, Margaret Lucetta Quick. That decodes as "Peggy" and I had a Nil Bag. Trust me. Would I lie to you? I am a college professor emeritus with an august face, tenure, and occasional students who return to the campus to regale me with their successes. The failures, I never see again unless the local news has a police blotter. I think, in retrospect, I'm one of the faces most of the people in this Ohio River town expected to see on a blotter of some sort. Then again, I had the Nil Bag, and all the magic I could use growing up!

They used to call me a "tomboy" and I took it as a compliment like my idol, Tom Sawyer. He and I had good hearts but our desire for fun was often misunderstood. Some of the events recounted in this memoir may never have happened; it's just the way I remember them or want to tell them to you. A good laugh is always worth a little exaggeration. Another role model was Buster Keaton whose magic on the 1930's movie screens made the Nil Bag possible.

As a professional "memoirist," I declare that no humans or animals were injured in these remembrances. However, I can imagine quite a lot of mayhem!

I may even get this work published in the academic journal.

Chapter One: The Nil Bag

Peggy, is that you?"

Who else would slam the kitchen door like that? "Yeah, Mom, it's me!" I answered.

"You' re late," she said. "Where have you been?"

"Tillie kept me in after school."

Mom looked up from the pan of beans she was snapping for dinner. "You must not call Miss Tarbrush Tillie! Show her some respect," she scolded a little.

Miss Tillie Tarbrush was my fifth grade teacher.

"What did you do?" Mom asked. She wiped her hands on her apron.

"Nothin'."

"The first week of school and you already have to stay after class? Come now, you must have done something." Mom looked at me in the funny way moms have. Sometimes a mom just won't believe a girl. Even her own dear daughter, like me.

"Well... Miss Tillie said I was day-dreamin' so she made me write twenty-five times, 'I must pay attention.' I done that—"

"Did that," Mom corrected.

"I did that. Then she made me write 'attention' twenty-five times 'cause I'd misspelled it."

"Well..." Mom smiled. "I guess day-dreaming isn't so bad. Not on such a beautiful day. If you are going to visit Gramps for the weekend, you'd better get going. But first, take out the garbage."

That's me! I always get the garbage. Why is it no matter what else happens in the world, kids have to take out the garbage? I went up to my room and got all my things together.

I got my pajamas and an extra shirt. I decided to forget my toothbrush. I stuffed everything inside a carry-bag and went downstairs. After I took out the garbage, I hurried to leave. Mom had a small package for Aunt Toot so I strapped it in the carrier with my own stuff and took off on my bicycle.

"Have a good time," Mom called as I left.

It sure was good to ride out to Gramps' place on a Friday afternoon. It made a girl feel really great. A whole weekend without school!

Gramps lives about three miles from us, on a small farm. Lots of weekends, I'd ride out there to visit him and Aunt Toot. Everybody says I look like my Gramps 'cause I'm tall and wiry for my age, just like he is. But my hair is light brown and Gramps' hair is white, and I'm a girl. So I don't look exactly like him. I'm not wrinkled either. Otherwise, being like my Gramps is a neat thing to be.

Gramps used to be way out in the country. The town just keeps growing out along the Ohio River towards Gramps' farm, so it isn't very far out to Gramps' place. You go three blocks down to the end of our street and turn left on the dirt road for about a mile 'til you come to the store at the crossroads. You turn left again and go about two miles along a dirt road when you come to the bridge. You go right over the small rise and there is the farm.

Gramps' farm is a neat, well-kept place. It has all the swell things farms are supposed to have. It's just like the ones we read about in first grade. There are animals, a hay loft, and an old horse to ride. There are lots of secret places in the barn where a girl can hide and just think. You can even day-dream without writing, "I will pay attention," twenty-five times.

I like to help with the chores. It's even fun to take out the garbage on a little farm. I just throw the table scraps into the pig pen. It's called "sloppin' the hogs." "Sloppin'" is one of those words that feels good when I say it.

The food is the best there is. Aunt Toot always bakes snickerdoodle cookies when she knows I'm coming. She makes real smooth mashed potatoes. She puts lots of butter and warm milk from Noodles into the potatoes. Noodles is their cow. I always ask for second helpings. Sometimes I get thirds.

On Friday night, we all went outside after supper to sit on the front porch. There was me and Gramps and Aunt Toot and Charlie Fupp. I love Gramps and Aunt Toot but I'm not so sure about Charlie. Charlie lives on the farm too. He helps Gramps with the farm work. Aunt Toot says Charlie is more like family than a hired hand. Charlie is okay, except he likes to tease. He teases a lot. He never knows when to quit. Sometimes he embarrasses me.

After dinner we all just sat on the porch. It was dark except for a few fireflies. They didn't know summer was almost over. They just kept flittin' around, but slower than usual.

"Gramps, tell a story," I asked. I knew Gramps liked stories.

"Oh no, not tonight. You've heard all my stories. Why don't we get Charlie to tell one of his." Gramps looked over to Charlie. "How about telling Peggy the story you told me?"

Charlie was sitting on the porch steps, just like me. He looked up at Gramps on the porch. "Which one do you mean?" he asked Gramps.

"You know the one, the one you heard about the Nil Bag."

I didn't much want to hear one of Charlie's stories though I had never heard about a Nil Bag. "What's a Nil Bag?" I asked.

"Well Peggy, it's just a story I heard," Charlie said. He looked up at Gramps again. I couldn't see his face in the dark. He sounded real serious. "Almost twenty years ago, in late 1917, I was just a young man. I couldn't wait to get away from home, from farmin', and mostly, from Ohio. So I was real glad to join the Army and go to fight in the World War in Europe. Yep, I was a doughboy—that's what they called us foot-soldiers. You've heard some of my other war stories, but I guess I never told about the Nil Bag." Charlie was gettin' real warmed up. "Now, I don't know for sure if it's true but this is how I heard it. And... soldiers who fight together aren't much for lyin' to each other. While I was in France, a soldier told me he had found a Nil Bag when he was a little boy. He sure wished he still had it. He said a Nil Bag was about the best thing a guy could have. When you wanted something real bad, I mean real, real bad, there it was! All you had to do was open the Nil Bag up and there was your wish."

Charlie looked right at me and went on: "Now, I didn't believe the soldier. I thought it was just a French story, him being French. I said he was foolin', but an English soldier was with us in the trenches. He said he knew it was true. He had found a Nil Bag when he was a boy in London." Charlie was really into his story tellin' now. I didn't say a word.

"So we put all the stories together. We decided there must be a few Nil Bags. They were spread out all over the world, being as so many people heard about them." He stopped speaking as if satisfied the story was done.

"Charlie, what are they?" I repeated.

"Well," Charlie answered. "As near as I can figure, they are some kind of magic little bag. All you have to do is find one and it is yours. If you tell anyone about it, it loses itself. I looked and looked, but I never did find one. Then the War was over and I came back to the farm. I guess I'll never find one now,"

"What did the Bag do?" I asked. I figured by now, Charlie was just teasin'.

"That's what is so special about the Nil Bag. It holds things," Charlie said, looking me right in the eye.

"What kind of things?" I asked right back.

"Whatever the finder wants most! It's different for each finder. The French fellow said his Nil Bag had a special potion so he could read other people's thoughts. It was something he really wanted to do. For the English boy, the Bag had a special powder. It made him run faster than anybody around," Charlie finished.

I thought I saw Charlie wink at Gramps. Charlie said, "If I found a Nil Bag it would hold lots of money. I could just sit back and relax and never work again." Charlie leaned against the porch post. "What would it hold for you, Gramps?" Charlie asked.

"I don't rightly know," Gramps said. "I'll bet Peggy would know how to use it. She's always thinking of good ideas."

"Oh, Gramps, you're just foolin'. Those things don't exist." I wasn't goin' to fall for their teasin'.

Charlie sounded hurt. "You don't believe me? Well maybe that's why there aren't any Nil Bags around anymore. If kids won't believe, I guess the Nil Bags just disappear. They lose themselves." Charlie stood up and stretched. "Goodnight folks, I'm turning in." Then he went to his room.

We all went to bed soon after. I was sure glad I didn't let them fool me about magic bags holdin' magic things. Charlie must have forgotten I was in fifth grade. I was too old to believe his stories.

We got up early Saturday morning. First, I helped with morning chores. After breakfast, Aunt Toot and I went out to her garden patch. There we got the vegetables for the day's meals. The tomatoes smelled good, but picking the beans made me itch. Aunt Toot saw me pick a bean, scratch and itch, pick a bean, scratch and itch. Finally, she started scratching just watching me.

"Peggy," Aunt Toot said. "You make a body all itchy just looking at you. Why don't you go gather the eggs for me."

"Sure, Aunt Toot!" I answered. I liked gathering eggs. I took the basket and set out.

"Watch out for the tom," Aunt Toot called after me. The chicken coop is built next to the barn. On the way to the coop I passed the old outhouse. Gramps was going to put in regular plumbing in the farmhouse. Aunt Toot had told him she wouldn't stay and take care of him without it. Then something called "The Depression" had started a few years ago. Ever since, people had stopped putting in real plumbing. They had stopped doing a lot of things. I don't really know why everybody was depressed but the grownups sure talked about it a lot. It had to do with nobody getting jobs and President Hoover. Then Mr. Roosevelt said we'd have a new deal when he was elected president. But everybody still talks about being depressed. So anyway, Gramps never did get an inside toilet. They had left the outhouse in the farmyard. It was run down now but it had been real classy when it was new. Gramps called it a "two-holer."

Gramps always raised a few turkeys. He had five hens and a tom. The son-of-a-gun tom turkey was a mean bugger and chased everything that moved. Especially me. I move a lot. It's why Aunt Toot had told me to watch out for him. The chickens were busy scratching for feed when I got into the coop. They hardly paid me any attention. Did you know if you find a cracked egg, you can just drop it on the floor of the coop? Those hens just gobble it up, eggshell and all. I never think of those cleaned chickens in the market being almost like cannibals. Things are different on a farm. There isn't any waste, even with cracked eggs. Still, I always hope I don't find a cracked egg.

I'd reach under the hens still sitting on their nests. I'd

feel around for any eggs. The feathers would tickle my fingers. Some nests had one egg. A few had two. The chickens just kept a-cluckin' and a-scratchin'. I had the basket about as full as I could handle without breaking the eggs. I started for the house. All of a sudden there was this noise. I looked around. There came the danged turkey with his wings flappin' and his wattle fiery red! I took off at a dead run. I saw he was gaining on me so I jumped into the two-holer and slammed the door shut. Just in time! That gobbler wasn't going to gobble me!

Whew! It was hot in there and it didn't smell too good. After a while I peeped out. He was still there, gobblin' and strutting around. I looked out several times. He was always there peckin' around or fluffin' his feathers.

I didn't want anyone to think I was afraid of the danged ol' bird, especially Charlie. I wasn't taking any chances either. I mean, a big tom turkey is a big bird. A very big, very mean bird. I just waited... and waited... and waited.

I don't know how long I was in there but it was long enough that I almost got used to the aroma. I was getting hungry and was afraid I would miss dinner. I didn't think anyone had seen me run in there. I didn't know how to get out without attracting attention. Or attracting Tom.

I needn't have worried though, for Aunt Toot had an eagle eye as well as a big mouth. "Okay, Peggy, you can come out now." I heard her say. "The big, bad turkey has long gone about his business."

I peeked out and there stood Aunt Toot. Boy, was I embarrassed! She had a grin on her face but she didn't say anything else for once. She just reached for the egg basket. Two of the eggs were cracked and one was already scrambled, shells and all. She shook her head and made the "tsk, tsk, tsk," sound aunts like to make. Then she went into the house. I followed closely behind, just like a shadow. I kept looking over my shoulder. I still wasn't taking any chances.

Out on the farm, the big meal of the day is at lunch. They call it dinner, and they call our dinner, supper. I don't know when they have lunch. Gramps and Charlie came in for dinner and were washing up at the kitchen sink. I heard ol' Charlie start to laugh when he saw me. I knew I was in for it. Charlie had seen it all. All through dinner and afterward he kept harping on me and the tom. It's bad enough for a girl to be chased by a turkey. I really didn't need Charlie too.

"First time I ever saw a turkey make a chicken out of a girl," Charlie teased. I knew he'd keep it up, saying how brave I was and all kinds of stuff. I didn't think I could stand the teasin' all weekend. I decided to just go home.

After I'd helped Aunt Toot clean up the table, I mumbled an excuse about having to go home. I got on my bike with all my stuff and left. Aunt Toot said she'd call my Mom and let her know I was on my way home. When I got to the bridge I saw some kids swimming in the creek. I sat down under a big ol' hickory tree to watch them. I was still feeling bad about the turkey. I didn't even feel like joining in with the swimming. I thought to myself, *Why is it that there's always someone around to laugh at a kid when she makes a mistake?* In my family, anyway. Sometimes I thought grownups just waited around to laugh at kids. I made enough mistakes to keep them fallin' on the floor! If only there was a way I could give them a dose of their own medicine! If I could just show them how hard it was being almost ten years old. It was awful havin' a body growin' so fast it kept knockin' things over.

There was also the "woman thing" coming for me. I just don't want to think about it. If only I could get a laugh on someone else for a change!

The day was warm but it was cool under the tree. I sat there for a long time, just thinking. I guess I was feelin' sorry for myself too. Finally, I figured I'd better go home. Mom would be expecting me. I had been leaning back against the tree and as I put my hand down on the ground, I felt something soft and smooth. I looked down at the object and couldn't believe my eyes. There lay a neat little Nil Bag!

It was just like Charlie said! A Nil Bag was real! Charlie said it was just about the best thing there was in the world. I mean, Aladdin's lamp was nothing compared to a Nil Bag. I never thought the Nil Bag was real. I never thought I would really find one. Yet there it was! In Ohio! Not France or England! It was just laying there waiting for me. I knew it didn't belong to one of those other kids. Their stuff was all over some rocks down by the water. And besides, no kid would leave a Nil Bag lying around. I was sure of that much.

The Nil Bag was about two inches square with a drawstring to close it. Being tiny didn't mean a thing. It could hold whatever a person wanted it to hold. It could hold lots of things at one time, even lots of big things. It could hold things nobody else ever dreamed. I opened it and found it was full of treasures. Everything you could think of. Everything I could think of, anyway. Like my Gramps said, I was a girl with ideas. I wouldn't have traded the Nil Bag for King Midas' touch.

Right off, I took to thinking. I couldn't tell anyone about it. If I did, the Nil Bag would lose itself. All the way home I was almost overcome with thoughts. With a Nil Bag, I could do all the things fifth graders wish they could do but can't.

Maybe I could get even with ol' Charlie for laughin' at me. I would get even with the danged turkey in a couple of months—on Thanksgiving—that tom turkey would be our dinner!

Chapter Two: The Truck

There were several things needing to be taken care of in our neighborhood. They were things everybody grouched about, like the Depression. But nobody did anything about them.

Halfway up in the next block lived a man who gave me and other kids a lot of trouble. He parked his old Model T truck on the sidewalk all the time. He could have put it in his driveway or just parked it on the street. No, he wouldn't do that. On both sides of our street, we have nice smooth cement sidewalks where all the kids liked to roller skate or ride their bikes. When you'd come to ol' Tuffy Tidbit's place, you would have to get off the sidewalk, into the street.

Once, on my bike, I tried squeezing between the truck and the thorny hedge Tuffy has in his yard. Out of nowhere ol' Tuffy came yellin', dressed in an old stained undershirt.

"Hey, you kid, get away from my truck!" he yelled. "You're scratching the paint!"

I don't know how I could scratch his old paint. First, I'd have to scratch through the rust before I could find any paint. I didn't feel like pointing this out to big ol' Tuffy with him yellin' and comin' after me. So I shoved on through, scratching my bike and leg on his danged hedge. I got out of there, fast! As I looked back, there was old Tuffy looking over his truck for scratches.

This day, Mom had sent me to the store for groceries.

Coming back from the market I had to get off my bike and walk it around Tuffy's truck. I tilted the bike a little too far and the quart of milk fell out of my carrier. The bottle of milk crashed on the pavement. Milk shot all over me and the street. Three million cats pounced on me, my bike, the milk, and everything. There I was in the street trying to pick up my bike, get the soggy bread back in the carrier, and fight off cats which I never really cared for anyway. As I looked up, there was ol' Tuffy on his front porch. He was in an undershirt scratchin' and laughin' like crazy. Immediately, I knew what I was going to do to old Tuffy.

Soon as I got home I went to my room to consult the Nil Bag. At first, I was afraid it couldn't help me. Then I found just the things I needed. I tucked the things into the Nil Bag until later.

The same night I was working on homework at the kitchen table but I was really thinkin' about Tuffy. About nine o'clock, I gave a big yawn. I collected all my stuff and gave another yawn. I even stretched this time so it would look more real. I told Mom and Dad goodnight and went upstairs to my room. I shut the door and checked to listen if anybody was behind me—nope. It was okay.

Out of the Nil Bag I took a little squirt bottle of Cantsee. I stood right in front of my dresser mirror and sprayed some on myself. A squirt and I simply disappeared! Just like in the movies: You can't see a person sprayed with Cantsee! I could see I wasn't there. Knowing I couldn't be seen, I had no trouble with Mom or Dad or anyone else stopping me. I quietly slipped out of the house and down the street.

When I got up to Tuffy's house, sure enough, there

was the danged truck on the sidewalk. Now, I am a careful person, you should know. I checked around the front of the house to make sure Tuffy wasn't around. His front door was open. Through the screen door, I could see ol' Tuffy in his undershirt listen' to a radio show. Every now and then he would slap his knee and laugh like crazy! I knew Tuffy and his undershirt would be busy until the show was over.

I snuck back to the truck. I didn't want to hurt the old rust-bucket. I just wanted to let Tufffy know what a problem his truck was. That's when I let the air out of all four tires! It was really easy with my little valve stem tool. All us kids carried them because bicycle tires had ways of going flat at the worst times. I poked the one end into the stem to release the air pressure; I sure didn't want the stem to shoot out and disappear. Inserting and twisting the little wrench end, all the air escaped. After seeing all four tires flat, I guessed I might as well do the job right. I let the air out of the spare tire too. It went so well, I came back and did this three nights in a row!

Each morning on the way to school, I'd see ol' Tuffy out in the street pumping up his tires with a leaky bicycle pump. He'd be cussin' like crazy. I'd just ride right on by, going way around his truck. I really tried to keep my laugh to myself.

On the last night, I came shovin' on down the street. I was feelin' pretty good about bein' invisible. Except there was ol' Tuffy sitting in his truck. He sat there lookin' around and around. He didn't see me. He couldn't. I had on my Cantsee. I walked right up to the truck. Then I got down and crawled over to the front tire. I let just a little bit of air out. Then I crawled all around the truck letting just a little air at a time out of each tire. It took me a lot of times around but Tuffy never felt the truck go down. When I left, there was Tuffy sitting in a truck with four flat tires.

On the next night, I sprayed on my Cantsee and went up the street for more fun. Tuffy wasn't inside listenin' to the radio. He was on the sidewalk telling one of our town policeman about the situation. I moved real quiet so I could stand right beside them and hear everything they said. They couldn't see me, of course. I really had to hold my mouth to keep from laughin' right out loud.

Tuffy was wavin' his arms and cussin' a mouthful. He was tellin' how the night before he had sat in the truck all night. He'd been alert. He hadn't seen anyone. Dang! In the morning again, the tires were flat.

The policeman stood there silently as he couldn't get a word in between Tuffy talking loud and cursing. The policeman had been writing in a little book all the while. After a time, ol' Tuff paused for breath. The policeman took his turn to talk.

He said, "Mr. Tidbit, did you ever stop to think that maybe someone is trying to tell you something?"

Tuffy said, "No! What?"

"It is against the law to park on the sidewalk. Parking there causes people to walk out into the street."

Tuffy screamed, "I have a right to park where I please!"

Quietly and patiently the policeman said, "No, you haven't a right to park against the law." Then he handed ol' Tuff a parking ticket to sign.

"No, I won't sign it!" Tuffy almost shouted.

"Okay," said the policeman. "Come with me and we will go downtown to the courthouse." The policeman was so calm, he was the cat's pajamas. He just looked down at the stains on Tuff's shirt and then stared Tuff in the eye and said, "The judge is waiting. Shall we go?" He tapped the ticket pad.

That did it. Ol' Tuffy signed the parking ticket. He scratched his head and went into his house.

As a grown up myself, I've thought about the attitude of our town policeman. Maybe it was because he knew the town, and he knew Tuffy that he could take such good care of the situation. I also wish he could have made Tuffy write, "I will park the truck on the street" twenty-five times.

After his ticket, Tuffy was a little more careful about parking his truck. Just a little.

Chapter Three: Miss Tiffany

There comes a time when a person, even a kid-person, even a girl tomboy, just can't take anymore garbage. I finally reached such a point with our next door neighbor. I'd had about all I could stand of Miss Tiffany. She is a tattle-tale and a nosey ol' busy-body. Being old isn't an excuse. From what I hear, she's always been that way.

Miss Tiffany lives in the little house next to us. She keeps her house and yard spotless and clean. She scrubs her front porch down on her hands and knees. She even scrubs the cement walk down to the front gate. She has old hair. It's from a scalp thing tying it back into a pig tail knot. She walks hunched over, probably from bending over scrubbing too much and she sounds like there's a frog in her throat, a bullfrog.

Miss Tiffany has a bulldog personality, a mean kind, except to her very own bulldog. She lives with Winston, her English bulldog. Winston is a ferocious-looking dog. He is big and white and his ugly face is covered with wrinkles. He has a big fang, sticking up from his lower jaw on either side of his mouth. His face is so flat, he almost has to stand on his head to eat. He is a well-trained dog even if he is ugly, flat-faced, wrinkled, and ferocious. He brings in the newspaper and he goes to the toilet in a certain place in the back yard. Winston even wipes his feet on the door mat. Miss Tiffany talks to Winston as if he were a person.

One other thing he does: He smashes down the geraniums, but I was the one who always got blamed for it. Whatever bad happened at Miss Tiffany's house, I got blamed for it. Seems like every time my friends and I played ball in my backyard, the ball went over the low fence and ended up in Miss Tiffany's yard. Miss Tiffany would come out from her house screaming at us to get the ball out of her flowers. Then ol' Winston would chase the ball and take it into her kitchen.

I had to give this a lot of thought. I didn't want anymore garbage from a dog!

One day I was playing with my favorite toy. You could wind it up tight then release a little thing, and the propeller shot straight up in the air. I always liked to see how high I could make it go. I let my toy go and the propeller shot up real high. A little puff of wind caught it and it went over into Miss Tiffany's yard. The danged dog, Winston, came crawling out of the geraniums and got it. He took it to the door and scratched. Miss Tiffany came to the door to let him into the house. When she saw what he had, she started screamin' at me. She ran over towards me with her little shufflin' steps, hunched over like she was, she couldn't help but see the geraniums. She blamed me!

"I've told you and told you to stay out of my flowers!

You evil girl, you mashed my flowers!" Miss Tiffany shouted at me.

"I didn't do it," I said.

"I saw you in there hunting for your toy!" she croaked.

Maybe I said a few things that sounded just fine to me. Words can sound different to grownups. She thought I sassed her! She thought I was talkin' back.

Mom heard it all, came out then, and made me go in the house. I had to sit on a chair in the corner for an hour for sassin'.

"Peggy, such behavior is not acceptable!" Mom said. She didn't say anything about the toy or the flowers.

While I was sitting in the corner, I got a good idea for getting even with ol' Winston. When my time was up, I started right out for the Nil Bag in my room.

It was another warm afternoon but it must have been cool among Miss Tiffany's flowers. Miss Tiffany had flowers everywhere. Flowers were around the fence and also in flower beds.

Looking out of the window in my room, I could see ol' Winnie snoozing among the petunias. I opened the ol' Nil Bag. I gave myself a good, big squirt of Cantsee so it would last a long time. I didn't want Miss Tiffany to see me.

I sneaked up on ol' Winston. Before he could smell me or hear me or know I was there, I gave him a good, big shot of BeQuiet. Ol' Winnie just sat there, being quiet. I painted him all over with a bright green vegetable color Mom used for St. Patrick's Day cooking so I knew it wouldn't hurt the quiet bulldog.

I didn't paint his eyes or fangs. I painted a circle around each eye in bright red food coloring I found in the other corner of the drawer. Yep, and I painted his fangs bright yellow. Food coloring is wonderful stuff! He just laid there looking like a big, ugly, fat, green, tomato worm.

Then I went up on Miss Tiffany's back porch to see what would happen.

Pretty soon ol' Winston began to stir a little as the BeQuiet started to wear off. He wiggled up onto the porch and scratched on the door.

Miss Tiffany opened the door and her eyes popped out. At first she didn't recognize ol' Winnie and was gonna shut the door. I guess she didn't want a ferocious green tomato worm in her house. Ol' Winnie gave a grunt. Then Miss Tiffany recognized her Bullworm.

"Winston!" Miss Tiffany began to scream. "What is the matter with you? Oh, you poor thing! What will I do? Oh! Oh! Oh!" Miss Tiffany bent down to Winston and said, "Winston dear, you must have eaten something to make you green." She petted him and petted him. Winston just wiggled.

"I know just what will fix you, Winston dear." Miss Tiffany started talking baby talk to the dog. "Mama will give her little Winnie a doggie dose of castor oil!"

Castor oil, ugh! Poor Winston. I knew he was in for a bad time so I went home. I almost felt sorry for Winnie. Then again, Winston wasn't my only problem with dogs. I had more trouble with cats, turkeys, and dogs!

About halfway up the alley lives a couple of dog lovers.

Mr. and Mrs. Doglover have a solid wood fence with about two feet of wire on top of it, all around their yard. They keep a ferocious barking dog. I have nothing against dogs even though they scare me to death. I only fear cats a little.

But this dog was B-I-G!

My best friend's name is Stinky Barnes. He lives one block up our street and over one block on the corner, where you will find him if he's home.

When I go to Stinky's house, I go up through the alley. It's closer and it's when I get all the garbage from the Doglover's dog.

Whenever I pass that house on my way to Stinky's, the danged dog lunges and jumps against the fence barking like a danged fool. He is a great big German police dog with fangs like an elephant's or bigger! All night long the dog barks at nothing.

One Tuesday, I was shovin' along the alley thinkin' about poor Winnie. Darn! The big dog hit the fence and scared the living daylights out of me.

"Well now, you stupid dog," I said from the other side of the alley. "I'll teach you about scaring people. Your dog-loving family can learn a thing or two."

At bedtime, I went up to my room as always. Then I used the Cantsee so I could go right out the front door. Holding my Nil Bag, I went up the alley right up to the Doglover's fence. The danged dog surely couldn't see me but I guess he could smell me. I hadn't done anything to stink about but dogs are pretty keen smellers. Of course, he barked and jumped on the fence.

I was ready for the dog. I had already taken a squirt can of BeQuiet out of the Nil Bag. As the beast lunged at the fence, I aimed the squirt can through a knot hole in the fence. He charged and I squirted the BeQuiet. That did it. The dog shut up and laid down on the porch.

By the light off the street lamp, I poked around in the

Nil Bag and there it was: A little Neet's Foot. There is nothing slicker for opening a door or gate than a Neet's Foot. I don't know what a Neet is but it has a clever foot. I opened the gate lock. The dog just looked at me from the porch. The BeQuiet was really working. I walked up to the back door and went inside. (People in our town never lock their doors, they only lock gates.)

It was an awful warm night so all the windows were open. I tiptoed through the house to look in the bedrooms. In the last room, I saw Mr. and Mrs. Doglover sound asleep in their double bed. They are big people. Their double bed just didn't have any room left over with them in it. I sized up the situation and knew what to do.

Out of the Nil Bag came a squirt can of SleepTight. I gave both Mr. and Mrs. a shot of it so they wouldn't foul up my plans by waking up too soon.

Quickly, I went back to the porch and lured the pesky dog inside. I hoped he had fleas. Maybe I could find some in the Nil Bag. No, it was all right. He had plenty of his own!

I coaxed the dog into the bedroom and up onto the bed. I whispered he should lie down between Mr. and Mrs. which he did. He was just so happy to be allowed in bed with the dog lovers. Not being a house dog, he didn't smell too good. Phew! I gave him a squirt of SleepTight. I pulled the covers up snuggly over all three of them. I even added a big wool blanket I found nearby.

It was a hot, humid, September night. I made sure all windows were closed tightly. I didn't want a cool breeze to wreck my work. I left the three of them, sweating, smelling, and scratching fleas.

I often wondered what happened when they woke up

the next morning. Maybe they changed their name to Mr. and Mrs. Doghater. From then on, the dog never jumped at the fence when I was going to Stinky's. I could see him looking at me and wagging his tail.

Chapter Four: Revenge on the Snot Twins

Down two blocks from our house, on the way to Gramp's farm lives these two snots. They're twins. I can't tell them apart. Neither can anyone else. They are two years older than Stinky or me and bigger. Their squeaky voices are just awful. They are sneaky buggers and do dirty tricks on me and Stinky all the time. They sick their dog on us or throw rocks. One afternoon when I went by their house, they were hiding in the bushes. I was riding my bike and goin' pretty fast. As I passed the bushes, they stuck a metal rod out through the hedge and it went right through my front wheel. The rod broke every spoke, the bike went spinning off, and I skidded into the gutter. I skinned both knees and tore my pants. Those twins just laughed like crazy.

Mom got after them 'cause that made her real mad. She went to their house and made them pay for the pants and the wheel. The new wheel made me feel pretty good. But I knew they'd really be after me from then on.

One Saturday morning I was going up the alley to Stinky's house. I saw the Snot Twins running away from the front of Miss Tiffany's gate. They were in such a hurry they didn't even stop to take a poke at me. I knew they'd been up to something. As long as I didn't get poked, I wouldn't worry about it. I went on up to Stinky's and forgot about them.

Under Stinky's back porch was a neat place to play

with our cars and little house and miniature horses. A real farm layout. There wasn't quite enough room for us to stand up under there but we didn't need to stand up. There wasn't any cement under the porch, just dirt. That made it perfect to make roads. You just scrape your hand where the road should go, sprinkle a little water on it and smooth the top as nice as you please. You've got a road! Me and Stinky had all kinds of things built under there. We had little towns, hills, and tunnels. There were rivers and everything. We made our stuff out of odds and ends and pretendin'. Even the cars were not real. They were just some little empty medicine bottles we'd collected here and there.

It was the most fun for Stinky and me. We especially liked it on a rainy day 'cause it was dry under there. At the end of the porch was a lattice. It was like a grill made out of wooden strips. We could close the lattice almost like shutters. No one would know we were under there. Better yet, no one would bother us. Whenever we finished playing, we'd close the lattice, leaving everything ready for our next visit.

On the Saturday I was talkin' about, Stinky and I had a great time. I forgot all about the Snot Twins. My stomach didn't forget when it was lunchtime. I started to get real hungry.

"See ya, Stinky," I said. "I'm going home for lunch."

"Is your dad home today?" Stinky asked.

My dad is a ticket-taker for the railroad and he has to work on the weekends sometimes. "Yeah, Dad's home, so lunch should be right on time," I answered. One thing about having a railroad man in the family, everything had to be on time. I don't know why. The trains never were.

I shoved on home and sure enough, Dad was there.

Boy, was he mad! The minute I stepped up on the porch, he called me to come into the house and quick! What had I done to make him so danged mad?

"What do you mean by nailing Miss Tiffany's gates shut?" He asked in a gruff voice. I knew he meant business.

"Her gates?" I asked, not understanding.

"Yes! She tried to run over here but she ran into the swinging gate that wouldn't swing. She nearly flipped over the gate on her head!" He almost shouted.

"Dad, I didn't do—" I tried to say.

"You not only nailed both gates shut but you wrote all over her clean cement walks!"

"No, Dad—" I tried again.

"And you wrote your name all over the place. It was after seeing your name on her walk that she ran over here. Or at least, she tried to run over with a shut gate in her way."

"Dad—" I tried one more time.

"Now you get yourself a bucket of water and some rags. I want you to get over there and scrub, and I want all the nails taken out of Miss Tiffany's gate, too!" Some of the red had gone out of Dad's face but he still sounded awful mad. "I will come over to inspect every inch of the place, so you'd better do a good job!"

Boy, did I wish Mom was there. Even though she sometimes punished me, at least she listened to me.

"Gee whiz…" I said.

"Peggy!" Dad said.

"Yes, sir," I answered. I went and did as he told me. I went to the back porch and got our scrubbing bucket. There were some rags in the rag bag and I took those too. Then I dug around in the tool box to get a claw hammer. I really trudged over to Miss Tiffany's house.

It took me a long time to get the nails out of the gate between our houses. They were pounded in from both sides. It was almost like two people had pounded them in. I used the claw hammer to pull out the nails and then threw the nails in the flower bed. The plants could always use a little iron. I wondered if plants liked rusty nail iron.

I filled up the bucket from the garden hose. I was going to squirt Winston with the hose while I was at it. Then I figured I was in enough trouble and this was no fault of his. I went around front to Miss Tiffany's sidewalk. The sidewalk was a mess! There were words and pictures all over it. They were drawn in chalk. There was my name all over it. PEGGY... PEGGY... PEGGY... PEGGY. I felt awful. I bent down and started scrubbing.

While I was scrubbing the chalk marks, Miss Tiffany came out of her house and said, "Now then, maybe, you will stop bothering me."

"But Miss Tiffany—" I began.

"I'm glad you signed your name," she went on talking. "There is no way to get out of your punishment today. You are a very bad girl!"

I was almost ready to cry so I didn't even answer her. I couldn't even think of a good revenge. I just felt like a sack of garbage had been dumped on my head and there wasn't a thing I could do about it. It was so unfair!

After I had finished the scrubbing, Dad came over. He looked everything over and then said very seriously, "All right, Peggy, you may go home now. I want you to go right to your room."

"Yes, sir," I answered. I put the bucket and stuff away

and trudged up to my room. I lay down on the bed but I didn't cry. After a while, I began to think things over. I remembered the Snot Twins running away from Miss Tiffany's gate. Of course, the Snot Twins!

I heard Mom come home from shopping. I could hear her ask Dad where I was. I couldn't hear the rest as their voices faded. They must have gone into another room. Parents always do that when they are talking about you. They murmur loud enough for you to know they are talking. Then they murmur soft enough that you can't understand what they are saying.

Criminitly, this life was awful! I didn't like it for Dad to be mad at me. I wished he'd let me explain.

He should have known....

I must have dozed off because the next thing it was getting dark when I heard a little knock at my door and heard Mom's voice saying softly, "Peggy?"

"Yes, Mom, come in," I said.

"I looked in earlier but you were asleep. Are you feeling better?"

"No. I feel awful!"

"Do you want to talk about it?" she asked.

I wasn't goin' to tell her. I was going to show her I could be stubborn too. But all of a sudden the words just tumbled out! I told her about being at Stinky's house, and the Snot Twins running away from Miss Tiffany's yard, and the bucket and everything. Mostly about those twins. Mom just listened. Mom's awfully good at listening.

When I finished talking, she didn't say a word. We just sat there for a long time. I felt better. I knew that she understood. Mom's quiet, but she understands. Everything.

Finally, Mom asked me if I was hungry. I remembered I hadn't had any lunch. Boy, was I ever hungry!

"I sure am, Mom," I told her.

"How would you like some hot dogs for dinner? On warm buns?"

Hot dogs and buns were what we had! Dad didn't have much to say at dinner. When it was bedtime, he went upstairs with me. He sat down on the chair next to the bed.

Dad said, "You know, Peggy, grown-ups make mistakes the same as kids do. Sometimes that means apologizing. I made a mistake today. I talked when I should have listened to your side; I am sorry. Sometimes I worry about my little girl getting into trouble. I forget you are growing up and thinking about things. Can we be friends again?"

"Sure, Dad," I answered. Gee, I really felt better now. I thought I might try for one more thing. "Dad, about all that work I did at Miss Tiffany's…" I began. Ol' Dad was ahead of me.

"Peggy, after all the pranks you really have pulled on Miss Tiffany, let's just call you even. That work is for all the times you didn't get caught!" Dad grinned at me in a strange way. I knew that he knew what I knew. I decided he was right. Miss Tiffany and I were even.

Getting even with the Snot Twins was a different marble in my sack. The Nil Bag could really help me there.

The next evening I was just shovin' around with nothing to do. I saw the two Snots comin' down the street. Real quick, I hid behind some bushes 'til they passed. Like I said, it's not that I am a coward. I'm just timid and careful.

After the twins passed, I went home and up to my

room. I wanted to think some thoughts. It was gettin' on toward bedtime before I got through thinkin'.

I got out my trusty Nil Bag and took a squirt of Cantsee. I thought I should be careful how much I used but the bottle seemed to be as full as I needed it. I slipped out of the house and started shovin' down the street where the Snot Twins with their sing-song voices lived. Their bedroom was on the ground floor. The Snot Twins' bed was close to an open window. That was handy for me. All I had to do was reach in and give them a squirt of SleepTight. I'm careful even when I'm invisible.

I crawled into their window. There those Snots were, both of them snoring with their mouths open. Now both Sing and Song had long, straight, greasy black hair which I hated. They wore it parted in the middle. It would hang down on both sides or in their eyes.

Out of my pocket, I took my trusty little scissors and really went to work. I cut off all the hair off the left side of Sing's head. Then I cut off all the hair off the right side of Song's head. Now I could tell one from the other. Maybe those sewing lessons Aunt Toot tried to teach me were useful after all!

Both boys were sleepin' flat on their backs. Not wanting to miss an opportunity, I squirted both their bellies with Stickem. Stickem makes anything stick to anything and is awful hard to unstick. I stuck the cut off hair all over their stomachs.

That was a good enough time for me to leave. I heard that their mother fainted dead away when she went in to call them for breakfast the next morning.

Chapter Five: Reciting at School

I could tell when I woke up on Friday that it was gonna be a dumb day, even if it was a Friday. Miss Tillie said we were having "reciting" on Friday. Poetry and such stuff. I just call 'em "pomes." I didn't know any pomes except maybe one. If she called on me, I'd let her have it. The pome I mean. I could hear Dad getting up so I'd better get to the bathroom first. I could hear Mom downstairs and smell the good smell of bacon frying. I got into the bathroom and wet my fingertips. Then I touched my eyes. No use overdoing this washing up. I finished in the bathroom and hurried downstairs and right into the kitchen.

"Peggy, please get the eggs out of the ice chest for me," Mom said.

The ice chest was in the entry way between the kitchen and the back porch. Every other day, the iceman would come and put twenty-five pounds of ice in it. We'd just leave the money on the top of the ice chest and he'd just leave the ice inside the chest. Mom sure wished she had one of those new fangled General Electric ice boxes. They had a big bird cage looking thing on top. You never had to put ice in them. They made their own ice! She would have to wait until the Depression eased up. Then maybe we could afford one.

I went to the entry way. Whoops! I slipped and almost fell. I had forgotten to empty the pan under the chest. The iceman might put the ice in the chest, but it was my job to take the melted water out. The darned ice melted all the time. It drained down a tube into a pan set on the floor.

Mom saw me slip and said, "Maybe now you will remember to empty the pan."

"Maybe now, I think I'll just cut a hole in the floor. Then we won't have to use a pan!" I told her. "We could just direct the tube into the hole and run a little hose to water your flowers by the porch."

"Hm," said Mom. "That's a good idea. I'll think about it."

While Mom fixed breakfast, I went to the dining room. There was the paper at Dad's place. We never saw my Dad at breakfast. He always hid behind the newspaper. I didn't know if he could read or not—maybe he just looked at the pictures. I looked at the newspaper and got an idea. Quick like, I whipped out my Nil Bag and found some Erase. I squirted all the pages of the paper except the front page. The words just erased themselves. The pictures erased too. I refolded the paper. The front page showed like always so I put it on the table where Dad could reach it.

It was almost time to leave for school, so Mom gave me breakfast. I ate in a hurry. I didn't want to be around when Dad opened the paper and found it blank.

I finished eating and was in the kitchen saying good-bye to Mom and getting my lunch sack. That's when the explosion came! Dad blew his top!

"Ellen! What happened to my paper?" he shouted.

Mom rushed into the dining room to see what was the matter. I knew what the matter was! Being a smart girl, I ran off to school.

All morning, we did the usual things at school. All morning I worried about the reciting coming in the afternoon.

After lunch, we all piled back into the classroom. My gosh, there was a mother there. Mary Helen Figlet, the smartest girl in class, had brought her mother.

Mrs. Figlet was a very stylish woman. So Mom said. Mary Helen's mother was a leader in society and a pillar of the church. I thought she was big enough to be a pillar all right. I don't know what the other stuff means.

Miss Tillie was all aflutter. She was so excited about having a pillar in her classroom! When we were all quiet, Miss Tillie called on Fannie Firpo. Fannie recited a pome called, "Our Flag." (Miss Tillie says "po-em." I just say "pome.")

Otto Pinchem was next. I don't know what dumb thing he did. Then, ol' Ima Goodie said one called, "My Doll." I was getting sicker and sicker of this mushy junk. Dad would call this stuff "sickening sweet."

Then, I got to playing with a fly. It was buzzing and crawling on my desk. I kept my hands real still and the fly would crawl up on my fingers. I didn't move. I was waiting for the fly to crawl down between my fingers. Just as I squeezed, the fly flew off!

Mary Helen was called on next. Her ol' mom smiled and nodded. Miss Tillie nodded and smiled. Mary Helen was tall and skinny. She had kinda reddish looking hair. I don't know if it was curly or not but there were a lot of little hair things hanging around her head. They were called "ringlets" by the girls but looked like weenies to me. They always bounced when she walked.

When Mary Helen got up we could see her dress was all caught up in the back. Mary Helen was prancing along and the kids were snickering. Mary Helen's mother called her back and fixed things except Mary Helen was so embarrassed, she started to cry. Miss Tillie and Mrs. Figlet got the tears mopped up and glared at the class. The kids shut up and Mary Helen started saying her pome.

"The tag at eve had dunk his still," Mary Helen misspoke. Well, what kinda talk was that? The kids howled again and Mary Helen flounced back and sat down. She was mad! Miss Tillie got the kids to shut up. She coaxed Mary Helen to try again. Mary Helen wouldn't budge. When her mother gave her a real mad look, Mary Helen went back up to the front of the room. The kids really tried to be quiet. Honest. We all wanted to see what might happen next.

"The stag at eve had drunk his fill," Mary Helen started her pome again.

I didn't pay much attention cause ol' Otto Pinchem got to poking me with his ruler. He kept sticking it up through the crack in my desk seat. I was looking in the Nil Bag to see what I could get him with, when I heard Miss Tillie call my name. Ugh! I don't know any pomes. I was so gunked, I didn't even think of the Cantsee. I started across the front of the room. Tommy Dunker stuck his dumb foot out and tripped me. The kids laughed as I almost fell down. Real quick, I turned and faced the class. My heart was thumping pretty hard when I started the only pome I could remember:

"I had a little dog,
his name was Rover.
When he died,
he died all over."

I snuck a look at Miss Tillie. She had a frown but she nodded for me to go on. So I went on. I recited:

"I had a little cat,
her name was Nell.
When she died,
she went to—"

"That will do, Peggy!" Miss Tillie cried out. "I can see

you are not very well prepared."

I was humiliated. I went back and sat down—mad. Why do teachers make you recite if they won't let you finish? Well, I knew I'd even things out.

Miss Tillie was sitting there at her desk watching the kids come up to recite as she called their names. Since I was in the front seat next to her desk, I could see her hands. (I think she kept my desk there on purpose.) She had her hands folded and layin' on the desk. While all the kids were looking at Bernie Wiffie recite his pome about trees, I opened my Nil Bag. I reached in and got just what I needed. I reached over and squirted one of Miss Tillie's hands with Cantsee. When she turned her head back again, she noticed, she only had one hand left. No one can see a hand squirted with Cantsee!

Miss Tillie jumped up screaming. Then she fell over in a faint. All the kids started screaming and hollering and throwing erasers and spit balls. I let ol' Tommy Dunker have a shot of Stickem. He couldn't get his feet off the floor. Otto Pinchem was still fooling around with his ruler. I gave him a shot, too, so Otto couldn't get off his seat.

By this time things were happening pretty fast. I saw Mary Helen's mother rush up to help Miss Tillie. But she bumped into a kid who fell down on Miss Tillie. Then Mary Helen's mother fell on both of them. They were all pretty well squashed by the pillar of society.

Two other kids must have decided to go for help. They started for the door just as the principal swung it open. Those two kids got smacked in the face with the door. The principal stood there with a real surprised look on his face. Just then he got a "splat" in the face with a spit ball. Another kid came running in with some water. He slipped and fell down, throwing water all over Mary Helen's mother instead of Miss Tillie.

I can't tell what else happened because the school bell rang. So, the other kids and I just went home. I didn't know reading pomes could be so exciting! Anyway, that's how I remember it. It wasn't such a dumb day after all. Even Dad didn't say anything special about his newspaper. At dinner, he just looked directly at me, winked and said, "You know, Peggy, there wasn't much news today, I wonder why?"

Chapter Six: Church and the Whappo

Mom said I had to go to church with her that Sunday. I didn't see why I just couldn't go to Sunday School—but no—I had to go with her and Dad. Mom said it was 'cause it was a special day—yeah, a special day of preaching and pounding.

The day started off bad when I tried to get dressed in Sunday clothes. My dress was too tight and too short! I guess I'd grown in one week. My good shoes didn't feel none too good either. I had a hole in the toe of my sock. I could feel my wiggling toe sticking out. We had to hurry. I just scrunched my skirt as well as I could and tried to ignore my toe. Dad insisted we get to church on time.

We walked up to church a little early. Everybody was standing around in front shaking hands with everybody else. You'd think they'd never seen each other for years. Mom and Dad got so carried away, they even shook hands with each other!

Pretty soon they got tired of all the glad-handing and we all went inside. We got a pretty good seat down front in the second row. After everybody settled down, the preacher came hippy-doing down the aisle. The preacher, Reverend Clarence Tocksenuff, went up on the stage where there was a small table with the book on it that he liked to pound. There was also a chair for him to sit on when he got pooped out or needed to think up some more to say.

On the same stage, but over to one side, was the organ with Miss Clara Clamshell sitting on the bench in front of it. I guessed she was going play it if she got a chance. Mr. O. P. Yew was the song leader. He went up and stood by the organ. Mr. Yew said, "We will now sing hymn number twenty-two.""

"What one?" I said to Mom.

"*The Old Ship of Zion,*" whispered Mom.

The old chip a dying? It sounded kinda crazy I thought, but Clara took off on the organ and everybody started in to singing. At the song's end, the preacher did some praying and here and there you could hear people saying, "Amen." But the preacher didn't take the hint. He kept right on talking. Finally, I guess the preacher got tired because he went over and sat down.

Everything was real quiet so I said to Mom, "What are we waiting for?"

Mom said Charlie Fupp was going to pass the "Confection basket." A confection basket is a long stick with a little basket on one end and ol' Fuddle Duddle Fupp on the other end. He shoves this in front of everyone. They have to put in their installment money.

Mom gave me a quarter to put in the basket but I wasn't going do it. I didn't know children had to go to Heaven on the installment plan.

When ol' Fupp got to me, he stopped. He said in a low

voice, "Okay, Peggy Pal, drop the two bits in the pot."

Mom gave me a poke in the ribs and I let go of the quarter—dang it! Well, I'd fix ol' Charlie. I gave him a squirt of Stickem on the hand holding the confection stick. Ol' Charlie took himself and the confection basket to the back of the church. Pretty soon we heard a crash that sounded like money falling all over the place. Of course, everybody in church looked back to see what was happening. There was ol' Charlie wrestling with the confection basket. Charlie couldn't let go of the stick because of the Stickem on his hand. Every time he would shake his hand to let go, he spilled money all over the floor. He looked up and saw everybody looking at him. Was he embarrassed! Pretty soon some of the Stickem wore off. Charlie was able to let go of the basket. Charlie tried to pick up the money but it would stick to his fingers. He crawled around picking up money and trying to pull it off his fingers like pulling taffy. When he got all the money back in the basket, Charlie stood at the back of the church trying to look like nothing had happened.

After the confections, Preacher Tocksenuff got off to a good start. I think he was mad at Charlie for dropping the money because he got to shouting and thumping the book.

I was getting mighty bored so I started taking out the stuff I had in my pocket. I fished out a stick of gum, took the wrapper off, and chewed it. I took out my whistle. I was about to put it in my mouth when Mom saw it.

"Don't you dare!" Mom said in a low voice.

The preacher didn't pay any attention. He just went on preaching. He was really having a good time.

Philip Philpots was sitting in front of us. Mom always said he wore a wig. I wondered if he did. The first chance I got,

I squirted the inside of his hat with Stickem. There was a fly crawling on Philpots' back. I chewed up the gum wrapper into a nice ball. I was gonna give that ol' fly the treatment. I was poking around in my Nil Bag for a rubber band. Instead I came across a Whappo. A Whappo is a handy thing to have. It is only about two inches square. When you squeeze it will stretch out and reach as far as you want it to go. When you unsqueeze it, it folds up into a little two inch square again. You can't even see it.

I took my gum wrapper spitball and stuck it on the end of the Whappo. I gave it a squeeze. Whap! I missed the fly with the Whappo but hit Philip Philpots on the ear. He jumped about a foot. He looked around to see what hit him. I just smiled back. I think I looked innocent in my Sunday dress. Mr. Philpots sat back.

I was getting pretty tired of listening to the preaching again. I guess we'd have been there yet if I hadn't found a show stopper in the Nil Bag. It was a little, tiny stink ball.

I put the stink ball on the end of the Whappo. I gave the Whappo a squeeze and it stretched right out. The Whappo laid the stink ball right on the preacher's book. It was the perfect spot. The preacher would smash it the next time he pounded his book. And he did!

Criminitlies! The stink ball was so small it didn't even make a mess when it got squashed. The preacher hit the book right in the middle of a speech. Whew! The stink ball was small but boy did it stink! The preaching came to a sudden end. I guess the preacher thought someone needed to go home. He eyed all the people in the front two rows. They were all eyeing each other. Everybody was wondering who made the awful smell.

The preacher looked over at Miss Clara Clamshell and her face turned red. Maybe he thought she was to blame. She just hauled off and struck a sour chord on the organ. With both hands!

When Miss Clara got herself together she took off playing. I think the song was "Onward Christian Sojers." Everybody got up and sang. Miss Clara kept playing the organ faster and faster. It seemed she wanted to get it over. Then we all got up and everybody left trying to get out to some fresh air. The preacher beat us to the door. As we left, he set everybody to shaking hands again.

Mom and Dad were so busy talking to their friends and shaking their hands that they didn't notice me. I was noticing everybody else!

When Philip Philpots got outside he put on his hat. He never noticed the Stickem I had put in it. He stood there looking for Miss Tessie Teapot. Mom always said he had a crush on her, whatever that means. Anyhow, when he saw her, he straightened his tie. He walked right up to her. When he got next to her, he snatched his hat off. The wig came too!

Miss Tessie was so stunned by the glare of Philpots' bald head, she took a leap backwards and stepped on Miss Dolly Doolittle's ankle. Miss Dolly opened her mouth in surprise. Her false teeth fell out. Then ol' Charlie Fupp spun around to see what was happening. Ol' Charlie stepped right on her teeth and busted them! I looked to see what had happened to Philpots' wig. I saw it lying there on the ground. I gave it another squirt of Stickem on the inside. Just as Philpots reached down to pick it up, Floyd Flatfoot stepped on it. There went Floyd, flopping up the street with Philpots' wig stuck on his foot.

Miss Freida Frump is always the last one to come out of church. She hangs back so she can talk to the preacher alone. Mom says she has designs on him—him not being married. Miss Freida came wobbling up on her skinny legs and high heel shoes. She was sure smirking at the preacher. I moved real fast. Everybody else was watching the wig being slap-footed down the street. I gave Miss Freida's shoes a squirt of Dissolve. Dissolve just melts anything away. Both heels fell off Miss Freida's shoes. She fell backwards just as the preacher reached out to shake her hand. As the preacher reached out to grab her, I couldn't resist it. I squirted some Stickem on their hands. They couldn't let go. It looked like the preacher and Miss Freida were dancing. There, in front of the church, they just couldn't let go!

About then, I thought it was time to go home for lunch. Mom was right, it had been a special day.

Chapter Seven: StopTime and the Garbage Cans

I really have to explain why I used the Nil Bag on my Mother. She's really a neat Mom. Really. In the summer, she ties threads on the legs of June Bugs for us kids. We bring her the beetles, she ties the thread, and we can hold onto the thread and fly the beetles. Kids all over the block know my mom can tie thread on the tiniest legs. She makes lemonade and popcorn for the neighborhood gang without any special reason. You see, my Mom's okay.

Unfortunately, my Mom has this mental problem. She thinks the only person in this whole house who can take out the garbage is yours truly, me. Right in the middle of listening to my favorite radio show, she says, "Peggy, please take out the garbage." I don't know how one family can have so much garbage! Sometimes I think she sneaks in garbage so I can take it out.

I have to carry the kitchen stuff out from under the sink, outside and around the house, over to the corner of the side yard where we keep the big metal garbage cans. Mom even has a special way I'm supposed to put the garbage in the big cans. If I just throw the stuff in upside down she starts yelling about garbage leaking all over the garbage cans. I ask you, "What else are garbage cans for? If you can't put leaky garbage in garbage cans, what good are they?" (I think when babies are born, their mothers promise the hospital to make them take out the garbage.)

I really hate to take out the garbage. Even if I start during a radio commercial, the show starts before I can get back. Sometimes I'm just lying on my bed thinking of things and I have to stop thinking just to take out the garbage. At night it's dark in the side yard and whenever I touch the metal cans, every dog in the neighborhood starts barking. Especially Mr. Doglover's dog. It's like a neighborhood announcement, "Hey everybody, Peggy is taking out the garbage. Her family sure has a lot of garbage. Where do you think they get so much garbage?" It's embarrassing.

I decided it was time I did something about my Mom's ideas about leaky garbage. One day, Mom was making dinner and I was laying on my bed thinking. It was important thinking about my Nil Bag.

"Peggy, please take out the garbage." I heard her call. "Peggy... now!" That did it. I knew what to do. I dug way down in the bottom of the Nil Bag and there was a little bottle of StopTime.

"Peggy, I'm talking to you," Mom had just finished saying as I rounded the corner of the kitchen. She reached down to open the cupboard under the sink. "Peggy, I want you to—" she started but just then—squirt! I sprayed a little StopTime on her. Mom froze like she was playing statues. She didn't even blink. I really had to hurry because I didn't know how long it would last.

I collected all the garbage under the sink cupboard. Boy, was there a lot! Mom can really pack it in. I hurried out the door, around to the side yard, put the garbage in the cans, right side up, ran back into the house, and casually picked up an apple. I slowly began eating the apple as Mom started blinking and finished her sentence: "—take out the garbage. Why do you always have to wait until I tell you?"

Mom opened the cupboard as if she had never been stopped by StopTime. The stuff really worked! Then she stared. There sat the kitchen sink and cupboard, all clean and neat.

"What did you want, Mom?" I asked real slow and casual. I almost stuffed the apple in my mouth to keep from grinning.

"Well... I... that is, I was going to ask you to take out the garbage but it looks... like... you already... have." She really looked confused but then she laughed. "Gee, Peggy, I was ready to nag you but you've already done it." She shook her head and stared like she had never seen an empty can before. Then she sighed, shut the cupboard door and went back to making gravy at the stove. Every now and then she would glance down at the cupboard. I think she expected to see the garbage jump out at her. I finished my apple and very carefully opened the cupboard door and dropped the core inside the garbage strainer Mom keeps at the sink. It went *thunk!* 'Usually I have to cram the core in because the strainer is overflowing. So this *thunk* was a new sound.

"Well, Mom, if you don't need me, I'll be in my room."

"Yes, Peggy, fine…" she said to me, but I think her mind was elsewhere.

The next day I had almost forgotten about using the StopTime. I was busy thinking about how to use the Nil Bag on Charlie Fupp when Mom called out, "Peggy, the garbage man comes today. It's time to put the cans out."

It's bad enough taking the garbage out to the metal cans. The part I really hate is taking the big cans out to the alley for the garbage man to pick up. The garbage men are supposed to come in our yard to get the cans, but ol' Davis says he has a bad back. If we don't take the cans out, he just sort of "forgets" to pick them up.

Miss Tillie says we should call ol' Davis a "sanitation worker" but we all know he's the garbage man. Every dog knows he is too. You can tell when the garbage truck turns the corner two blocks away. Each dog warns the dog in the next yard that the garbage truck is coming. Except at Bernie Wiffie's house.

Bernie lives with a crazy aunt who has two geese. She says they make good watch dogs. When the garbage truck gets near the Wiffie's house, those watch-geese start honking and squawking. Those geese set off the dogs who had already quit barking because they had forgotten why they were barking. Yeah, there's lots of excitement in the neighborhood on garbage day. If I was a garbage man, I would spend my day off driving my truck around and around in circles until every dog and goose was hoarse.

Mom was at the window. She didn't see me so I moved up behind her and—squirt! There she was, stopped by StopTime. I would have paused to look at her statue, but I knew I didn't have much time. I ran out to the side yard and carried the first can out to the alley. I ran back to pick up the second can. Whew! I could hardly budge it. Mom had really outdone herself with garbage for the can. I would waddle along two or three steps. I would drag the can. All the while I kept checking the kitchen window to make sure Mom was still a statue.

There! I got the old can out to the alley and ran back into the house. I was just coming in the door when Mom started blinking. I just stood there smiling as if I had just heard her call me.

"Yes, Mom," I said. "Did you want me?"

"Peggy, you know what today is." She stopped short. There, out in the alley, she saw our garbage cans. Her mouth fell open. She was really surprised.

"Yeah, Mom, it's Thursday."

"Peggy… I… that is… Peggy?" She looked awfully confused. "When did you put those cans out? I would have sworn they weren't there a minute ago."

"Why, Mom, I just took care of my chores this morning." I thought I sounded innocent but Mom looked very suspicious. Moms just don't know how to trust a kid when she's doing what she's told before she's told. It drives them crazy.

"Well," she said looking out the window again. "Thank you for getting the cans out early."

That was Thursday. I decided to keep my StopTime handy.

On Friday, Mom started to tell me to clean up my stuff on the dining room table and as she pointed at the table—squirt! By the time she started blinking and moving, the dining room was clean enough for company. Even Mom's company.

Saturday was a real challenge. I knew Mom would tell me to clean my room. On Saturday, moms all over America are telling their kids to clean their rooms. It's another one of the Mother's Laws. I was worried about one squirt of StopTime lasting long enough for me to get my room even started. I was kind of afraid to give her too many squirts in a row. I didn't know if time would ever start again for Mom. Instead, I got up real early Saturday morning, before Mom and Dad. I shut my door and got to work. I mean, the room was a mess! I got my pajamas out of the storage box, found underwear on my closet floor, got my shoes out of my sock drawer, crammed my games into the game shelf, and took more shoes off the coat hook. I knew one way to get Mom for sure was to clean under my bed without being told. I even got under there and found stuff I hadn't seen for months.

About two hundred hours later I heard Mom moving around the house. I jumped up on my bed and began reading a book. Mom knocked on the door and said, "Peggy, are you up?"

"Yeah, Mom, come on in." I had my StopTime ready just in case.

Mom opened the door and her face was surprised and pleased. "Why Peggy, your room looks wonderful!" Wouldn't you know it? Mom was overwhelmed with my clean room until she looked around and saw the full wastebasket. I had to put my stuff somewhere! If you can't put waste in a basket, why have wastepaper baskets in the first place? As her eyes looked at the old sock and cardboard tube hanging on the rim of the basket—squirt with the StopTime! I swooped up the basket while Mom stood with her mouth open. Her finger pointed to the space where the basket had been. I really had to run to empty the basket. I didn't want Dad seeing what I was doing. I made it! Out my door, down the stairs, out through the kitchen, around the side yard to the metal cans, emptying the basket, back through the kitchen up the stairs, and finally back into my room.

I got the basket in place as Mom blinked and said, "Peggy... the basket... oh.   It's empty.... I thought I saw an old sock but it's empty." Then Mom kind of rubbed her eyes and shook her head. "Peggy, I don't feel well, I think I'll sleep in this morning." With a last puzzled look at the wastebasket, Mom said, "Good job on your room." Then she went back to her bedroom.

Sunday and Monday went the same way. I got my chores finished on time. If there was something I missed, I'd use my StopTime to hold Mom frozen until I got it done. By Tuesday, I saw Mom checking all the wastebaskets in the house every time she passed one. When she fixed dinner, she put some wrappers and an empty can into the kitchen garbage. She almost glared at me. All the time she was working in the kitchen, she kept an eye on the garbage. When the paper boy came to the front door, Mom went to get the money to pay him. I quickly picked the can and wrappers out of the garbage and disappeared around to the side yard. *Plunk!* The evidence was in the big cans. I didn't go back in by the kitchen. I went through the gate and walked in the front door. I was getting pretty good at casual strolling by now. I strolled into the kitchen.

Mom was back in the kitchen and she just looked at me. This time she didn't look confused. She just grinned at me the way mothers do when they know something you don't know and they aren't about to tell you.

Mom kept grinning all the rest of Tuesday and Wednesday. Then it was Thursday—the day for Big G, Garbage Day. I was dragging the big cans out to the alley when all of a sudden I realized something important. I hadn't used any StopTime for the past three days. Instead, I was doing all my chores on time. I had even done a few things ahead of time— not very many but a few. Mom had been grinning for days. I had a feeling this wasn't turning out as I had planned. I turned around and saw Mom standing right behind me.

"Peggy," Mom said. "I have to admit I was confused last week when things started getting done without my nagging. Now, I'm sorry I was suspicious."

"Aw, Mom…" I started to say. Mom had the sermon voice she uses and it embarrasses me. Especially after the trick I had played on her.

"No, let me finish. I'm very proud of the way you have been doing all your chores. You are really growing up and being responsible. I'm especially pleased with how you got the garbage out." Then, she gave me the real clinker. "Now that we both know what a good job you can do, I'm sure you'll keep it up!" She reached down and hugged me. Right there in the alley with all the dogs barking, my Mom hugged me for doing a good job. Criminitly! What can a girl do? I mean, she was smiling so proudly. I felt awful. I mumbled something. Mothers are used to girls my age mumbling a lot and she just patted me, saying, "You are becoming quite the young lady." Then she went back into the house.

So here I was. Instead of teaching her a lesson, I had made her proud. Now she would expect me to keep all my chores done. I had proved I could do it if I wanted. For the rest of my natural life, I would be taking garbage cans out to the alley. There wasn't enough StopTime in the world to get me out of this. Maybe, I thought, I better be a little more careful how I used my Nil Bag!

Chapter Eight: Just a Regular Day

Weenies! They are so good! I like them with catsup and mustard both. And onions. And sweet pickle relish. And a long, long weenie bun. That's what I had for lunch the day in October. Mmm! That must be why I felt so good. I knew it was going to be a real good day. We were having a late summer. It meant kids still wanted to go barefoot because the weather was so warm. Moms kept saying you should wear shoes because it was *October*!

After lunch, I planned on making myself scarce. I didn't want to be around home because Mom was having her lady friends over to play cards. Ladies are silly. They always ask the same silly questions or say silly things:

"Do you like school?"

"My, are you still growing?"

"What's your teacher's name?"

"Why, you're almost a young woman now."

All that silly stuff! I just took off my shoes and left the house before they got there. I was just going to have a regular, good old day. Of course, I took my Nil Bag with me.

I was just strolling along down the street thinking a few thoughts. Halloween was just a few weeks away. Then was my birthday. This year, Thanksgiving Day fell right on my birthday! I'm not sure just where it fell from. Once, when I was little, I remember my birthday and Thanksgiving being on the same day. I thought everyone in the country was celebrating my birthday and being thankful I was born. I felt really special. The next year my birthday stood by itself. It takes a while for a little kid to understand why the calendar keeps changing days. I'm not sure I understand it yet. Yep, it was a really good day.

I was thinking about Halloween when I heard a noise behind me. It was just a little noise. I turned around and there came ol' Sing and Song. Those Snot Twins were bigger than me but I wasn't afraid of them, I just ran away to be on the safe side. I ducked around into the alley. Real quick like, I got my Cantsee out of the Nil Bag, took a squirt, and disappeared!

Ol' Sing and Song came ripping around the corner. Sing stopped short when he got to the alley. Song was running so fast he almost ran into his brother. The two of them looked around.

"Where'd she go?" asked one twin.

"She was just here!" answered the other.

They didn't know I was just standing there between them! They were looking and looking. I pulled a stick out of the Nil Bag, an invisible stick. Whack! I let one of them have it right on the rear end.

"What'd you do that for?" the twin yelled at his brother.

"What?" asked the other.

"That!" said the first twin as he gave his brother a kick in the pants.

"Hey!" yelled the second twin and the fight was on.

It seemed like the perfect time for me to stroll on

down the street. Once those twins got fighting each other, which they did often, they didn't need any help to keep going.

It was an awful good day to walk clear downtown. All the way to town I could watch people who couldn't watch me watching them. I walked clear down to the town square. It was a nice little park with all the stores around it. There were benches to sit on. Mostly there were people to watch pass by. Kind of fun. Some looked happy, some sad. There was an old man sitting on the bench next to me where I sat down. Course, he didn't see me. He had a bag of popcorn in one hand and he was feeding the birds with the other. It was almost like he was holding the popcorn out to me. He'd take a handful of popcorn and I'd take a handful. He'd take some popcorn and I'd take some popcorn. He sure looked surprised when the popcorn disappeared so fast. The birds and I ate it all!

I noticed a lady pushing a baby buggy. People were stopping to look at the baby. I supposed it was a baby. I decided to go see for myself. Being invisible, I just went over to have a look. Sure enough, it was a baby.

The baby's mother was busy talking to a friend. I got busy with my Nil Bag. I took out a nice soft baby-safe black grease pencil. First, I drew a nice bushy mustache on the sleeping baby's face. It didn't look right. The round little face needed something more. Then I knew what. I drew fuzzy eyebrows on the baby. Perfect! It made the baby's face look just right!

I was just beginning to think about adding a mole or a beard. I heard the friend say to the mother, "Let me see the darling baby of yours."

The lady looked into the buggy with a sickening sweet

smile on her face. One look at the baby and her whole face screwed up with surprise. She was determined to say something nice so she said, "My, your baby certainly has a lot of hair!"

"Yes," the mother answered proudly. "He looks just like his father." Then the mother looked into the buggy. Wow, did she let out a squeal when she saw the baby. She began fussing and fussing over her baby with a handkerchief. The baby woke up from the rubbing and he started crying! I thought it was a good time to go back to my bench. I wondered if the baby's dad really had bushy eyebrows and a big black mustache.

It was such a nice Fall day, lots of people kept walking through the park. They went back and forth doing their Saturday shopping and visiting with each other. I saw two people grin at the lady with the hairy faced baby. It made their day!

Going back to the park, I wanted to see if the man had bought anymore popcorn. I saw a little ol' girl with messy hair blowing bubble gum. Each bubble seemed to be bigger than the last one. She was good! She started working on a real dilly of a bubble—the biggest one of all. I was impressed! Then I couldn't stand it. I reached over and just tapped the bubble. It busted! The bubble settled down on her fluffy hair. What a mess! She must have chewed three chunks of gum to make a bubble so big. She had three times the mess to clean up!

I went over and got a drink at the water fountain. I was really wishing I had an ice cream cone. I would have loved a double-decker. Being invisible was a problem. I couldn't just walk into a store and say, "A double-decker, please." Goes to show you there are even problems with being invisible.

Things were pretty slow in the park for a while, I didn't have anything else to do so I went into Tessie's Tick Tock Shop. I wanted to see what time it was. Gee! What a lot of clocks. There must have been a million clocks in the shop. Big ones, little ones, all kinds and all running, ticking and tocking, tocking and ticking. Miss Tessie was in the back of the shop. She called out, "I'll be with you in a minute."

Looking at all those clocks, I wondered who wound them. I still wondered what time it was. They all pointed to a different time. Most of all, I wondered what kept them all going. I knew how to stop them. It was easy. I opened the Nil Bag and took out the StopTime. Squirt, squirt, squirt. Every clock stopped telling time. Miss Tessie came out from the back of the shop. Was she ever startled by the silence! She stood perfectly still as if she couldn't believe her eyes... or ears. I never did find out what time it was. I did decide it was time to leave.

I started towards home. Surely those silly ladies would be gone by now. Anyhow, I was getting hungry. Criminitly, I hoped there would be some chocolate cake left. I could hear the women's voices as I walked up to the front door. I gave myself an extra dose of Cantsee and went in to see what all the noise was about.

The ladies were all playing pinochle. It's a card game that sounds like "pea-knuckle." The rules were pretty silly as far as I could see. You have one hand as full of cards as you can hold. When it comes your turn, you reach out to the middle of the table where some more cards are stacked. Then you lay down a few cards on the table in front of you. If you lay them all down, the other ladies get mad and they start to gripe. The ladies were all divided up, four to a card table. Our whole parlor was filled with card tables. It wasn't very exciting.

I thought these ladies needed something to make the afternoon special. I decided to look into my Nil Bag. There he was. Something special. The cutest little mouse you ever saw. He was just looking up at me, begging me to take him out of the Nil Bag. For some reason, I paused. I could imagine laying him very gently on the top of the cards. He would wiggle his cute nose, and some friend of Mother's would reach out for a card and touch him instead. She would startle, the mouse would startle, and a whole ruckus of screeching women would startle each other as an innocent little mouse would be running and cards would be flying and I would be laughing. My pause grew longer. I simply stopped. I just didn't want to hassle Mom's friends.

Maybe—just maybe—Mom was right. I was getting "responsible." I was growing up. That was a disturbing thought as I tucked the Nil mouse back in the bag. I went upstairs to my room to let the Cantsee wear off. I never did get any chocolate cake. I didn't know "growing up" was going to be so hard.

Chapter Nine: Halloween

Halloween is the best time ever in the world for having fun and getting even with people. I knew it was going to be a special Halloween because I had the Nil Bag for a magic night. I couldn't wait 'til it got dark! I got started early in the day since it was a Saturday.

I looked in my drawer for something to help pass the time until folks let us kids start trick-or-treating the neighborhood. I found the best little gadget tucked in the drawer, way in the back. It would be just the thing to give Miss Tiffany. It looked like a little flashlight. But when you pressed the button to make it light, a long snake jumped out. Perfect!

I gave myself a squirt of Cantsee and went over to Miss Tiffany's house. I knew she kept her flashlight on a shelf in her kitchen. I was able to slip into her kitchen. I traded my flashlight with the rubber snake, for hers. I put her flashlight out on the shelf on the back porch near her gardening things. I knew she'd find it later. I went home and wondered when Miss Tiffany would need a flashlight.

By dinnertime, I was gettin' pretty excited about it being Halloween. I could hardly sit still at the table. I wasn't payin' much attention to Mom and Dad. I was busy thinkin' thoughts. Then I heard Mom say, "Oh, I was at Miss Tiffany's house today. You should have been there."

Dad smiled and asked, "What happened?"

I just kept quiet. I stirred my gravy and mashed potatoes.

"Well, Miss Tiffany had asked me to come over to check a dress hem for her," Mom said. "When I got there, she dropped her thimble. It rolled out of sight under a low cabinet. She couldn't see the thimble so she went and got a flashlight. When she pressed the button, out popped a big green rubber snake! I jumped! Miss Tiffany put her hands over her eyes and hollered, 'Oh, no!' I had to leave because I was going to laugh!"

Dad laughed 'til he could hardly get his breath. Mom laughed too. Every time they thought about a rubber snake jumping out at Miss Tiffany, they started laughing again. Funny thing, though. Neither Mom nor Dad said a word to me.

I wonder if they suspected. I wonder if they cared.

By this time, it was dark and Halloween could really get started. I went upstairs to get dressed. I had an old black blanket and I cut a hole in the middle. I pulled the blanket over my head so it hung over my body. Just my head stuck out. Next, I took an old silk stocking of Mom's. I pulled it over my head and face. Weird! My face was all twisted up by the stocking. I reached in my old toy chest and pulled out some glows-in-the-dark paint. Lookin' in the mirror was hard because my eyes were a little twisted. I managed. I painted a big, wide, white circle around each eye. Then I painted a wrinkled circle around my mouth. I could move my face and the painted circles changed shape. I could really scare people!

I went downstairs where Mom and Dad were reading. Both of them laughed at my costume. They told me to be careful and have fun. I was planning on it! I rushed outside with my Nil Bag safely under my blanket. It was Halloween!

The night was cold and cloudy. The moon kept popping in and out among the big puffy clouds. There was a creepy feelin' in the air. I was feelin' pretty good until I heard a loud scream and a dog howl. Ooo-whee! It was dark all right. I got kinda nervous so I decided I better have some fun to... uh... take my mind off bein' scared, I mean. I knew Mary Helen Figlet was havin' a party and I could have fun there. First, I thought I would stroll by Miss Tiffany's.

When I got outside Miss Tiffany's gate, I took a big squirt of Cantsee. I squirted my whole body, blanket and all. All but my head. My head with the twisted face and glowin' circles was all that could be seen. I went up on Miss Tiffany's porch, rang the doorbell, and waited. I rang it again and kept ringing it 'til she opened the door. There was just enough light from her hallway to shine on my floatin' head out on the dark porch.

Miss Tiffany didn't say a word or make a sound. She just looked at my glowing head, floatin' there on her porch. Then she slowly closed the door. I heard a loud *thump*! Like a body fallin'. Oh my gosh, I was about as scared as she was! I thought, I've killed her! She died of fright right behind the door. I didn't mean for that to happen. I had to help her! I opened the door real quick to see if I could help her. To tell her I was sorry. But there was no body behind the door.

All of a sudden I heard a scream, looked up and there came Miss Tiffany! She was swingin' a broom at my bobbin' head and screamin' like a panther!

"I'll get you, you bodyless ghost! Get out of my yard," she screeched. "Get it, Winston! Get the ghost!" *Bam*! She almost hit me as I ran out the door and off her porch. She moved awful fast! If I wasn't so scared, I would have been surprised at how fast she could run. I didn't know Miss Tiffany could run so quick. I ran out of her yard and down the street as fast as I could. I didn't stop until I was way down the block and could hide behind a tree.

I rested behind the tree until I was sure she had stopped chasing me. I'm not sure, but I think I heard her laugh as she went back inside her house. I think she laughed a lot!

By the time I got my breath back I realized I was near the Snot Twins' house. I knew Sing and Song were invited to Mary Helen's party. She always invited the whole school. I almost didn't want to go to the party because of them. Then I got to thinkin' some thoughts. What if the Snot Twins didn't get to the party? Maybe I should just keep them at home. They didn't deserve any Halloween fun. All they should have was

Halloween garbage!

I squirted some Cantsee on my head and disappeared all together. The Snots were just comin' down the steps of their house when I got there. I could have guessed they would be dressed like bums. They had no imagination. Anyone could be a hobo or tramp. All it took was some old clothes.

I waited 'til they started across the yard where there was a big tree and some bushes. I gave each of them a big squirt of StopTime. There they stood, two hobo statues stopped in time!

Now I was feelin' better again. I started back down our street so I could go to the party.

Mary Helen lived in a big white house with lots of trees and bushes around it. Part of the house was built like a tower on a castle. It was covered with vines and looked spooky. There weren't any lights on in the whole house. The moon went behind a cloud just then and it got awful dark. I thought I heard chains rattle up in the tower. I wasn't gettin' scared but I was awful careful. With all the bushes, it kept gettin' darker as I walked up to the house. I wished Stinky was there with me. There were jack-a-lanterns along the path leading around the house to the basement door. These weren't happy jack-a-lanterns. These were mean lookin' pumpkins. They watched me. I know they did.

I finally got to the basement door, where the party was to be. I was so scared, I had a notion to go home. Some weird sounds were comin' out of the bushes. I spun around and swear I saw a ghost disappear around the corner of the house. I started to run back but I tripped on my blanket. I fell towards some bushes and I landed on something that moaned, "Ooo-aaah-ooo!"

It was enough for me! I got up quick and ran to the basement door. I wanted in! I started banging on the door... the door slowly opened on its squeaky hinges. It opened all... by... itself. I thought I'd die right there!

By the time I stopped holding my breath I saw a dim light at the bottom of the basement steps. Real slow... my legs walked real slow... I went down the stairs... real slow.

The basement was the scariest place I'd ever been. There were no bright lights, just spooky dim lights were glowin'. There were great big corn shocks and pumpkins in every corner.

I almost jumped out of my blanket when I turned my head. There was a naked skull glaring right at me! Something looking like cobwebs hung down from the ceiling. My gosh! What a place! When my eyes got used to the darkness, I could see a few other kids sitting around. I went over and sat down on a low stool. More kids began to come down the steps. No one even said a word to me. They just stared around the spooky room. I couldn't tell who they were. They were all dressed up like pirates, clowns, devils, ghosts and everything. They kept whisperin' and giggling to each other.

Some of the goblins must have been as scared as I was; I could tell from the way they acted. One clown came over and sat down on my invisible lap. She screamed, jumped in the air a couple of times while her big clown feet ran in mid-air. She scared me and I jumped up and howled too. I didn't know what was the matter. I just couldn't stop howlin'. It started all the kids howlin' and screamin' and scarin' each other.

I realized I was still invisible. No wonder no one spoke to me. No wonder the clown was scared when she sat on a body that wasn't there! The Cantsee was wearin' a little thin though as I was beginning to see my own hands. I must have looked like a shadow in the dark room. I went behind a corn shock and gave my body another squirt of Cantsee. I wanted to stay invisible.

I had a little more glow paint in my pocket so I painted my hands and face. I tucked the Nil Bag under my invisible blanket. Only my "floating head and hands" could be seen. I slowly came out from behind the cornstalks and started to move quietly around the room.

Hot doggies! My floating head stopped the party cold for a minute. All at once everyone was yellin' and fallin' down again. I was gonna try something really scary but before I could think, Mrs. Figlet snapped on some lights. She must have been afraid all the kids would scare themselves to death. As soon as the lights snapped on, I sprayed my head and hands and completely disappeared. Thanks to Cantsee, I was invisible.

Mrs. Figlet fussed around and got the kids to playin' games. They started bobbing for apples in a big tub of water. I got to tappin' their heads and goosin' around. Whenever a kid wondered who touched them, I would whisper, "A ghost." Some kids spent the whole party with a scared look on their face. They kept lookin' over their shoulders, but they never saw me.

I figured it was gettin' on towards eatin' time. Mary Helen's mother came down with doughnuts and a big pitcher of apple cider. She set the pitcher down on a long, decorated table. I knew I couldn't eat with the other kids. Watchin' the doughnuts disappear into thin air might get all the kids screamin' again. It might end the party before I could finish eatin'. I followed Mrs. Figlet upstairs to the kitchen where all the food was!

There was a great big kettle of weenies on the stove boilin' away and smellin' so good. There must have been a thousand weenies in the pan! Mrs. Figlet took a big tray of buns and went back downstairs. I stayed with the weenies.

I got a plate—no—I got *two* plates. One wouldn't be enough. I took charge of five—no—*six* weenies. I scooped up one gob—no—*two* gobs of potato salad. Mrs. Figlet started comin' back up the stairs. I ducked into the dining room and got under the table.

The Figlets had one of those yappy little German weiner dogs. The dog looked like a hot dog without a bun. The dog came sniffin' right under the table after me. He tried to get my food! He kept wigglin' in and out until finally I bonked him on the head with a weenie. That was a mistake! The danged dog ate my bonkin' weenie! Before I knew it, he had eaten all six of them.

Mrs. Figlet quit fussin' around the kitchen and went back downstairs. So, I went to get six more weenies. I also got two chocolate covered doughnuts and some baked beans. I hurried back under the table. The dumb dog had eaten the potato salad. Between the danged dog and Mrs. Figlet comin' and goin', I wasn't getting much to eat!

Real quick, I went out to the kitchen and found a tray. I loaded it up with hot dogs, baked beans, potato salad, doughnuts, some pickles, peanuts, and a glass of cider. I went back under the table and the dog just wagged and wagged his tail. He didn't care if I was invisible; he was my friend for life.

Between me and the dumb dog, we ate everything in sight. The dog could hardly walk. He just kind of laid on his side with his feet sticking straight out. The little weenie dog looked like a bologna loaf! I wasn't much better off myself.

I heard the party downstairs breaking up. Maybe they ran out of food. I figured it was about time for me to go home too. I crawled out from under the table. I felt, just maybe, I had overdone the eating. I was able to slip by Mary Helen and her mother at the door. It wasn't easy. I was bigger than when I came in.

I waddled down the street until I felt sick. I made a run for some bushes and really threw up. It made me feel a little better. I hoped the hog of a dog got sick too.

I remembered the Snot Twins who were trapped in the StopTime. I went on down there to let 'em go. I was still covered with Cantsee. When I got to the twins' house, the StopTime was just wearing off. I heard one of the boys say, "We'd better hurry or we will be late for the party!"

I had to laugh 'cause they didn't know the party was all over. All the food was gone. Oops, I was getting sick again.

Chapter Ten: The Only

One day, I felt just terrible when I got home from school. I was all mixed up inside. Dad always said it was all right to cry if you save crying for important things. I didn't know if this was important enough. I went up to my room and searched and searched through my Nil Bag. There wasn't any Feelings-Straighten-Outer in the bag at all. Tucking the bag away in my pocket, I lay down on my bed and felt bad inside.

"Peggy?" Mom asked, knocking on my door. She hadn't said much when I came home. She just watched me.

"Come in, Mom," I said.

Mom opened the door and looked in. I didn't even care if she saw how messed up my room was. She didn't even mention it.

"Bad day at school?" she asked.

"Yeah...." I said. I didn't really want to talk.

"Well," Mom said. "Why don't you go out to see Gramps for the afternoon. Aunt Toot phoned to say she was trying a new cookie recipe and could use a taste-tester."

I thought to myself, *No sense letting hurt feelings get in the way of good cookies.* I slowly sat up. I've found when you feel sad it'd better to move slow. Otherwise, no one will notice how bad you feel. "Okay... Mom," I said real... slowly.

Mom smiled, patted me on the shoulder, and said, "That's a good idea, Peggy. We'll be having dinner late this evening, so just be home before dark."

I must admit just riding my bicycle out to Gramps' place made me feel better. Sometimes moving around makes you feel better than laying on your bed.

I passed the place where I had found the Nil Bag. I didn't even stop. I rode into the farmyard just as Gramps was going out to milk Noodles. Usually, I jump off my bike and let it roll to a stop against the fence. On this sad day I got off the bike slowly, set it upright, and even put down the kickstand. I wanted Gramps to know how badly I felt too.

"Hey Peggy, I'm glad you came out," Gramps said. He put his arm around my shoulders as we walked out to the barn together. "Your aunt's cookies should be ready by the time we get the milking done. Come on and keep me company."

"Sure, Gramps." We walked along, not talking. Gramps knows how you're feeling even without talking about it. We went into the barn where Noodles was waiting. Gramps put some hay in the manger for the cow. He hooked a leather strap around Noodle's neck. She stood there in her stall munchin' and chewin'.

I got up on some hay bales and picked out a long strand of hay to chew. Meanwhile Gramps sponged off the cow's udder. He got his milkin' stool and put the milk bucket under the cow. Then he started the squirt, squirt, squirt of milking. I always liked the sound the milk made squirting in the bucket. First there was a high squirt. Then, real quick, there was a low sounding squirt. There'd be a little pause. Then the high sounding squirt would start all over again. The sounds changed as the bucket filled with bubbly milk. By the time the bucket was full, it'd be making sounds like: "Swish, swoosh... swish, swoosh... swish, swoosh."

I was just sitting there sucking the straw and listening to the bucket fill. Gramps squirted milk into the mouths of the barn cats who always came around at milking time.

"Peggy," Gramps asked, "how'd school go today?"

"Not so good," I answered.

"I've had those kind of days, too," Gramps said. He never stopped the milking.

"Yeah," I said. Now, I was ready to tell somebody what had hurt. "It's those ol' Snot Twins again!" I confessed. The twins had been pretty good for a few weeks after I got the scissors to their hair. Their mother had cut what hair was left 'til it was real short. Boy, were they ever embarrassed with their funny looking heads. Then one twin, Sing I think, started telling kids that they really had a Mohawk haircut. Those Sing Song twins started prancing around like they were special. By the time their greasy black hair grew into stubble, they were meaner than ever.

"What did the twins do?" Gramps asked.

"They called me names."

"Must have been pretty awful names to make a girl feel so bad," he said.

"They said I was an 'only child'!" I could still hear those sing-song voices yelling: *Peggy's an only chi-ld! Peggy's an only chi-ld!*

"That bad, huh?"

"Yeah...." I answered. I remembered standing there in the schoolyard wanting to yell back at the stubby-headed twins but the words wouldn't come out right. I had just shouted, "Yeah, you... *you twins!*" It wasn't much answer to being called an only child.

"Then maybe I'd better feel bad, too," Gramps said and surprised me. I thought he would try and make me feel better. Now he was just going to be miserable too.

"Why should you feel bad, Gramps?" I asked, taking the soggy straw out of my mouth.

"If being called an only child, which you are, makes you feel badly, then I should feel bad because I'm your only Gramps!"

"Yeah...." I started.

"And your mother should feel badly because she's your only mom. Boy, I hope your dad's miserable. He's your only father." Gramps looked up at me from milkin' and I almost thought he was teasing except he looked serious.

"That's different!" I said.

How?" he asked. He looked right at me. I knew I better think out my answer.

"Well, being my only Gramps—it makes you special."

"Oh..." Gramps said slowly. "What about your only

mother? Shouldn't she feel sad because she's an 'only'?"

"No, Gramps, Mom's special... just because she's Mom. Dad, too. I like having only one mom and dad."

Gramps looked confused. He stood up shaking his head. He hung the stool back on its peg and put the milk bucket out of the way so Noodles wouldn't kick it. "I don't understand, Peggy. Are you upset because they called you an only child, or because you are one?

Now my feelings were really mixed up. I was beginning to think this was important enough to cry about.

"Both, I guess...." I answered.

"About the name calling: It's something you kids have to work out for yourselves. You can let it bother you or...."

"I know," I said. "Sticks and stones... but names will never hurt me."

I remembered how my very best friend Stinky got his name. His real name is Alfred. His mother always bought him some funny kind of socks. Sometimes he wore rubber tennis shoes. Whooee! When Alfred took his shoes off, you could smell his feet clear across the room. Even with his socks off, Alfred's feet were pure poison. We always called him Stinky and he said he didn't mind. He thought "Stinky" was a better name than "Alfred." Most kids would get mad being called such a name. But Stinky liked it. Even when Alfred's mother started buying him cotton socks, we kept on calling him Stinky even though his feet smelled fine now. He's still Stinky to us. His mother just calls him Alfred.

I looked up at Gramps. "I guess we can let names hurt us. Or, if we want, we can like the name."

Gramps nodded. He sat up on the bale with me and picked out a chewin' straw for himself.

"Being an 'only' can be special," he said and sounded proud.

"An 'only'? "

"An only anything! Being the only man to fly solo across the Atlantic Ocean made Lindbergh special." Then Gramps looked at me. "Being the only girl in class to get an A on your homework would make you special," he finished.

I hadn't thought of it that way. "Are there other onlys?" I asked.

"Everybody is an only of some sort."

"Gramps, that's not true." Now I knew he was teasing me.

"Yes it is. Your best friend is an only."

"Oh, Gramps," I said sadly. "Stinky has two older brothers and two younger ones."

"But he's the only one in his family with red hair and freckles. He's also the only middle child of his family."

Gramps was right. Still, being the only redhead didn't seem as bad as being the only child.

"How about Miss Tarbrush?" I asked.

"The only fifth grade teacher at your school," he answered quickly.

"How about the preacher?"

"He's the only preacher at our church."

"Oh."

"You see, it's up to you to find the special reason for being an only," Gramps said and then he sucked on his straw. He looked as if he was real pleased with himself.

"But being an only child can be lonely," I said.

"Only if you make it so," he answered. "Did you know I was an only child? I was always glad."

"Why, Gramps? I hear people say things like, 'Tsk, tsk, tsk. Too bad she's an only child.'"

Gramps winked at me and poked his elbow in my ribs. "It's because they don't know better. Or else they're jealous!" He grinned.

"Why, Gramps?" I wasn't feeling nearly so low now. I really wanted to know.

"When you're an only child, you're also the oldest. You get all the privileges of the oldest. You get to ride your bike to school or out to here to see me. At the same time, you are also the youngest child. You get the special attention the baby of the family gets. And you don't have any older brothers picking on you like Stinky has…"

"…and you don't have to babysit younger brothers or sisters," I added now since I thought about it.

"That too," Gramps agreed. "Best of all, I think, is that you learn how to make everybody your best friend. Think about Stinky. He's your best friend. He's just right. He's not too old, like an older brother who might be interested in other things. He's not too young, so that you couldn't do any fun things with him."

"Best friend…" I repeated.

"Making good friends is just as important as being close to your family."

"Why, Gramps?"

"Even with family we love, sometimes brothers and sisters get separated."

"Yes," I agreed. "Like Alice from school. Her parents separated when her dad couldn't find any work in our town because of the Depression. Alice's father and brothers moved to another town to get work at a mill. She only sees her brothers in the summer."

"Some of the other students may have more than one mother or father or grandfathers and grandmothers or aunts and uncles. There are families with all sorts of people, because the important thing is *family*." Gramps sounded very pleased with himself. He went on talking: "You can always make good friends. A brother may grow up and move away. You can't just make a new brother but you can always make another new friend. That's special too."

"Did you make friends when you were an only child, Gramps?"

"Did I? I'll say! I had some distant cousins, Lauren and Mike. They were my best friends. The three of us just loved sweets, especially fudge. The only one who loved fudge more than us was my dog, Sadie. One time my mama was working in her garden. The three of us kids got to working in the kitchen. We were younger than you are now, and I didn't rightly know how to make fudge. I just mixed a tiny bit of vanilla powder with lots of sugar and water and stirred and stirred. Lauren and Mike took turns stirring too. It was awful runny. We stirred more and more sugar into the mess until I poured it into the pan Mama always used. But we had put so much sugar in our fudge one pan wasn't enough. I kept filling up pans until all my fudge was put up. Then we hid it in my closet. Next time Lauren and Mike came over, I took them upstairs. We all three climbed into my closet and had the grandest time eating fudge. Sadie, too. The fudge was as hard as a rock! Pure sugar. But we thought it was wonderful. It was our secret. We'd have a fine taste whenever they came over.

"There was a lot of fudge for three kids and a dog. One afternoon, Sadie came stumbling out of my closet. I had left the door open when I went to school. Sadie had shoved the door open and eaten most of the remaining fudge. Sadie was one sick dog!" Gramps laughed remembering his old dog.

I laughed too. Ever since Halloween, I knew about dogs who eat too much.

"Come on," Gramps said. "Enough talk. Let's put this milk away. Then we can go up to the house and eat some cookies."

Gramps had one arm around my shoulders and the other carried the milk bucket. We walked over to the spring house. The little building was built over a natural spring. We had lots of springs like this in Ohio. The water would bubble so clean and cold out of the rocks. Then it would dribble into a concrete trough. It's like a little ditch. Gramps set the bucket in the cool water. Later, Aunt Toot would skim the cream off the top and pour the milk into clean milk cans to keep it fresh until we needed it. Even in the summer, the spring house was a cool place.

After we put the milk to cooling, we went up to the house. Outside the kitchen door, we could smell the warm cookies that Aunt Toot was baking.

Gramps stopped, wiped his feet on the mat, and looked at me. "You know, 'only' is not the same as 'lonely.' You can let things get you down, or endeavor to persevere. It's up to you."

I smiled back at him. There are times when an "only Gramps" is even better than a Nil Bag.

Chapter Eleven: Thanksgiving

I could hardly sleep the night before Thanksgiving. I was

excited about my birthday being the very same day this year... and staying overnight at Gramps'... and well, just about everything!

My whole family went out to Gramps' farm on Wednesday night when Dad got off work. It was so Mom and Aunt Toot could get an early start on all the cookin' for the big Thanksgiving dinner on Thursday. I got to sleep in my favorite place. It was a big feather bed way up in the attic.

A feather bed is like sleepin' on a big, big, feather pillow. You can pull a feather comforter on top. It's as warm and soft as can be, even on cold November nights. A girl can just sink down in the bed and think and think.

I knew why I couldn't sleep. I was too busy thinkin'. On Thanksgiving Day, I was goin' to use all the tricks in my Nil Bag. It was my birthday too and I'd be the big ten years... a decade old. I still felt like the whole country was celebratin' my birthday. I was goin' to celebrate a Nil Bag Day. It would take planning so I went to bed early. I lay up in the attic thinkin' about all the things I could do with the Nil Bag.

Ol' Charlie Fupp look out! My Nil Bag Day would get him. First, I could squirt Cantsee on myself. Being invisible I could go down to Charlie's room. I could turn his clock ahead an hour so he'd be sure to get up early. No, that wouldn't work. On the farm everybody got up early. Especially the rooster. In school they always tell you how roosters crow at dawn. Well, Gramps' rooster didn't read the books. He crowed all night long.

I thought of sneakin' into Charlie's room and sewing his pant legs shut. He wouldn't be able to get his feet through. He would jump up in the morning, jump in his pants, and jump all around the room trying to get his pants on. His feet would get plenty cold.

Later, I could imagine Charlie at dinner. He would be lickin' his chops over a turkey drumstick. Knowing how Charlie likes drumsticks, I would spray the turkey legs with Stickem when no one was lookin'. When ol' Charlie got his favorite drumstick, he couldn't let go of it! I could put a big green worm on Charlie's salad. When he helped himself to the gravy, I'd give the bowl a bump. The gravy would spill down his shirt front and into his lap. Whew! That would be funny! When he stood up to mop himself, he would see he was sittin' in apple butter.

Aunt Toot would probably come with a wet cloth to help clean Charlie up. I could give the cloth a squirt of Stickem. Their hands could get stuck on the cloth. They would both be pullin' on it. The rag would tear in two! Aunt Toot would fall on the table knockin' a dish of cranberry sauce all over Dad. By this time ol' Charlie would be gettin' pretty wild. He'd hit Mom in the eye with his elbow while she goosed him with a fork!

Jeepers! What ideas! I got to laughin' and laughin' up there in the attic. Peggy girl, you've got quite a brain! Just thinkin' about all those jokes made me laugh some more. I'd be even with ol' Charlie Fupp, for sure. I just kinda went off to sleep thinkin' good thoughts.

The next morning I got up real early. Real early for me, I mean. The rooster had been up all night crowin'. I decided it was time to see what he was crowin' about. After all, it was the special day of my birthday. I got dressed and went down the back stairs. I wanted to get out to the outhouse without anyone seeing me. When I was younger, the outhouse was kind of a novelty. Now, it kind of embarrassed me to go there.

I was sneakin' down the back stairs when I heard Mom and Aunt Toot talkin' in the kitchen. I stayed back in the stairwell. I could hear what they were sayin' but it wasn't really eavesdroppin'. I was just sort of gatherin' information in case they had any birthday surprises!

"I sure hope Peggy likes this cake. I made it special for her," Aunt Toot said.

"Of course, she will!" Mom answered. "Your applesauce cakes are the best in Ohio. They're Peggy's favorite. Next to your home-grown pumpkin pies!"

"I've noticed a difference in Peggy this year," Aunt Toot said. "She's still the jokester but there's something else." She sounded real thoughtful.

"Oh yes, she's growing so fast, we have to keep letting her hems down: Skirts and pants."

"It's more than that. She just seems... well... *older* I guess," Aunt Toot finished.

"I know what you mean," Mom said. "We're so proud of the way she's doing her chores. We don't even have to remind her. The garbage is out on time. Her room is cleaned up. She's doing her part, and she'll be a young woman any time now."

That really embarrassed me! Mom and I had talked about changes coming for me. I knew all about the "M word," and hormones, and stuff. It was just hearing her talk with another woman about it made me feel funny.

"She's really a special, creative, and caring girl growing into a beautiful young woman."

Oh, wow, now I was super embarrassed. Here I was planning Stickem tricks on Aunt Toot while she and Mom were talking about how grown up I was. I thought: I *won't be using my Nil Bag on Aunt Toot or Mom.* It didn't seem fair.

Real quiet, so they wouldn't know I was listening, I went out the back door to the outhouse. Then, I went on into the barn to do some more thinking about my Nil Bag. It was still early morning.

The barn had a sweet fresh hay smell. I climbed up in the hay loft and got a straw to suck on. It was very quiet except for the sounds of the animals getting up for the day.

I heard voices coming into the barn and was about to call out when I realized the voices were talking about me. I was a pretty popular subject this morning. I wonder if grownups always talk together about kids? Or is it something special on birthdays? I decided to stay hidden in the loft and just listen.

"Peggy will like middle school. For a while I wasn't sure she'd be grown up enough. But this year, she's begun using her head. She's more responsible," Dad said.

"I know," Gramps agreed. "She's thinking about things more seriously now. We've had some nice long talks." Gramps' voice sounded so friendly. "I'm really proud of my grandaughter."

"So am I," Dad said. His voice sounded as pleased as could be. "Peggy keeps coming up with new ideas to help the family—like taking care of the water from the dripping ice chest."

"Oh, Peggy—" Gramps started to laugh.

Dad interrupted: "Gramps, I've just thought of something. It might be time we stopped calling her, 'Peggy.' She might prefer to be called Margaret or Margie or Maggie."

"I think you're right," Gramps agreed. They kept right on talking but went outside. I couldn't hear the rest of what they said. I knew I liked what they said. Margaret? Mmm. Margaret sounded pretty good. Stinky would probably call me Maggie, but it was all right.

What wasn't all right was my using the Nil Bag on Gramps or Dad. "Peggy" might do that. But Margaret? Nope, it just couldn't be done.

After Gramps and Dad left, I climbed down from the loft. I strolled back into the kitchen. Everybody was there and feeling good.

"Happy birthday!"

"Happy birthday, Margaret!"

"There's the birthday girl."

"Happy birthday, Margie."

Everybody greeted me. It was downright embarrassing.

We all had a yummy breakfast of eggs and bacon, muffins and corn meal mush. There was fresh butter and homemade preserves and cold milk from the spring house. What a way to start a birthday!

"How does it feel to be ten years old?" Charlie asked. He was busy finishing his breakfast.

"It feels just fine," I said as I buttered just one more muffin. "How does it feel to be forty-two years old?"

"Haw, haw." Charlie started laughing. "You know, Peg... er... Margaret, that's what I've always liked about you. A lot of kids can't take teasing but you can take it and dish it right back! You've got a real sense of humor. Happy birthday, pal." He got up from the table, gave me a tap on the arm, and went outside to do chores.

That did it! Now I couldn't even use the Nil Bag on ol' Charlie—no applebutter on his chair and no Stickem on his hand. I mean, Charlie really liked me! It was kind of a surprise to find out grown-ups can tease a kid just because they really like them. Maybe there wasn't as much garbage in life as I used to think.

Later in the afternoon I was exploring up in the attic. I found some old toys of mine stored there. They were baby rattles, things like that. Boy, were they ever silly! I guess I liked them once. When I was little. It's funny how you outgrow even toys. There were even some baby clothes in an old trunk. I held them up to me. I couldn't believe I was ever that small. No wonder Mom kept saying, "You're growing so fast!"

I was just putting the things away when Mom called: "Margaret, it's time for dinner."

I started to go downstairs. First, I felt for my Nil Bag. It was there, in my pocket. I took it out and gave it a long look. A real long look.

"Margaret...?"

Real quick I hurried back to the trunk. I lifted the lid and tucked the Nil Bag inside, right next to my old favorite teddy bear.

Thanksgiving dinner. The whole family and some friends would be there, too. And I was ten years old, almost a young woman!

Epilogue

Memoirs are supposed to take the writer from where they were or what they've been through or what they've learned, to a resolution of sorts. I'm going to end this epic now with these lessons learned:

1. Growing up can be hazardous to your health.

2. Sometimes the best of friends can be the best of everything all life long. Stinky was one of the many boys who went to war after Pearl Harbor. We wrote letters but never saw each other again until after WWII changed everything, including "Stinky" into "Alfred." I was in college working toward my doctorate and Alfred was using the G.I. Bill. We found each other again and have been together all these years with children and grandchildren who often bring back the memories of Peggy and Stinky.

3. Bulldogs love to lie in petunias.

4. Church is a time for quiet meditation or else your brain will over-stimulate.

Sincerely,
Margaret L. Quick
September 18, 1979

CANTICLE IN BLACK AND WHITE
TIME FRAGMENT 2025 CE

What the heck are you doing in this dungeon? You look like a nerd hunkered over a gaming keyboard!" Nathan admonished his sister while pulling the drapes to allow the autumn sun to filter through the room.

"Stop, Nathan! I've got work to do and all the light does is reflect the dust in the air. Leave me alone," Lauren said without looking up from her computer screen. She was used to her older brother telling her what to do, and also to ignoring him.

"What are you doing besides blue-lining and editing other people's work? You haven't done any work of your own since Kyle's death." Nathan was relentless. This conversation had never coaxed his widowed sister from her grief before. Today, he was stepping up the pressure; he was desperate for her.

Nathan missed Lauren most of all. Growing up, there were thousands of pictures of 'the twins.' Even Nathan and Lauren would see pictures of themselves and say 'the twins.' Nathan always assumed the big brother role because he was a few minutes older. The two were not identifiable as twins. Lauren was short and slim; Nathan was tall and burley.

Lauren's soft brown hair was luxurious and shoulder length' Nathan's was prematurely thinning. Their dispositions were different as well as Lauren was quiet and reserved with Nathan being boisterous and outgoing. People thought Lauren looked like their mother, and Nathan, their father.

It was their devotion to each other that noted a special sibling relationship. They had grown up playing together, reading the same books, going to school and college together. Always, they confided in each other. Their paths only diverted with Nathan specializing in global climate changes. He was ensconced in the sciences and gained his doctorate in climatology.

Lauren was working toward her doctorate in Speech/Language Pathology when she met her brother's best friend, Kyle. Her quiet demeanor was complementary to his enthusiasm for everything. Lauren and Kyle married because they could not bear to be apart. Nathan was Best Man to Kyle and devoted brother to Lauren. Always, the twins remained each other's best friend. The three joked they needed to find a woman for Nathan who could complete the quartet.

The foursome was never realized. After three short, wedded years, Kyle was diagnosed with early-onset Prostate Cancer. As horrendous as cancer is for the patient, it is equally devastating for the caregiver—watching a loved one struggle with the medical regimen and pain.

Kyle, the love of Lauren's life, left her exhausted and alone with his death. All the compassion and support from family, friends, and colleagues insulated her as she withdrew more and more. Gradually, she isolated herself to proofing manuscripts and theses for the college. It was enough for her, but not for Nathan!

"Lauren, I've had enough of this 'poor me' stuff. You are a vibrant woman; that's why Kyle fell in love with you. You had three blissful years together; most marriages don't have so long a honeymoon. Remember Dad's saying: 'I cried because I had no shoes until I saw the man who had no feet.' You may be barefoot now, but you still have your feet! It's time for you to find yourself some shoes." Nathan's tone was intense. He needed Lauren to see how concerned he was. Now, Nathan only wanted for Lauren to live again.

Lauren finally looked up from her screen, surprised to hear the forcefulness of his words and see the frustration in his face. Her hands began to tremble and she pulled them away from the keyboard. "Nathan... you don't know...."

"You're right, I don't! But Kyle was my best friend—"

"He was my reason to live...." Lauren whispered.

"I just know there's a whole life ahead of you. Kyle will always be a part of it. You must know he would want you to take your memories into the world, not hide away from it."

Nathan's sincerity reached his sister's heart. Tears welled in her eyes matched by the single tear on Nathan's cheek.

Lauren paused, her fingers tracing the edge of the laptop until she took a deep breath and closed the lid. She said, "I love you, Nathan. Where can I find some 'new shoes?'"

Standing on the foredeck of the Antarctic research and expedition ship, the *Shirley Keene*, Lauren laughed as Nathan joined her in the crystal January air. "When you encouraged me to get a new pair of shoes, I had no idea they would be Antarctic boots to match insulated snow pants, and a down parka with a faux fur hood!" The look on her twin's face turned her laugh to sympathy. "Still a little seasick?" She asked. The rough waves of Drake Passage to the southernmost continent had isolated many of the passengers in their cabins.

"Oh, it's better. I kept breakfast down; the motion sick patch is working. A little more time and I'll have my sea legs." Nathan sounded optimistic.

Lauren swept her windblown bangs aside. "Considering how you would get seasick on the ferries at home, I was surprised you arranged a tour to Antarctica on a boat."

"A ship!" he corrected her. "This grant opportunity came up for the Foundation Climate Research for me since the original grantee was sick. Because the ship books guest travelers as well, it was a win-win opportunity for us both. I'm glad you came." He attempted to keep the horizon in sight in spite of the ship's motion through the waves.

Lauren turned back to the railing, taking in the expanse of ocean before them. Crossing the Passage was relatively mild this day. The air was pristine and she had no sense of limits on the horizon. The colors of the ocean blended into the sky where clouds wisped. 'Expanse'? No, that word was too limiting to describe the scene before her. The bow waves and vibration of the ship were the only clues to her movement through space. Lauren held the rail and took a deep breath as pure as any she had ever experienced in her life. *If only she could share it with Kyle....*

Nathan interrupted her thought. "Lauren, I've got to set up my monitoring equipment, are you okay on your own?"

"Oh, yes, I'm fine. I'll just wait for the other 'guests' to settle in and come up to share this view. Maybe I'll read in my cabin. We still have travel time before we start the ice and mammal views."

Nathan swept his arm over the sea water swells. "What can you *read* that will match this?" He smiled and repeated, "I'm really glad you came with me. I'll see you at dinner—if the seasick patch is still working." The 'climatologist' in him took over and Nathan left to tend to his data equipment.

Alone again, Lauren anticipated the next days on board. Basically a research ship, travel guests were encouraged to increase the positive impact of scientific endeavors. Experiencing the world outside encouraged protection of the oceans and conservation of wildlife. It also aided in funding research projects. Research scientists, like Nathan, became teachers in the most appropriate classroom—the real world.

Lauren hesitated to leave her observation post. She snuggled deeper into her coat and wrapped a scarf about her throat. It might be January, but it was summer here approaching the Antarctic Circle. The amazing sea ice was a swath of diamond crystals, each floe a prism of shapes and colors. Because of its angle, the sun cast patterns of awesome beauty. Returning her eyes towards the horizon, she gasped.

Forward, just before the bow, a spectacle surged above the waves. She knew the Killer Whale by reputation but was breathless at the sight. The magnificence of the enormous sleek animal leapt from the powerful waves. The white and black image curved above the sea, pausing at the apex of the jump as if giving gravity a chance to catch up. Then, the Orca fell into the surface with saltwater spray over the ship in an orgasmic explosion of joy.

Instinctively, Lauren wiped her face of spray and looked to the railing to share the excitement, but there was no one there.

Dinner was informal because this was a working research ship. Guests and specialists intermingled, coming and going as necessitated by the individual projects. Lauren was seated with the group at the captain's table. The chatter dealt with the transportation issues getting to the port of debarkation, the weather, family matters, and the excitement and anticipation of the days ahead.

"Captain," Lauren asked. "I saw the most fantastic Orca today; will there be more?"

"Oh, yes! Always more! They are our star performers."

"I saw a killer whale doing tricks at a marine park once," said Patricia, a gray-haired woman accompanying her daughter, a film producer.

Captain Freya Aberg replied: "Breaching is part of their natural behavior. 'Killer whale' is actually a misnomer. They are Orcinus orca, the largest of the dolphins. Instead of keeping Orcas in marine parks as prisoners, what you'll see here are wildlife in their natural habitat. They roam all the oceans, and people like yourselves, come to their world to evaluate and appreciate."

Patricia remarked, "You can't get millions of people on tourist boats."

"We reach out to them through documentaries like your daughter is developing. Technology brings the glory of the Orca's natural world to the living room, the classroom, the theatre, the orchestra, the gymnasium, the park."

"The orchestra?" Brian, an older man from

Chicago asked.

"The sounds of whales have been made into orchestral symphonies. You can access them in your cabins." Gently touching her mouth with a napkin, Captain Aberg continued, "For this voyage, you will have sightings with penguins too numerous to count, nurseries of thousands. There will be views of whales, dolphins, sea birds, and seals. Our itinerary supports the research projects on board, and there are always surprises awaiting the next ice floe." With that promise and a smile, she excused herself for her evening duties. She was a tall woman of Scandinavian background and wore her formal captain's uniform with dignity. As she walked toward the ship's bridge, a little black ball of fur scurried out from beneath the table and followed the captain through the door.

Patricia blinked in surprise and asked, "What was that?"

The steward laughed. "That's Callie, the Captain's Schipperke. The 'little captain' follows Captain Aberg everywhere."

"I've heard of cats onboard, but little dogs?" Patricia shook her head. "I'm learning a lot already and we haven't even reached our destination yet."

Nathan slipped into the empty seat and touched Lauren's shoulder. His expression showed excitement to be gathering data in his favorite topics. Seasickness was forgotten. "Lauren, this is perfect! I no more than got the monitors installed when data began collecting. For whatever people think about climate, there's more than sitting in an office making weather predictions!"

The smile on her brother's face was a pleasure to see.

Lauren said warmly, "And I've seen an Orca and Schipperke in their natural habitats! I'm becoming *really* glad I came as well!"

After dinner, Lauren strolled on the afterdeck, again relying on the guardrail for balance. Above her, a single white bird glided in the ship's draft. It was an albatross, its long wingspan allowing it to float over the ocean, not even flapping its wings. Hovering so close to the ship, the legendary sea bird appeared to look Lauren in the eye; she did not look away.

In her single cabin bunk later that night, Lauren tried to put the pieces of this trip together. Lauren was surprised by the fatigue she felt just maneuvering around a ship buffeted by waves. She reminded herself the Passage had tortuous currents. It said so in the book she'd read. She had so much to tell Kyle, so much she wanted to share with him. She imagined watching the Orca with him, cuddling and talking in the cabin, being intimate with his warm body in the crisp night air. She was trying to live again, but it was without her beloved.

Reaching the Antarctic peninsula on schedule set more shipboard activities into action. Researchers manned their computer and satellite connection around the clock. Zodiak rubber boats were launched with particular assignments depending on the research being conducted. Guests watched from observation decks, explored the ship, or rode in the Zodiaks. Patricia was enthralled watching her daughter take footage of the rugged snow covered peaks and ice floes of the channel. Brian was exhilarated by the marine life he could recount to his grandchildren back home.

Nathan guided Lauren to the data room where

computer monitors brightened the dark.

"Lauren, I want you to meet Dr. Miguel Ruelas," he introduced her to the sound technician. The man never looked at her, just waved and mumbled while gesturing to be silent. He wore headphones and stared intently at a screen showing waves of sound. His fingers clicked the keyboard as the sounds progressed. Pausing to touch his beard, he turned to look up at Nathan and Lauren.

"Hello. Can't visit now; we're tracking a pod of humpbacks, and they're singing!" He did smile at that and re-arranged the headphones on his dark curly hair. Giving the two another glance, he clicked on the speakers and Lauren could hear the sounds so exciting to him. It was the symphony the Captain mentioned last night: Melodious, haunting, and somehow emotional.

'Where's Mark?" Nathan asked about the other researcher on the team.

"He's in the raft with the microphones. It's a great recording!" Dr. Ruelas' attention never wavered from the screen.

"We'll come back later," Nathan said as he guided Lauren to his own work station for climatology.

"So this is your home away from home," Lauren chided as she eyed the technology instruments. "I love what you've done with the place." She never quite understood the passion Nathan felt toward the measurements and complex data but she was proud of his work. He wasn't just researching climate change; Nathan was involved in the science to understand and survive with those changes.

A *plink* from Nathan's computer drew his attention and Lauren knew his tour guide talk was over as he slipped into place by his monitor.

Lauren smiled at her brother then walked around the room, nodding to the others involved in their own work. The whale songs drew her back to the sound technician; he had left the speakers turned on. Standing behind Dr. Ruelas, watching the blips on the screen, the sounds were mesmerizing. She closed her eyes and imagined the behemoths in the sea singing for miles.

"Beautiful, absolutely beautiful, isn't it?" Dr. Ruelas asked as he looked over his shoulder. "I have a hard time ever pulling away from it; it's even richer sound here than in the Zodiac."

Lauren opened her eyes to see the specialist looking directly at her and waiting for an answer. "Oh, Dr. Ruelas—"

"Miguel, please. We're all friends here."

"All right, Miguel. Tell me what I'm hearing. Are these just natural calls or something more? Are they moaning or communicating?

"Both; we just don't understand their language." Miguel's dark eyes showed the same degree of interest in her questions as he had previously shown his monitor. Just then, the sound band changed and there were clicks and whistles. Miguel turned to adjust the recording levels.

"What's that? Why did they change?" Lauren asked.

"They didn't, it's a new sound. There's a pod of Orcas moving by. They have distinct sounds to differentiate pods!"

"Like local accents?" Lauren was intrigued.

"Exactly! They're dialects." Miguel was torn between Lauren's enthusiasm and his need to decipher his data.

"You go ahead; I can wait, the whales—the Orcas— won't. We can talk later." Lauren backed away and Miguel was already lost in concentration. Fascinated by the concept of communication, Lauren had many more questions and would search out Dr. Ruelas' answers.

Walking to her cabin through the myriad of passageways, Lauren passed the boat launch area. Brian was climbing out of the research inflatable and helping Patricia. Their faces were flushed with the sea air and excitement of the excursion. Patricia's daughter and her co-photographer were unloading the video equipment into the launch bay. They told the boat crew they had been able to film the whale pods. It was the same encounter Lauren had seen and heard in the data room. She felt totally involved in the science of the voyage.

At the afternoon buffet, passengers, crew, and researchers all shared their stories. Lauren just listened. She enjoyed exploring the ship yet felt restless without some concrete work to do. She thought about editing some manuscripts in her cabin then dismissed the thought. It was something she could do at home, thousands of miles away. With the long daylight hours, the ship was alive with chores, research, visiting, and adventures. It was difficult to differentiate between waking and sleeping. Meals were available to accommodate the schedules and the surprises. Fortuitous encounters with the whales were interwoven with research as well as the routine projects of taking samples.

Passing the launch area again, a breath of air verified it was too early to end the day. Lauren climbed up to the foredeck to watch the sun ride along the horizon. She knew at this season, in this place, there were no daily sunsets... like she and Kyle had once watched.

"It just keeps rolling along...." a deep voice said behind her.

"What?" she asked in surprise, turning to see the person joining her.

"I was thinking about a song about a river. At this latitude, there really isn't a sunset. The sun 'going down' is a quirk in our habit of thought." Miguel stepped beside Lauren and they watched the sun together. "I'm sorry you didn't come back to the data room. We got some great recordings."

"And the photographers got some great video, I heard," she answered, snuggling her coat, then holding the rail.

"Tomorrow is my turn for recording in the boat. Would you like to join me?" Again, Miguel looked directly at her. "We can talk about whale clicks, whistles, and pulsed calls. Whatever you like. Later, we'll be in one of the most beautiful channels on Earth. We can see it from the observation decks after we return." He paused, waiting for her answer.

Made uneasy by his attention, Lauren wasn't sure what she should say. She hadn't said 'yes' to many invitations since Kyle had died, and it wasn't as if Miguel was flirting with her. He was just asking her to ride in a boat with other people to see spectacular ice floes and hear whales sing. *Nathan was right, I have become an isolated nerd... and a paranoid wimp.*

"Yes, Dr. Ruelas—I mean, Miguel. I would enjoy going to sea with you." Her expression was as surprised as her words.

At the breakfast meal, Patricia slipped into the chair next to Lauren. "My dear, what are you up to today? This trip is so wonderful! Debra, my daughter, will be doing some editing today so Brian and I will be whale watching again. He's such a delightful travel companion. He's been everywhere in the world and to think we met at the bottom of the Earth!" She hardly paused for breath. "I saw you wandering around the ship with that nice young man, Nathan. Otherwise, you are always alone…." Patricia paused to eat a muffin. "I'll tell you, Lauren, it is such a pleasure for a widow like myself to meet such a nice gentleman as Brian. A woman can get very lonely for a companion, and just between you and me, traveling with a bunch of old ladies just isn't the same. I think—"

Lauren interrupted the discourse. "Nathan is my brother, a climatologist, who's on board with a research grant and invited me—"

"A brother?" Patricia confirmed then went on talking. "I should introduce him to my daughter. Is he married?"

Lauren shook her head but before she could explain more, Patricia was distracted and turned to the male passenger across the table. All the while eating between words, she asked, "What are you up to today? My name is Patricia!"

Lauren just shrugged, finished her food, and rose to prepare for the Zodiak trip.

In the passageway to her small cabin, Lauren almost collided with Nathan.

"Whoa, little sister, where are you going? Have you been on the Zodiaks yet?" He kept looking over her shoulder as if eager to get to the breakfast meal.

"No, I'm going today. We're checking out the whale songs and I—"

"Great! I'll touch bases with you later!" Nathan gave

her a quick kiss on the cheek.

Lauren noticed his stubble before his disappeared down the passage, and thought ruefully: *Beards must be a statement for researchers in the Antarctic. And I'm getting use to not finishing sentences! I wonder if whales have the same problem with their sentences?*

After dressing in her cabin, Lauren felt like an ad for pillows. Walking the passage to the boat launch, she wore her brightly colored coat, insulated pants and boots rated for the Arctic. She manipulated her fingers into her gloves and tried to remind herself this was summer! The life jacket the crew helped her put on just added to her bulk. Watching the little inflatable bobbing in the port doorway almost changed her mind about leaving the security of the ship for a floating raft on an icy sea.

Already settled in the boat with his technical devices, Miguel saw her hesitation and stood to assist. He reached for her arm and they each grabbed the other's wrists. It was the stronger hold the crew had briefed the new passengers about, but with the rhythm of the choppy waves, she almost fell into the boat. Miguel caught her, holding her for a few seconds next to his chest to steady them both. He smiled at her look of surprise then pulled her into her assigned seat. His enthusiasm for the day was evident as the inflatable sped to the planned location for the afternoon. He kept looking back at Lauren. She was immediately glad of the insulated gear she wore and pulled the hood up to hide her flushed face.

Her embarrassment at falling into the researcher's arms soon dissipated with the excitement of flying over the ocean and breathing such clean, cold air. Lauren felt the momentum of the motors, the waves beneath, and the wind.

She had to admit to herself, she felt more alive than ever before! Her senses, her thoughts, and even her memories were amplified through the experience. She felt the extreme of every sense. She thought her ability to feel such emotions had died with Kyle. *If only... if only....*

Miguel switched seats at a calm interlude and offered Lauren a mug of hot chocolate from his thermos. "Lauren, you look absolutely enthralled, and we haven't even reached the Orcas yet."

Grateful for the chocolate and his words, Lauren sipped the warm liquid and tried to remember her questions. "Yesterday, you said the Orcas have different dialects. How do you know they are speaking to each other?"

Again, Miguel was encouraged by a chance to share his work. "There are recordings of pods from all over the world and we recognize the patterns, just not the individual words. There are even differences between residential or transient pods."

Excitedly, Lauren said, "Yesterday, the clicks of the Orcas reminded me of a code. I won't say Morse code but possibly an Orca code? I've studied language and am fascinated by the idea of another species, as intelligent as the whales, being able to communicate. With all the emphasis on Artificial Intelligence, I wonder if it's Natural Intelligence that could give us the answers we desperately need."

"What answers do *you* need, Lauren?" Miguel's voice was so soft, she could barely hear him. His eyes never left hers.

"Oh, I don't know the answers because... I'm still sorting out the questions." Lauren paused and looked starboard to hide her confusion. They were entering a field of pack ice as their boat skillfully piloted in and out of the chunks floating about them. When she turned back, Miguel's attention was on his devices.

Once the excursion returned to the ship, Lauren changed clothing into warm fleece and took her jacket to the dining area. Avoiding Patricia and unable to find Nathan, she hurriedly gathered hot lobscouse and hardtack. With the sea air and excitement, she hungrily ate the traditional stew of meat and broth. She was eager to watch the sun ride the horizon and left quickly to climb to the observation deck. The Captain was just leaving there with Callie following her to the bridge.

The foredeck was almost deserted; most passengers were in the galley dining area after their active day. She saw Miguel at the railing and thought she'd return another time. Before Lauren could leave, he saw her and quickly motioned to join him. With binoculars, he was intent on ice off the port side. "Look at this! The Orca pod is chasing a seal onto the floe. I hope Mark has the recorders going. They would be clicking up a storm!" He pulled another set of binoculars out of his pocket and handed them to her.

Adjusting the eyepieces, she saw a single seal swimming through the floes being chased by a pod of Orcas. The seal floundered then reached a larger piece of ice and maneuvered to wiggle upon it. Immediately, it moved to the center of the floe, now bobbing in the water. Around the edges of the ice, the pod circled.

Lauren held her breath. The seal looked so alone, so isolated. She identified with it immediately. "Is the seal safe now?" she asked Miguel as they both watched.

"Seals are never safe when there's a predator hunting them, whether it's human or Orca. And this pinniped has the equivalent of a wolf pack after it."

"But the seal is out of reach. Won't they give up and find another meal?" Lauren desperately wanted the isolation to be the protection the seal needed.

"Orcas are the apex predators of the sea. This isn't a stunt at a marine park. This is the real world." His eyes never left the scene unfolding before them.

In this real world, the Orcas moved away briefly. Lauren thought: *This is the end of the hunt; the seal will live another day.* Movement caught her eye and she fastened her binoculars on the pod of Orca turning together, swimming in close synchronization directly towards the floating ice. Their bodies and tails created a wave that washed over the floe as they dove beneath it. The seal was sliding off the ice floe, then waddled to regain its position and flopped back to the center. Again, the wave washed over the floe as the pack continued its moves. The seal was almost washed into the sea but paddled against the wave. With the third pass, the Orcas were moving faster, side by side. The force pushed a larger swell over the top of the ice and they dove beneath it. Washed over the edge, the seal lost its berth. Immediately, the Orca leader came up beneath the flailing and exhausted seal and pulled it beneath the frothing water. *This was the real world.*

It was too overwhelming. Lauren backed away from the railing, rigidly gripping the binoculars, and rushed to the safety of her cabin. Dismissing her coat and boots, she climbed under the down comforter and curled her knees to her chest. She could hardly breathe. She identified so closely with the lone seal that she was devastated by the result of the hunt. Intellectually, she knew the Orcas had to survive; they helped keep the other marine species healthy. Their ingenuity to reach the seal demonstrated a brilliance in the natural world. The pod unity and communication gave them strength. The seal never gave up. At another time, on another floe, another seal would escape. While human sciences monitored and collected data on the climate status, the species of Earth adapted to their survival mode.

Lauren's trembling ceased but her emotions were confused. Was she grieving for the seal or for herself? Would she return to the hermit she was prior to this trip or to the woman she had become while married to Kyle? She had known the magic of a loving marriage, had endured the tragedy of caring for a beloved, and she had lost her goals in life. She had survived! She wasn't a lone seal. She was a woman with family support and loving memories. She was experiencing an adventure of exquisite beauty just outside a porthole. Lauren had a life ahead of her to appreciate; it was time to begin it. Would she? Could she? At that thought, she looked to her insulated boots and coat in the corner of the room. They were the answer to her questions.

A quiet knock at the cabin door accompanied Miguel's call, "Lauren, are you all right?"

His warm concern brought her thoughts back to the present. Without opening the door, she answered, "Yes, Miguel; I'm just thinking. Let's meet after dinner on the afterdeck."

At eight bells, Lauren was at her usual place on the afterdeck. On this evening, researchers, off duty crew, and passengers had staked out their favorite viewpoints. The promise of the

Lemaire Channel was fulfilled! Words were useless, too mundane to describe the towering basalt peaks, the icebergs and the still waters. Statuary of ice, light, motion and colors were fashioned by the ocean, the Master Sculptor. Forms of water and ice curved and danced as reflections of the fading light. Indescribable, the channel could only be felt in the air and sensed through the visual images surrounding the vessel. Awed by the stillness and grandeur, Lauren experienced peace and clarity.

Behind the ship, a cleared wake was quickly smothered by ice fragments and floes. A single bird, like a winged spirit, hovered in the air currents above. *Just like life,* Lauren thought. *We make our passages and move on. The albatross could be a soul watching over me.*

Miguel stepped next to the railing but respected Lauren's silence. When she initiated speaking, it began an evening of long conversation. She told Miguel about her family, about Kyle, of her previous studies in communication. She included Nathan's urging her to take this voyage. In turn, Miguel promised the joy of watching thousands of penguins on islands, of hiking on ice fields, and more Zodiak excursions. This time, when he took her gloved hand in his, she did not pull it away.

"Miguel, after this voyage, I'm returning home to finish my doctorate, but with an expanded approach. My emphasis will be on communication between the Orcas. I think my speech and language background will be helpful and maybe, just maybe, I'll be able to break that Orca code." She smiled at the encouraging expression on his face. "Maybe, I can become an intern on one of your research projects?"

"I'll be ready when you are," Miguel answered

sincerely. "You may even be able to complete your theses online with a research project from here. Field work—ice fieldwork—is essential."

Lauren turned around slowly taking in the panorama. She took a deep breath of the cold air and felt the vibration of the ship. From behind an ice covered cliff, the sun poured its twilight colors over the glaciers. Like mirrors on the surface of the sea, the water created depth to the experience. Yes, Lauren thought, *this is the real world, and I have my boots.*

FINAL CURTAIN
TIME FRAGMENT 1955-1995 CE

Howard wasn't acting. He really was dead. He would be that way—dead—for the service to follow. If he hadn't been dead, he would have objected to the smarmy way the funeral director looked down at Howard's body. The director sighed as if he were sad and looked out at the small chapel gathering. The director was acting. He began with a facial expression and voice tension he always used to begin:

"Welcome, friends, to the celebration of the life of Howard Rhodes. Born 1917. Died 1995. As Howard would agree it's appropriate, we will appreciate him in three Acts. Family and friends? Please begin." Another sigh, and a gesture to a small woman to come up to the podium, started the proceedings. The director sat behind the coffin and seriously perused the memorial program.

Act One: Eulogy
by Millie Rhodes

This Eulogy is for Howard, the man who shared one third of my life, who cared for me and our child, and who eventually left us to find his dream. The dream may have been there all along but life had a way of distracting him.

We met at the Community Theatre in our Southwest metropolis. I was a starry-eyed college student spending my summers working crew in the theatre, acting in plays, and running errands. It was the magic that comes from audience applause and hometown newspaper reviews. It meant working with people who loved the theatre enough to give their very best, *pro bono publico*.

Howard was already established in his father's accounting firm the summer we met. It had been a destination all his life. Howard always found it easier to go along than confront a situation or disappoint his father. It was the call of spread sheets, debits and credits, receipts, expenses, and tax forms which confirmed his entry into accounting. He was an accountant because it was what his father wanted.

When the Firm needed a volunteer to do 'community service,' Howard found himself keeping the books for the Theatre in the Round. Suddenly, Howard's accounting had a purpose. He had been introduced to the theatre by a few Humanities classes in college. Now, Howard kept the invoices. Costumes were borrowed or rented. Props were dug out of basements. Tickets were to be printed, sold, and box office sales tallied. The play must go on!

Howard was a sober young man with a facial expression that might turn to dour as he aged. He was plain but pleasant at his post-college age. At rehearsals, between scenes, I would sit and talk with Howard who seemed to know all the lines of all the characters and we would talk about characterizations, great dramatists, and preferred plays. Once, the director even called Howard to play a small part as a businessman and the acting bug bit him.

The community players put on four plays during the summer to an after-dinner crowd in the hotel ballroom-turned-theatre. Light drama and comedy—perfect plays for warm summer nights in an air-conditioned venue.

I was taken by Howard's seriousness and willingness to let me talk about becoming an actress, about roles I would play. As a tiny, red-haired actress, I needed to search plays for my niche. My venue was comedy and I was usually cast as a maid or a silly friend. Howard was a mature, solid man of thirty with a worthwhile job. Occasionally, he would fill in a part as a man of substance. He always had stage presence no matter how small the role. Through the summer, I talked and talked and he listened. Gradually, he talked and I did the listening.

With the closing curtain, I returned to my senior year at the local university. The college 'boys' seemed so young and flighty. Howard and I continued to date, attending theatre productions, or just being together. I had major decisions facing me. At the time, college women were recommended to be teachers or work for the telephone company. Perhaps I should get a teacher's credential and teach Drama?

The decision was made for me... for us. I was pregnant by the end of the Fall semester. I can say that easily now but at the time it was a conflict of emotions and embarrassment. Without hesitating, Howard asked me to marry him. I tell this in the eulogy, as a former wife, because this man is one for you to know, as I did, once.

As Howard expected, his father accepted the situation and insisted he would love being a grandparent. We were married at the courthouse; I quit school to build a nest for us.

We still participated in summer theatre. At first, there

were a few obvious stares, friendly jokes, and best wishes for the couple who had met in the round. In my last trimester, I mostly participated by watching, while Howard continued to help wherever he could. He was also trying out for various and more difficult parts.

Our next experience was not as pleasant to recall. Our son, Robert, was born with severe problems of anoxia. We brought him home with high hopes but knowledge of possible complications. I was a stay-at-home mom for our dear little child. In spite of everything and our loving care, it soon became evident that something was very wrong with our little boy. He went into seizures, did not react to sounds, and instead of a healthy cry, he would whimper. The specialists could do nothing but tell us young parents to 'enjoy the little tiger while they could.'

While we could. It became our challenge and we pursued the next years with our sick child. As he grew, his problems became more severe. We tried different doctors and organizations, yet no one could do more to help us. There were frequent hospital stays for his respiratory difficulties.

In addition to the medical care from Howard's good health insurance, every spare dollar went to pursuing a cure. By Robert's eleventh birthday, the family was bankrupt both emotionally and financially. All the failed excursions to medical clinics, psychological studies, and clinical trials could diagnose but not cure Robert. Howard and I felt we had failed. Howard had ulcers from work. Robert seemed to think he wasn't good enough. Otherwise, why did his parents keep trying to change him?

Howard and I ceased doing things together. One of us would always need to be home with Robert. We still participated in the summer theatre, but always singularly. We dismissed recommendations of in-patient hospital care even though there were medical facilities available. Howard began to broach other care possibilities. I wouldn't hear of it. Robert was *our* son, and we would *make* him better.

With strong urging, we finally agreed to let Robert take a 'vacation' at a group home for disabled children. When we returned days later to reclaim Robert, we found him with a cluster of people in the garden. He had a smile of contentment we had never seen as his parents. The attendant assured us he'd had that expression the whole time he was there.

"He wasn't isolated or made aware of his disabilities. He wasn't medically invaded," the attendant explained. "He was with other youngsters, enjoying appropriate activities, and respected for what he could do, not pressured for what he couldn't do."

Robert's smile made the decision. It was time to let go, not for our sakes but for Robert... and we did. Robert became a resident at the care home. Howard and I returned to our empty house as strangers. After all these years, we were more housemates than a married husband and wife.

I resumed theater activities; I was a story lady at our library. I volunteered at local charities. I helped in the local hospital when they needed someone to hold the preemie babies and rock them for human contact. Howard became more involved in business clubs. We never participated together; we never shared a bedroom. In the summer, we avoided trying out for the same play. Other than casual information, we never talked any more.

One night, at a cast party, as the lead in a difficult

drama, Howard was giving a speech to the cast and crew. He announced he was resigning from the accounting firm he had inherited and going to Hollywood to work in television! With the bombshell causing complete silence, he took an exit, stage left, and departed without any explanation.

If it was a mid-life crisis or last chance at a dream, I don't know or begin to understand. He was over fifty years old and left me without income or resources. The sale of the accounting firm paid off our home and debts with a trust fund for Robert's care. I was always a volunteer, so my job skills and opportunities were limited. Personally, I had to rent rooms to college students. I appreciate the concerns and help all his friends have offered me. When the divorce became a reality, I felt abandoned. Howard followed his dream... now I must create my own.

Act Two: *Memoir*
by Howard Rhodes
(written post retirement)

The following epitome might be called a "memoir" or "autobiography" or even a "confession." I'm only writing it because my wife, Allysia, believes I need something to do to keep me home and sane. My wife is like that. She prefers a sane, retired husband. As a continuity director, she's still working on television scripts from our home now that we're back in Arizona.

I consider myself to be a stable, serious, and responsible man. It may have started with my youth and being the son of a CEO of his own accounting firm. It could also have been my lack of imagination to find any other occupation besides accountant in my father's firm. I grew up in Arizona, carefully maintaining my mediocre grades in school until I went to the local university and graduated in the middle of my class. I was scooped up by my father's firm and established a workaday career. I was average height, medium build, brown-haired, and an accountant. When I tried dating, I was considered boring. Even the women accountants in the firm declined my few invitations. Reaching age thirty, I wanted to be more; I just didn't know how.

The "how" was decided for me. Our firm assumed the charity work of accounting for the local Theatre in the Round. It looked good for the firm and my father picked me for the assignment. Perhaps, he thought no one would miss me for the extra time I would spend on the *pro bono* project?

Imagination which had been dormant all my life was sparked the evening I walked into the hotel ballroom. It was being transformed to a theatre-in-the-round for the summer. There were people talking and laughing, sets and props being constructed, actors reading scripts aloud, lighting technicians on ladders, other techs checking sound levels, and a director blocking out positions. The platforms holding the seats for future audiences were being used as needed workspace. I could almost hear applause as I was introduced around the busy areas and left to my own table to spread out my worksheets. I was part of it! I was part of the *theatre!*

The summer sped on through four after-dinner plays. I found myself filling in for actors in minor roles. In-between the accounting chores, I could interact with the others. I discovered I wasn't so boring when sharing ideas about a play or particular role. I also found the young women liked to talk to me because I would actually listen. Millie was such a person: Delicate, red-haired, and eager to talk. By summer's end, we were together outside of the theatre, and I was experiencing the pleasure of her company. In the Fall, Millie returned to her classes at our hometown college, and we could still see each other. I returned to the mundane routines of the firm with the nagging feeling there was a decision to be made.

The decision was made for me... for us. Millie was pregnant.

My father and I were in his private office when I apprised him of the situation. The staff outside could sense the tension between us as they surreptitiously watched through the glass wall. I sat in the chair across from him at his large walnut desk.

"How do you know the baby is yours?" was my father's first reaction: No query about Millie, no surprise, just a demand.

"Mine? I just know it is!' I almost shouted at him. "Millie and I have been exclusive all summer and I'm an old enough man to be sure of this. She and I have discussed this and we're going to be married."

My father gasped! "Marriage! Why marriage? There are other possibilities, including putting the baby out for adoption. Why... why... marriage?!" His face was turning red and he slammed his fist on his desk. "You don't know..." he began, but I didn't wait.

"I know this is my responsibility and I'm sorry you don't think I'm man enough to take care of a wife and child but you're wrong." I was ready to let loose with a soliloquy on being a good father—unlike him—but I gained control and let a dramatic silence hang in the air. I had never confronted him so forcefully before. His mouth was open in astonishment.

I turned to see the staff scurrying outside the glass and thought to myself: *Now they know I'm man enough as well!* I never told Millie about the conversation with my father.

Millie and I were soon married in a small, private ceremony. With my accounting salary we could afford a pleasant house and Millie quit college to make a comfortable home for us and the new baby.

The next part of this confession is difficult. Allysia thinks I need to increase the tension in this summary of my life. It would make a better story arc. She's worked as an editor on scripts her whole career, so I respect her ideas. Increase tension? I want to forget the tension, not increase it. Let me just outline the years and not relive them.

Our baby Robert was born with great difficulty. The doctors didn't think he would survive to come home to the nursery Millie had so lovingly prepared. After two weeks of agonizing visits to the hospital nursery, we brought him home to a stringent medical routine. It was a regimen that would last him, and us, for all of his fragile life at home.

Millie and I took turns with outside activities. I had my accounting work. She had Robert and a cadre of medical experts. When summers came around, we would each volunteer for a play. Never together, as one of us would be home with Robert. Some friends even complimented me on my fatherly devotion, saying they would not have the endurance I did. They did not know the disappointment each time a "cure" was unsuccessful. Being with Robert was easy; it was the medical world that was hard. The doctors would try to hide their real thoughts, but their faces showed their hopelessness.

It was the grinding pressure of working at my job that sucked all joy from my morning wake-up. Someone wrote, "Love your job and you'll never work a day in your life." I don't believe that person was an accountant. Those numbers marching across the page or tabulating on the computer screen had become ticks of time marching through my life.

The community theatre was my respite, my delight. Beside keeping the books, I started trying out for bigger roles. With make-up I could play a variety of ages and surprised myself at how easily I could relate to different characters. Comedy was more difficult than drama. I learned it was all dependent on timing.

Professional movie companies often stayed at the hotel while filming the old western town in the nearby desert. It was originally built of adobe with a stagecoach station, a church, and a boardwalk of stores. Many westerns were shot there. Some of the young actors were real dimwits or so full of themselves they would look down on our theatre. I got to talk to some of the production crews and a director or two. They took my business acumen seriously. In my forties, an agent with one company came to watch me perform in a profoundly serious drama and talked to me after the play. He said there was a need for mature actors who could meet the range of emotion I had demonstrated. He gave me his card.

It was difficult when Millie and I finally allowed Robert to move to the group home. Millie and I were torn between wanting the best for Robert, and our wariness of a future without him at home. Was I shirking the responsibility I boasted about to my father? Or was I allowing my son to experience a more contented life? Questions, always questions.

When my father died, I had another decision. Should I remain the primary owner of the firm? Should I sell to the local competitor who was eager to enlarge his office? Should I continue going to luncheons with business cohorts? Should I play golf on my next weekend off? What had I accomplished in my life that I sincerely wanted to do? I couldn't even remember any of my dreams as a young man to know if I had fulfilled them. I guess my tension was part of a mid-life crisis. I didn't run away with a girl half my age or buy an English sports car. I just kept grinding away in my daily work and wondering what the next twenty years would bring; I was a responsible man.

The stress of actually running the firm was greater than I anticipated. My ulcers started acting up again, and I became anxious over the slightest business detail. The day I received notice of an IRS audit, I experienced a full blown attack in my father's—my—office. I felt my heart beating with chest pain and couldn't catch my breath. My assistant found me crumpled at my desk, sweating profusely, and unable to speak because of the tightness in my throat.

With the whole staff watching through the glass walls, 911 was called and I was wheeled out to an ambulance and emergency room. After hours of waiting and tests on machines, an incredibly young doctor advised me: My heart was fine, I'd just had a panic attack. I should consult my regular doctor and try to relax. *Relax? How? I had responsibilities!*

Getting dressed to go home the next day, I finally realized it was *my* turn to answer the questions and make the decisions. The nursing attendant helped me into a wheelchair, required for discharge. Into my lap, he put a potted plant sent by the firm.

As the attendant wheeled me out to the hospital parking lot, I found myself counting the numbers on the rooms—backwards. Fifty-one, my age; fifty, forty-nine, forty-eight, forty-seven. Where had the years gone? By the time I reached the exit, I had my answer.

I could be responsible to myself! Millie had her own life, Robert now had his, and my parents were dead. I could sell the accounting firm to finance my excursion to the next half of my life. I was going to create a dream for now, and seek... whatever it was... that would make me happy. Now!

I confess. I knew what would make me happy. I had a business card with an agent's name. I was going to where the movies and television series were made. I would accumulate credits and work my way up to more substantial roles. I had acted all my life as a mild-mannered accountant. Now, I just wanted to be a movie star!

Will this memoir end with my great successes and lessons learned? Will it solve the mystery of a man's change of life? There are more than enough stories of people overcoming great hardships to become better people and advisors on the meaning of life. This isn't one of them.

I do think it's never too late to create a dream, but you need to be very careful how you achieve it.

Act Three: Obituary
by Alan Caldwell Stone

I knew Howard Rhodes from his early love of theatre, and through his working years as a professional actor. Some major stars can make or break a movie in the millions of dollars.

Others can afford to be jerks to the "little people"—to the crews, character actors, and extras. Howard belonged to that special cadre of professional actors—the character actors and supporting players. The ones who last the longest are the actors who play the game, the people who get along with the crews. They work hard and steady. They are the ones who last the longest in filmdom because of their professional approach to acting, their dependable performances, and knowing the value of team effort. They're the actors who pop up in your favorite motion pictures and television shows. They are the names filling the lists of credits. Sadly, Howard was never satisfied with this role.

Originally, I met Howard when he was the financial manager of our nonprofit summer community theatre. He kept the financial records of purchases, costs, ticket sales, program printing, and general expenses. He was an older, married man and sometimes played more mature parts. Gradually his accountant's heart was won by the call of the theatre, and he became an actor in a number of plays through the 1950s and 1960s. He came in contact with an agent who was scouting the old western town. Movie crews often stayed at the same hotel where we performed.

I lost track of Howard in the mid sixties. I graduated from college and left our town to try my own hand at professional acting in Hollywood. It was a lot more difficult than volunteering at our community theatre or trying out for plays at the university's Drama department. I was young, living cheaply, making contacts. Gradually, I worked into a number of roles, steady enough for fans to recognize me from "The TV Show." Most importantly, I was doing what I loved— acting, and making a living at it.

In the 1970s, Howard followed his own dream to work as an actor in television and motion pictures. With some unexplained personal decisions, Howard sold his accounting firm. He unilaterally divorced his wife, Millie, leaving her stunned. He began a new career for twenty-three years and I ran across him on a Hollywood set. We occasionally crossed paths and would talk about the old days. He didn't miss them at all and appreciated the excitement and fulfillment he felt. He did have a bitterness toward the small parts he was able to get. He once told me the first half of his life was spent grinding away for other people. This last half was meant to be a celebration for him. Instead, he was now grinding away for the front office. He re-married. His wife, Allysia, was a continuity director on the TV series where he was a minor character. Howard often played a judge whether in the old West or modern metropolitan courtrooms. His longest lasting supporting role ended after thirteen seasons with the television series' finale. He and Allysia retired to the desert.

Howard is survived by his wife, Allysia Rhodes; his son Robert Rhodes, and the actors who have appeared with him. In lieu of cards, any contributions or memorials should be donated to the Rhodes Care Home Foundation in honor of his son. As for Howard, he has left the building....

Final curtain.

THRESHOLD
TIME FRAGMENT MARCH 31, 1945 CE

The big man sat tensely on the small stool, concentrating on the worksheet in front of him, trying to pay close attention to the lines and squares he'd been penciling in since the aircraft took off the runway from Thorpe Abbotts Field. The control tower was silhouetted beside Quonset huts, the taxiing aircraft, service trucks, and military personnel all hurrying to duty. The deep signature roar of engines dominated the runway area. Above the field, the early morning formation of bombers marshaled into position. Assembled from various U.S. Army air bases across the English countryside, the Allies slipped each squadron into its designated place to perfection. From that altitude, the greening fields below resembled the spring farmland of Iowa; it was another reminder the B-17 bomber was leaving home. When all aircraft were in position, the command sent the whole formation thundering across the English Channel waters to Germany.

Sighting the ocean waves below, the navigator, Dale Westridge, allowed his mind to briefly slip away and remember...

With Army flight training, he and his bride, Harriet, had traveled together around the United States to various airfields. They had never been so far from the Midwest before. The excitement of the country was palpable for the war effort; the mood of the nation hungered for victory. They were a part of it all: traveling by train, investigating new towns, meeting new people, being together. The passion of young, married love meant grasping each chance to be intimate—a treasure of a break in training or overnight pass. Such a moment meant his dearest Harriet became pregnant. She was beginning her third trimester when Dale was finally deployed to England. Staying with her mother in Iowa, Harriet would only have her husband's letters for comfort. Following military directive, Dale never wrote details about his missions, but personally he could write:

"I sure wish I was there to be with you. I keep thinking I should be there when the baby comes. I feel as if I have deserted you, my beloved. I'm so tired after a long day over the 3rd Reich. During that time, I'm too busy to worry about things at home but I think of you at night in my bunk. I have been sweating it out over here though and at night I wonder quite a bit. I love you, darling."

This March morning at the navigator's table, Dale smiled and touched the cablegram inside his flight suit. Arriving just days before, it announced he was the father of a baby girl, Janice. He loved the name and was glad for a little girl just like the niece he adored. The thought of a wife and daughter waiting for him was heartening. The channel below changed to land, crossing the Continental Coast; enemy resources were waiting, and the real work lie ahead.

This day's mission to a Zeitz, Germany, oil field was

almost routine for this late time in the war, March 1945. The Allies were hammering Germany's resources, front lines racing toward Berlin. The Luftwaffe was immobilized for lack of fuel. The 'little friends' of Allied fighters accompanied and protected the formation part way. The squadrons approached the target oil fields from the south because of the headwind. It required their prolonged steady flight over the target. The togglier was experienced in controlling the flight for the Norden bombsight. The level flight was imperative for hitting the objective. The Mighty Eighth Air Force slammed bomb loads with grid bombing because extensive smoke screens covered the target area. Outlines of features were glimpsed and coordinated with the primary points on the charts. The steadiness necessary to complete the mission gave the German flak operators surrounding Zeitz time to calculate the altitude and configure the fuses for the anti-aircraft shells. They had the bomber formation range and altitude and fired their battery of cannons. The flak started immediately as the toggliers controlled flying the aircraft to release their loads. Deadly bursts carpeted the sky and engulfed the formation.

Looking at the charts helped distract the navigator from the flak explosions which rocked the B-17, thundering in the aluminum frame, even above the roar of the engines. He didn't want to sweat... not a good idea at this altitude where even the electric flight suits had a hard time keeping a man from freezing to death. The navigator station was in the lower nose of the aircraft. The togglier seat and the Norden bombsight was suspended in front of the Fortress in a Plexiglas nose bubble. It allowed a panoramic view of the gravel field ahead of the squadron. Except, each piece of gravel was an explosion aimed to destroy any chance of a flight home.

The B-17 earned its designation as a 'flying fortress' from its gunners: a ball gunner hanging below the fuselage, a top turret gunner above the pilot and a tail gunner covering the tail behind. Armaments at portholes were designed to protect the bomber on its daylight missions. At first, the young gunners were buoyant from the mission completion, then silent. There was nothing to shoot at, no action to pursue. This was the hardest time of all, sitting in a B-17 Flying Fortress without any defenses at all. The crew members just watched the myriad of explosions around them, watched for other aircraft, and held on to the contents of their stomachs. One of the waist gunners wasn't even supposed to be on this mission. He had replaced a sick crewman. From the intensity of the flak, he certainly wished he'd been the one sick instead.

Dale kept his mark on the chart feeling the nearby concussions in the unpressurized fuselage when he was almost knocked off the stool, his shoulders jammed into the sight over the worktable. He heard the explosion at the same time the fuselage lurched, and knew this was it: they were hit! He instinctively grabbed his chest and mask; he was still breathing oxygen through the face mask. He righted himself in a crouch and his legs were still working. Quickly he looked to the nose compartment and saw the togglier was shaking from the concussion. He yelled towards the crewman then looked out the starboard window to see the Number Three engine was completely gone. The entire nacelle had been ripped off the wing like a pocket torn from a shirt. He heard the pilot and co-pilot above him, shouting, giving directions when another explosion slammed the craft. The yelling in the earphones checked the crew, the Number Four engine was feathered, its blades turning to create minimum drag. With no starboard power, the Fortress began losing altitude.

This was the pilot's last required mission, he could go home, stateside, if he could just get the bomber back to Thorpe Abbotts, back to the base in England. Struggling with the controls, he made his decision... he was going to try and make it to friendly lines. The Russians were within a few miles of Berlin. It was a chance! He and the co-pilot fought with the controls; they attempted to hold altitude, but the port engines drove them to the east, curving away from the formation, towards Russian lines... and towards the ground.

Dale wasn't sure if he heard the pilot ask for 'position' or just knew it was needed. He shouted coordinates to the pilot as the plane was holding together heading for the under-cast of clouds separating them from the earth below. Already the clouds were engulfing the damaged aircraft as its elevation diminished. In a moment of clarity, the navigator thought of his young wife standing and waving to him. She wore a dark skirt with decorated suspenders over a white blouse. Her blond hair was curled and waving in the wind. She was waiting for him; he had to get home. The vision vanished as he concentrated on the charts and direction the plane was heading. He shouted the coordinates again and confirmed them.

The pilot commanded, "Bail out! Jump!"

Turning in the tight area, Dale looked back along the fuselage to see crewmen struggling to check their parachutes as the cabin filled with smoke. Helping the stunned togglier with his chute, the navigator pictured the close proximity of friendly lines on the chart and hoped his chute could take him there. He pushed the togglier out their escape hatch and followed. Blackness overtook him due to lack of oxygen.

The Fortress disappeared in the under-cast clouds. Radio transmissions were conflicting from the B-17s already headed back to England. The bomber formation witnessed yet another aircraft disappearance... more painful because the war was in its final death throes. World War II was over for another U.S. Army aircraft, a casualty of the Bloody Hundredth Bomb Group.

A child in a German garden saw the parachutes, like little mushrooms descending slowly to the ground. In the quickness and madness of the war, there was something almost peaceful, serene, even in their lazy about their fall to the earth. She thought they were quite pretty. She knew there were men dangling at the ends of those great mushrooms, it never entered her thoughts until the soft clouds of silk touched down. A shout came from inside her home and she ran towards her mother at the door. The sound of trucks on the road made her turn. The S.S. in the Opel-Blitz troop carrier truck heading towards the touchdowns paid no attention to the small girl running through the broken garden.

Weeks later, in a side yard in Iowa, Harriet tucked a letter stamped with its six-cent airmail postage in her pocket and started to handle the wet laundry. She was still a bit weak from the difficult delivery, but at least she and baby Janice were at home. After the diapers were hung, she would take the baby and walk down to the corner to post her daily missive to her husband, Dale. She hadn't received recent letters from him and worried when the backed-up mail would finally get there but she kept sending hers.

She was uneasy this morning because of a dream that had reoccurred these last few weeks. In the various scenarios she was always trying to find her husband. She would see him walking away in his Army officer's uniform with his relaxed natural ease. He was whistling an Irish melody. Running as fast as she could, the dream held her back in slow motion and she could never catch up with him. Alone, the young mother would awaken in tears. The previous night, the dream was different. She ran after her husband calling to him and he stopped, turned, and faced her. His face was almost expressionless as he said, "Honey, I've got something to tell you." That was all. She awoke weeping.

The wet diapers were suspended one by one in the April sunshine. Clothes pins lined up like little soldiers holding them in place. She paused when the Western Union telegraph boy stopped at the gate, opened it and slowly came up the walk. Her breath tightened as the boy wouldn't look her in the eye. She signed for the message and slowly placed the telegram into her pocket next to the letter that would never be mailed. The diapers needed to be hung to dry... her fingers trembled as she affixed each clothespin... then she read the telegram:

17 APRIL 1945
THE SECRETARY OF WAR DESIRES ME TO EXPRESS HIS DEEP REGRET THAT YOUR HUSBAND SECOND LIEUTENANT WESTRIDGE DALE F. HAS BEEN MISSING ACTION OVER GERMANY SINCE 31 MARCH 1945. IF FURTHER DETAILS OR OTHER INFORMATION ARE RECEIVED YOU WILL BE PROMPTLY NOTIFIED.

J.A. ULIO, THE ADJUTANT GENERAL

AN INTERVIEW WITH J.W. CAPEK

When did you start writing and why?

I'm not really a writer—I'm a storyteller; it began with my Grandmother's stories and listening to radio programs. By second grade, Sister Magdalene would have me tell stories to class when our work was finished. I told stories on live television in the fifties and had conversations with puppets, Squeaky and I Am. In high school and college, I could act out plays and stories. When I was teaching high school, stories were one way to engage students in learning.

I tried writing *Deerwhere* science fiction in the seventies but rejection letters convinced me I had no audience—as far as publishers were concerned.

In these latter decades, I re-discovered the true joy of writing for the mental stimulation, and the surprise interpretations I receive from readers. I also think the readership is now ready for my story of the Uniales, the third sex with their own pronouns and relationship to human males and females. I would tell you their story here but it is already available in *The Deerwhere Codex.*

Which authors or books or media influenced you the most as a writer?

I definitely go to the master storytellers with an eclectic collection of classics. If the books affected me personally, their influence would emerge in my writing. My personal philosophy relies on seven decades of experience, and reading stories is a part of that. Beverly Cleary (*Pollyanna*) Charlotte Bronte (*Jane Eyre*), Erma Bombeck, John Steinbeck (*Grapes of Wrath*), Robert Heinlein (*Stranger in a Strange Land*), Mark Twain (*Roughing It*), Zane Gray (*West of the Pecos*), George Orwell (*Animal Farm*).

Which authors or books or media had the biggest impact on you as a person?

Pollyanna established her "glad game" with me very early, and continuously directs me. It enhanced the concept of "I cried because I had no shoes until I met the person who had no feet." There are reasons why proverbs continue to explain events of our lives. They prove their truth over their long lives. Current events are actually explained in *Animal Farm*. Carl Sagan's *Cosmos* opened the universe to me. I enjoy current writers, but they usually remind me of the classics. I've also discovered new perspectives by re-reading books which I treasure.

Which of your original twelve *Prompt* stories are you most pleased with?

Peggy and the Nil Bag. Years ago, I collaborated with my mother-in-law to create a story about the 1930's. We had fun with the fantasy, typed it up, and put it on a closet shelf for half a century. I thought of the story when working in *Prompt* because it wove the characters into another time fragment very different from our current era. The theme of pure fantasy was a novel approach as was the character of Peggy as well. Editing and developing new characters was an experience of enriching an old draft. I had to evaluate adapting outdated terms and culture for a modern readership.

Which of your original twelve *Prompt* stories did you find the most difficult to write?

Originally taxing, it was the March story, "Charandos." The uniale canon was already established in my *Deerwhere Codex* trilogy. Exposition of sci-fi world took three books to establish including the pronouns of nhe, nes, nem. It was challenging to squeeze such a complex fiction into a short story in 25 days' time. One of the uniale characters, Li Mor, disappeared in Codex Awakening and I decided to give nem a personal tale... this story.

I returned to the *Deerwhere* saga to extend the character, now Alyx, a uniale with a blanked memory in a colony of all uniales. The new setting created a need to carefully edit the events in the story arc. With Alyx's first person narrative, I also described how the male and female characters were perceived and observed from the uniale view. It was demanding to chose between elaboration or minimizing of events. My characters and their situations tempted me to expand to a longer manuscript.

What book on writing do you recommend?

In your reading, find a compatible author to your voice and style. Try their writing book. Authors have their own recommendations in books, interviews, or blogs. Go to your local library, or a writer's group. Trust your instincts. If you are creative enough to be a writer, you can choose advice that will work and discard superfluous information. Remember, you can always quit the book and libraries don't charge for unread books

What advice would you give an unpublished writer?

The mental process of creativity in writing has to be experienced to be understood and appreciated. I am amazed by the number of people who have said they "always wanted to write." I don't know the scientific reasoning, but w-r-i-t-i-n-g is different than just thinking about a story or talking about it. Write your journal, your letters, your round-to-it list and the Great American novel. Just do it! Build upon what you know. Enjoy! A caveat, be very wary of online promotions, it's a jungle out there. Be aware that "writing" is only part, it's easy. "Marketing" is hard! And… don't quit your day job! With the competition of writers, basic income is usually necessary.

Do you have a "dream project" as a writer? What would it be?

My plan is to complete *Fragments of War,* a book I have been composing for my whole life but never had the emotional stamina to write. *Fragments of War* will be an historical memoir of the search for my father who was killed in World War Two. I have been overwhelmed with the completed research and never able to get past the first chapters. Now it is my time fragment to write the actual memoir. I believe the discipline garnered in *Prompt: The Second Generation* will enable me to write the book in 2023.

Your stories are published in the seasonal *Prompt* anthologies but also as a collection of just your own work. Did you have a conscious theme for your personal collection?

For the first three months, I was responding directly to the prompts. They would trigger scattered ideas to narrow down and define the story. By April, I recognized an emerging theme in my stories. My title, *Fragments of Time,* became the dominant idea as all the stories reflected characters being affected by the times they lived. I recognized the variety of times influencing my characters with their emotional responses to the events happening. As short stories, they were fragments.

You have a body of work outside your *Prompt* stories. Share why those other works are important to you and how they differ from your *Prompt* stories.

The uniale was inspired by the tumultuous period of the sixties and seventies when I was a young bride and mother attempting to make sense of my place in the world. Americans were dying in Vietnam while others walked on the moon. There were influences of assassinations, political infighting, gender fluidity ascending, racial conflicts, emerging drug cultures, overpopulation, global pollution, border wars, and an energy crisis. Unable to fathom a solution to all the dissension, I created the Uniale—an amalgam of the best attributes of humanity, a hope for Utopia in the twenty-fourth century.

The Deerwhere Codex was a definite science fiction trilogy forecasting a future with three distinct humans: uniales, females, and males. The most important facet for the uniales was the development of their personal pronouns that gave them their true separate identity: Nhe-subjective, nem-objective, nes-possessive. This depicted their humanity.

Exploring gender stereotypes and gender roles was ground-breaking in 1978 and I was unable to interest any publisher. I did not know how to market such a manuscript. Now, as a mature woman writing in science fiction, I was finally published by Hagengard Press (2017) and Blue Forge Press (2018.) My time frame shows younger generations aren't the only ones looking at these core issues of humanity.

With the *Prompt* stories, I began with the prompt but then my thoughts expanded to a specific situation and time.

Characters developed to comprise the cast. The characters and events fashioned the story rather than a plotted outline. The theme of fragments and times supported the universal theme of "humanity abides" through the collection.

Who do you write for and how does it drive you to create?

I create stories because I can! I have used storytelling all my life for entertainment, for teaching, for remembering, for sharing, and for personal enjoyment. I write to tell stories as were told to me and gave me the blueprint for my life. Being a high school teacher, I found I could make better contact with my students by connecting stories to the concepts I was teaching. Characters come first, and they participate in the creation of the time frame, the settings, the events and conflicts, and the resolution.

That said, there is a difference between writing or "telling a story" to an audience of one or a whole theatre. In talking, you have personal interaction. You can adjust the story length, read the listener's expression, and change the pace according to the response you receive. Is your audience receptive, laughing at the jokes, or hostile to the words you are using? With "writing" you are never sure who is going to read your work, or when, or the reception of the particular words you have constructed. With one *Prompt* story, I received totally different reactions from the beta reader and the editor. Neither was what I had intended. I can do my best work expressing my thoughts but wonder how they will be interpreted. I appreciate that I have a bookshelf with my published stories and those of my writer friends. For anyone who loves to read, the physical realization of "my book" is enthralling. The mental stimulation of the writing process is a great way to approach the decades ahead, and that drives me to create.

Optimally, we're always growing and improving as authors. Talk about how you grew or changed as a writer over the course of the year.

 Knowing the *Prompt* stories would actually be published was extremely encouraging. The impetus was to create towards the goal of publication. There also was tension and turmoil in being committed to the creation of a short story each and every month. I wanted my work to be my best. I became very aware of the construction of the story. Some sentences that were "perfect" needed to be placed differently. Technically, style based on fundamental grammar and language, became easier with the process. The discipline of monthly submissions, of deadlines, working with beta readers and the publisher, meant I became more productive. Through the process, I could see the concrete result of my work. As a writer who waited through years of rejection, the *Prompt* project gave me confidence in my creativity.

My basic folders for each story included Resources, graphics, Characters, drafts, Blue Forge directions, and story statistics. Story plus characters plus time plus setting plus events equals the *Prompt* story of the month!